# A BIRD IN THE HAND

# Ann Cleeves

# A BIRD IN THE HAND

MACMILLAN

First published 1986 by Century

This edition published 2023 by Macmillan
an imprint of Pan Macmillan
The Smithson, 6 Briset Street, London EC1M 5NR
*EU representative:* Macmillan Publishers Ireland Ltd, 1st Floor,
The Liffey Trust Centre, 117–126 Sheriff Street Upper,
Dublin 1, D01 YC43
Associated companies throughout the world
www.panmacmillan.com

ISBN 978-1-0350-0805-6

1 3 5 7 9 8 6 4 2

A CIP catalogue record for this book is available from the British Library.

Typeset by Palimpsest Book Production Ltd, Falkirk, Stirlingshire
Printed and bound by CPI Group (UK) Ltd, Croydon, CR0 4YY

MIX
Paper | Supporting
responsible forestry
FSC® C116313
FSC
www.fsc.org

Visit **www.panmacmillan.com** to read more about all our books
and to buy them. You will also find features, author interviews and
news of any author events, and you can sign up for e-newsletters
so that you're always first to hear about our new releases.

Dear Reader,

*A Bird in the Hand* was my first completed novel, and like most first novels it took a long time to write. There were times I was convinced that I'd never get to the end. It was started when my husband Tim and I were living on the tidal island of Hilbre, in the Dee. We were the only residents, we had no mains electricity or water, and I really wasn't into birds or birdwatching – despite the subject matter of this book. I'd given up my work as a probation officer because I was pregnant with our first child and this, I decided, was the time to write. There was little else for me to do, except whitewash the former coastguard building, which was our house, and feed our hens.

I had never been to a creative writing class and had met no published writers, but I'd read voraciously and widely. My first attempt had been a literary novel, set around an adventure playground, using my experience as a social worker. It had been hugely depressing and almost without a plot. It was never finished. My comfort reading had always been crime fiction, however, and in crime I found the structure to ease me to a conclusion.

Technically, this book is not without its faults. The point of view jumps from character to character within the same chapter, and because of this, I can see that there should be more depth to the internal monologue. If I were writing it now, with the benefit of experience, I'd let in some space and some light. The storytelling would be clearer.

However, I enjoy the depiction of the world of obsessive twitching as it was then, before mobile phones and pagers, when university education was free, and students roamed the country to look at new birds. I still believe in the characters, probably because many of them were based on people I knew. There's also a youthful energy about the writing. The settings move at great pace from Norfolk, to Cornwall, to the Scilly Islands and to the Highlands. It's a novel by a young woman, desperately wanting to tell the story, never believing she'll actually be published, and certainly never thinking that she would still be writing thirty-five years later.

I hope that you enjoy meeting George and Molly Palmer-Jones. I am very fond of them.

Ann Cleeves

# Chapter One

IT WAS A WARM May evening, a Saturday, and a small boy was playing with a home-made model boat at the edge of a pool. The land was flat; water and reeds and marsh stretched to a shingle bank and beyond that to the North Sea. Everything was quiet and the village seemed a long way off. The sun was low, so when the boy stood up to reach across the water with a stick to untangle his boat from the reeds, the long shadows made him look very tall. He was playing very intently, and his father, dozing with a paper in the sun, watched and only smiled as the boy waded into the pool until the water began to spill into his wellingtons, poking further into the reeds with his stick.

The boy watched a lot of television, liked American thrillers, and it was with certainty that he had turned to his father, his Norfolk voice not showing excitement, even if he felt it, to say:

'Dad, there's a body in the marsh.'

His father rose to look, not believing, still dazed by the sun. When he saw the figure, surrounded by rushes like an

1

animal in its nest, disgustingly, obviously, dead, he could think quite calmly:

*At least it isn't one of us.*

He did not need to look at the face to tell that the young man lying in the shallow water at the edge of the pool did not belong to the village, because on the mud beside him, the strap still around his neck, lay a pair of binoculars.

'Dad,' said the boy again, very quietly. 'It's Tommy.'


Tom French had known that something would happen on that Saturday, that it would be a special day. He had planned it, prayed for it. He had planned it the day before, as he listened to the shipping forecast on his radio. He had decided then that he would go out early onto the marsh, well before he was due to start work at eight. He knew that he often made plans to get out early, but that he rarely carried them through. More often than not he was shaken awake by Dennis, the breakfast chef at the White Lodge. Tom had no incentive to get up for work: he was employed as vegetable chef, but worked as kitchen porter, cleaner, sometimes even as waiter. He hated the White Lodge. It kept him away from the marsh. He lived in a tiny room at the back of the hotel. In the mornings he would move silently about the kitchen, boiling water, setting tables, while Dennis, huge and tattooed, swore at the waitresses and sang Led Zeppelin loud. Often hungover, sometimes still drunk, Tom would move in a dream. Only between breakfast and lunch, as the kitchen grew hotter and the noise of singing and pans louder, would he begin to become alive. Then he would regret his failure to get out onto the marsh before work.

But on the Friday night he knew that he would go the next day. He was a twitcher, and as he listened to the shipping forecast he knew that he would go. He claimed that he had given up twitching, retired because of his work and his commitment to Sally. But he was still a twitcher. At one time he had travelled all over the country to see rare birds. He collected the sight of them as other people collect stamps or train numbers, but the pleasure in the rarities was not only in the collection, in the addition of a species to a list, but in the beauty of the birds themselves, in the delicate differences between them. He told himself, and other people, that for him birdwatching was an aesthetic, almost a spiritual, experience. He did not travel far now to see rare birds, but his passion for them was as deep as it had always been.

It had begun when he was a child, living over his parents' grocery shop in Kentish Town. He could remember vividly his first awareness that the world was inhabited by anything other than humans. He had been seven and a half, and he and some other boys had broken into a derelict house, still frightening and empty after the war, but showing no actual sign of bomb damage. There was only one piece of furniture in the house: a wooden cupboard which stood in the corner of the living room. Inside it was a stuffed kestrel. He had known that it was a bird, but he had never before seen a bird like it. It had fascinated him and he had fought off the other boys for possession of it. He had taken it to his schoolteacher who had named it, magically, and had introduced him to the local natural history society, where she made him a junior member.

Birdwatching became a secret passion, shared only with other birdwatchers. He could never have admitted at school,

3

especially at his grammar school, what he did at weekends. As it was, he never quite belonged there. It was a relief to find other people who were as interested, as fanatically interested as he was, and he spent more and more time watching birds or travelling to see rarities. His only close friends were birdwatchers.

Then he had found Rushy. He had come there first, of course, to see the birds, hitching most weekends from London in the spring and autumn, sleeping in the hut near the putting green or in the ladies' toilets. But he liked the place too. He felt that it was his place. It was small enough to know well. He made trips to Shetland and the Scilly Isles, but there he always felt a tourist. He always came back to Rushy. It had always been known as a good place to see big numbers of common migrants, but Tom found rarities, occasionally he found spectacular rarities, and the reputation of the village grew and spread. Rushy became the property of every bird club and Young Ornithologists group. The dudes and the RSPB members, the wealthy amateurs of the bird-watching world, who stayed in the hotel where he worked, did so because they hoped to see golden oriole and wood-chat shrike, the rarities for which he had made the place famous. He felt that it was a responsibility and he missed the old freedom.

Now, ironically, he only ever saw other people's birds. It was true that when the last guest had finished lunch and only Terry was left in the kitchen, and he walked into the Blue Anchor, just on closing time, all the twitchers knew him; gathered round him to ask his advice, to tell him what had been seen. Very rarely did he miss anything good – someone would leave a message for him at the hotel if there was a bird in the area which was known to be new for him. Very rarely did he have to buy his own drinks. But at every rarity there would be a gaggle of birders with tripods, telescopes and cameras; he was always one of a crowd. He missed the excitement and the glory of being the first to see a rarity.

Now it was May and the wind had been blowing from the south-east all week. A wind from the south-east in spring brings migrant species from Europe and Africa and Siberia, and it brings vagrants, birds with no reason to be in this country, arriving only by accident and because of the wind. Even on the bad days, when he worried about Sally and money, and worked overtime in the afternoon, making tea for the children, Tom knew which way the wind was blowing. On the Friday night, listening to the shipping forecast on his cheap transistor in his small and dirty bedroom, as he heard the bland, objective voice report the possibility of mist and fog patches at dawn, he knew that the next day would be special. It mattered more to him that night than anything else that he find a rare bird, more than caring for Sally and Barnaby, more than finding work that he enjoyed.

He phoned Sally in Fenquay, explaining that he would not be across to see her. He had tried to be tender, sympathetic, but she had been offhand and indifferent. He had considered cancelling his plans, because she frightened him more when she was distant and cold than when she was hysterical. When she had taken the overdose, she had been deadly, icily calm. But even while he thought about taking the bus to Fenquay, staying the night in the cottage with Sally and Barnaby, he knew that he would not do it. Because the wind was blowing from the south-east, and the night migrants reaching the coast at dawn would meet and be grounded by a bank of fog, and there was nothing more compelling than spring migration in perfect conditions.

The night porter saw Tommy leave the hotel at five forty on the Saturday morning. It was very foggy, and although the porter was watching, he could not see which way Tom went once he left the building. He was a nervous man, and was more worried about his drive home in the fog than about Tom's destination. Later he was to tell the police that Tom waved and called to him, but did not mention that he planned to meet anyone. He guessed that Tom was going birdwatching because he was wearing wellingtons and carried binoculars and telescope. He did not know that under his anorak Tom was wearing a thick, striped sweater, not really suitable for birding, which he always wore on special occasions, because Sally had knitted it and he thought that it was lucky. The porter was the last person to admit to seeing Tom alive.

When Dennis called for Tom at seven forty-five, the room was empty. He swaggered swearing into the kitchen, and shouted to Terry, who had a learning disability, who had been working in the hotel for ten years and was still paid the same wages as when he started: 'You'll have to start on the teas. Tom's still in Fenquay.' Terry grinned dutifully. Despite himself, Dennis smiled back with a vague, rude, envious gesture.

When the Fenquay bus went past at eight thirty and Tom was not on it, Dennis shouted to one of the Spanish chambermaids to phone Sally's home to find out where he was. He had been late before. He was too soft on that temperamental bitch. The girl returned to say that there was no reply. When Mr Yates, the manager, discovered – despite the kitchen staff's attempt to hide the fact – that Tom had not turned up to work, he was not surprised. Casual staff were so unreliable.

There were no birdwatchers in the Blue Anchor at lunch-time. They were too busy counting the bluethroats and wrynecks, the red-backed shrikes, too busy peering through the fog, checking every willow warbler trying to turn it into a Bonelli's, every whitethroat in the hope that it would become a spectacled warbler. Only the landlord missed Tom. It was unusual for him not to come in for a pint before going out on the marsh.

It was the sort of day that confused the village. At the peak of migration the birds had been kept on the ground by the fog in huge numbers. Yet the birdwatchers seemed dissatisfied. There was an air of frustration, of frenzy. It seemed impossible that among so many birds there was nothing unusual, but no rarity had been found. Villagers who noted the large numbers of birds and expected the twitchers to be pleased were hurt by the frantic bad tempers. It was as if Rushy had let the birdwatchers down.

The village expected the birdwatchers now every spring and autumn and though it complained of their presence every year in a gentle, pleasant way which had become a habit, it was happy to exploit them commercially. Few of the locals understood them, or made any effort to know them well. They sold books and food and pictures to the birdwatchers – birdwatchers staying in their homes extended the bed and breakfast season – but the intense enthusiasm, the fanaticism puzzled them. The village was red-stone, flint-faced, like many others along the coast, and its inhabitants wondered in a bewildered, accepting way why it should have been chosen for special attention by the birdwatchers. And yet, in spite of the detachment, the occasional hostility, there had been some impact on the local population. The excitement of twitching was infectious. That morning Ella, owner of the Windmill Cafe, glorious in black nightclothes, had looked out of the bedroom window, and exclaimed to her husband:

'Look at that wind and that fog, Jack. We'll be busy today. They'll be motoring in from all over the country.'

Her dark eyes had flashed at the drama of it all, and she thought of the profit which would be shown at the end of the day.

So, there was a strange feeling in the village, sensed by locals and birders alike. The thick fog which had rolled in from the sea at dawn would not clear. The cars moved slowly and people stopped and remarked on the weather, and remembered other times when the fog had lasted a week, and throughout the day odd young people in disreputable clothing, carrying telescopes like offensive weapons, rushed through the village to the marsh, or back from the marsh to the copse. Later, older and more respectable people arrived in cars, and politely asked their way. All day, shut in by the fog as the strangers arrived, there was a feeling that the village was under siege and under invasion.

It was late afternoon when Adam Anderson found the 'big one', the rarity for which they had all been waiting. Adam was still at school, one of the younger generation of twitchers, most of whom were still regarded with suspicion because of their wild claims and lack of respect for tradition and the order of things. But Adam was nervous, quiet. He was dedicated and spent more days in the field than he did at school. Because of his long hair, his jeans and Indian cotton shirt, the older twitchers, who had been his age in the sixties, felt at ease with him. Adam knew, as all birdwatchers of any experience in Rushy knew, that he must get his information to the Windmill.

The Windmill was a wooden hut on a piece of flat derelict grassland below the shingle bank, next to the coastguard station. It had been built by Ella and Jack when there had been talk of developing the area for the tourists, plans for a funfair and amusement arcade. Perhaps the developers had been dissuaded by the bleakness of the place, the talk of flooding, the pressure of the conservationists, because there was no more building. If tourists went to Rushy they seldom wandered out onto the marsh. So Jack had gone back to work, driving the school bus.

Before the arrival of the birdwatchers, Ella had sat alone in the hut, making an occasional cup of tea for fishermen and bait diggers. Now, as on most weekends in the migration season, the Windmill was packed. Most of the birders, hungry, dampened by the fog, had given up the dream of finding the big one, and were drinking tea, sharing information, waiting for the phone to ring with news from other parts of the country. Ella, who had been growing middle-aged, grey, with the failure of the business, had been rejuvenated by the twitchers, and expressed her gratitude by promoting their image in the village. She was a big, handsome woman, whose grandfather was said to have come to Rushy as a tinker. She had adopted the twitchers' code as her own, once banning for a season a birdwatcher who had kept news of a rarity to himself. She mothered them and spoiled them and made a lot of money out of them.

On a day like this she felt the birdwatchers' depression personally. They seemed to have brought the fog with them into the building. The windows were misted with it, and there

was a smell of damp. Every class of birdwatcher was represented, and although the hierarchy within an ornithological
society would not be noticed by an outsider, it was recognized
by Ella. Until Ella knew his name, where he lived and what
work he did, a twitcher did not properly belong.

The person who most obviously belonged in the place was
a young man, scruffily but carefully dressed in a sailing smock
and worn cord trousers. He stood behind the counter, in the
kitchen, and lazily helped himself to a cup of tea. He had a
stubble of beard and began to roll a cigarette, in a calculating,
self-conscious way. He was always showing off. He seemed
to be cultivating the image of a South American revolutionary.
From a corner, loud but nervous teenagers watched him with
envy. One of the teenagers, who wore an earring and dyed
orange hair, made a teasing comment which was obviously
uncomplimentary to the man pouring the tea, but he made
it as a gesture of defiance, and there was little laughter from
his friends.

An elderly couple, the man dressed immaculately like a
country gentleman, the woman in a tweed skirt and wellingtons, pushed open the door of the cafe and stood just inside.
Ella was busy and had her back to them. The young revolutionary smiled broadly, but the gentleman put his finger to
his lips and winked at Ella's back. When she turned round
he was standing behind the counter beside her, eating a piece
of her fruit cake. There was a real pleasure in her surprise,
and when he took her hand she blushed before she sent them
both to the customers' side of the counter, saying that they
were in her way.

'Now, now, my dear,' said the country gentleman. 'That's
surely no way to talk to the oldest twitcher in Rushy.'

'Mr Palmer-Jones,' replied Ella with great spirit. 'I shall talk to you how I please and how you deserve.'

Then, affectionate and angry, she turned on the young man:

'If I catch you behind here again, Robert, with that filthy tobacco, I'll ban you for a month.'

Unrepentant, the young man refilled his cup and led his friends to a table to sit down. As he stood to let them past him, he noticed that the sun was shining.

The fog had remained dense throughout the afternoon, when suddenly, at five, like a vast blind rolled back to the sea, it cleared. So the line of observers lying against the shingle bank, their telescopes unused on their knees, could see Adam running along the straight flat track from the main road. His running was thrown out of balance by the optical equipment he was carrying, and he ran like an excited schoolgirl, legs flying. They sensed his urgency and slid down the shingle and ran too, towards the Windmill. The few people still walking slowly and hopefully through the marsh saw the line of black figures on the bank disappear and they also began to run. When Adam pushed into the hut with so much energy and excitement that it seemed that the room could hardly contain him, there was a crowd behind him jostling him further in. Adam tried to speak, but he was out of breath and the background music was so loud that no one could make out what he said. Ella knew what was expected and turned off the radio. Then there was silence. They all heard when, still fighting for breath and with a slight stutter, he said:

'Bimaculated lark. On the lawn behind the hotel. I'm sure it is.'

With tolerance and affection Ella watched the snack bar

empty and, on her knees to sweep up a cup and plate broken in the confusion, said to her assistant:

'You'd best get some more bread out of the freezer, Sandra. We'll be busy tomorrow.'

Then: 'He's such a gentleman, Mr Palmer-Jones. He was a civil servant before he retired. Do you know, he used to work for a minister? He told me once. Fancy young Adam finding a bird like that.'

All the birdwatchers went inland, to trespass on the parkland surrounding the hotel, and there was no one to disturb the peace of the marsh, where a little boy was playing with his boat in the sun.

Mr and Mrs Palmer-Jones lived in a pretty and tidy village in Surrey. Their house was neither pretty nor tidy. It was a red-brick Victorian vicarage with flaking paint and a garden of tangled undergrowth, with a pond full of newts and toads. A battered old swing had been left to rust on the lawn for the benefit of grandchildren, and the latch on the front gate was always sticking. Mrs Palmer-Jones shocked the village by standing unsuccessfully each year as a candidate for the Labour Party in local authority elections and going on CND marches. Over the years these idiosyncrasies were forgiven, but she refused to join the WI, and that never was. Until she had retired at the age of sixty she had worked as a senior social worker in Guildford. This had been viewed as a respectable occupation for an elderly lady, like working for the WRVS, until Molly Palmer-Jones had made the mistake of describing some of the details of her work. Then it became common knowledge in the village that she worked 'not with the needy or old ladies or orphans, but, my dear, with youths, criminals and drug addicts.'

Mr Palmer-Jones was a naturalist of the old-fashioned type, who knew about plants and butterflies as well as birds. His weekly article on natural history in the local paper made him something of a celebrity in the village. He was a founder member of the Surrey Conservation Trust. But even he began to behave a little oddly as he grew older. He went to India in a Land Rover. When he retired he sold his Volvo and bought a Morris Minor van, in which he and Molly travelled all over the country looking for and watching rare birds. Strange people were seen to visit the house, people who were dropped in the village by lorry drivers after hitchhiking from the motorway, young people, carrying nothing but a sleeping bag and a battered telescope. Yet unlike his wife he maintained decent standards of dress and speech. There was sustained criticism by a member of the Conservation Trust with journalistic ambitions of his newspaper articles, which now reflected his trips to see rare birds, but he continued to be respected. He had an air of authority, of sadness, which encouraged people to keep their distance. They were, perhaps, a little frightened of him, despite his polite friendliness.

Clive Anderson was also something of a local personality, in a conventional, squire-like way. He was a magistrate. He could be seen in church and at county functions. He had travelled into London on the same train as George Palmer-Jones before George retired, so the men were acquaintances. Molly Palmer-Jones had fought with him and pleaded with him in the juvenile court where he had often sat as chairman. The families had been neighbours for many years but there had been no contact between them; they had nothing in common.

It was with some embarrassment that Molly opened the door to him, just as it was growing dark on the Thursday after their return from Rushy. Anderson was a small, slight man, whom Molly had sarcastically described after a particularly hard-fought battle in court as 'a typical psychopath, totally devoid of affection or emotion.' His diffidence, his obvious discomfort now were so unusual that Molly forgot her hostility and automatically, professionally, tried to make him feel more at ease. He moved into the house with the contained energy of an athlete, and she realized that although he was in his mid-sixties he was very fit. She remembered that he had been a member of one of the Everest expeditions. He did not look at her, but moved impatiently, restlessly, as she spoke to him. Not recognizing that they had had any previous contact, he interrupted her and asked abruptly to speak to her husband. With uncharacteristic tact she left them alone in the big, cluttered kitchen where George was reading the final proof of the *Surrey Bird Report*. With distaste, Anderson refused a glass of home-made beer, but he accepted a Scotch.

'My son tells me that you're one of these twitchers.'

There was accusation in his voice, as if Palmer-Jones had betrayed their generation.

'But not, I'm afraid, in Adam's class,' Palmer-Jones replied immediately and smoothly.

'He never talks to me about it. He's good at it then, is he?' Anderson spoke blandly, but could not quite disguise his interest.

'He's the best birdwatcher of his age that I know. He found a bimaculated lark at the weekend.'

The praise pleased Anderson, and seemed to give him the

confidence to admit to an interest in his son's activities, though he hid his curiosity in aggression.

'Perhaps you could explain to me what a twitcher is. Adam seems to think me incapable of understanding.'

George Palmer-Jones ignored the sarcasm and replied as carefully as if he were presenting a paper at an academic seminar.

'Twitching is derived from the Wessex phrase "twitching like a long dog", which Hardy used and which is still common today in rural counties. A long dog is a greyhound. It could be interpreted as "straining at the leash," perhaps. So a twitcher is a person who is in that state when he hears the news of a bird which he has never seen before, and remains in it until he has "ticked it off" – another birdwatching term – derived, I suppose, from the habit of placing a mark by the new species in the field guide.'

'It never seemed much of a hobby to me,' Anderson said. 'Perhaps I never encouraged him enough. He took no interest in the things I cared about. I thought he did it to spite me. Like the long hair and running away from school. He's in the local comprehensive now, and doesn't spend much time there. They tell me he'll pass his A-levels, but he won't apply for university. He's only just eighteen.'

Then quite suddenly:

'His mother left, you know, when he was a child. She was a lot younger than me, of course. Things were different then, and because she left, because of the circumstances surrounding the separation, I got custody. I don't know if it was the right thing. We've never been very close. Sometimes I wonder even if he's my son. He's always been a weak sort of boy.'

Palmer-Jones sensed the disappointment of the man whose

whole life had been competitive, who had needed to prove that he was fitter, stronger than his friends and whose son would not or could not compete with him at all.

'I'm sorry. I don't understand how I can help you.'

'Adam and I don't pretend to be very close, but I'm not so insensitive that I can ignore him when he's distressed. This business in Norfolk has distressed him. I can tell that. I want it cleared up.'

There was a touch of petulance in his manner. He was used to getting what he wanted.

'I see,' said Palmer-Jones lightly, 'and of course it would be very embarrassing for you, a magistrate, to have Adam involved in a murder inquiry.'

'Of course it's embarrassing.' The man's voice was still flat, reasonable. 'I've survived more than embarrassment in my career. I'm not asking for your help on my own account, but because of my concern for my son. I seem to have little authority over him, but if you discover any illegal or unsavoury element in this twitching, which wastes all his time and energy, I'll prevent him from further participation. In my own way I care about Adam. He's not the sort of boy who can look after himself. You're an intelligent man. I know the kind of work you were doing in the Home Office. Clear up this matter for me. If you come to the conclusion that no birdwatcher had any part in this young man's death, I'll trust your judgement. That's all I want to know.'

Despite a residual cynicism about the man's motives, Palmer-Jones was impressed. It was not easy for Anderson to ask for help. Yet he said:

'Surely you, of all people, can trust the police not to make a mistake.'

The magistrate's quick, almost hysterical response showed, for the first time, the extent of his anxiety.

'Have you heard these birdwatchers talk to each other? It's like another language, as if they belong to a secret society. When I listen to Adam talking on the telephone to one of his friends, I can't understand a word. How could an outsider persuade one of these fanatics to talk to him reasonably and rationally?'

'And as a fanatic myself, you feel that I may have more success?'

'I want to know what happened. Because Adam is unhappy and because you appear, in some way, to be a friend of his, I'm asking for your help.'

He stood up and spoke with stilted formality, as if he were in court. He had already given away too much.

'If you do agree to act for me in this matter, I will of course pay all your expenses and any fee you consider to be reasonable.' In a mocking voice, talking almost to himself, Palmer-Jones said:

'I could extend my list considerably with unlimited resources.' He stood too, and said quietly in an offhand, dismissive way, 'I'll think about it and let you know.'

# *Chapter Two*

IT DID NOT TAKE George Palmer-Jones long to decide that he would accept Anderson's offer. He was not even sure that there was a decision to make. He wondered for a short time if it was sensible to become involved, but knew that the speculation was pointless, because he already was. He would accept Anderson's offer as an investment against boredom. It seemed sometimes that a fear of boredom had shaped his entire life; he felt that he was haunted by a childhood of unrelieved tedium.

He had been brought up in a small town in Herefordshire, only a mile from the Welsh border. He was the only child of a moderately prosperous local solicitor. His mother had died when he was an infant, but the town seemed peopled by elderly female relatives who enjoyed the sacrifice of caring for his father and himself. The countryside in the district was magnificent, but until he was old enough to explore it himself he hardly saw it. With his wife's death his father had become preoccupied with the trivial events of the town, the safe everyday events. George still remembered with dread Sunday afternoons in the gloomy parlour, the identical spinster aunts, his father lifeless and grey, becoming animated only when the aunts began to gossip about petty misdemeanours, property and wills. If the talk approached scandal his father would withdraw, bring the conversation to a close, and George would be left with a tantalizing sense that he had missed something of interest. There had been a clock in that parlour with a loud, distinctive tick. When he experienced the panic of approaching boredom George could still hear the clock ticking in his head.

He had married Molly because he had known from the beginning that she would never bore him. He had chosen his work for similar reasons. His last post had been particularly demanding, because of its ambiguity: he had been neither policeman nor civil servant, but the decision to retire from it was the most difficult he had ever taken. In contrast, although he knew that his position as unofficial investigator would be awkward, his decision to accept the magistrate's offer was made almost immediately.

The morning after Anderson's visit he made two phone calls, both of which Molly disapproved. He still had influential friends in the Home Office, and from a contact there obtained the promise of the most recent police report on the French murder. The ease with which this transaction was completed shocked Molly. She would have felt easier if he had lied to gain the information. She gave him a lecture on corruption and privacy, but they had had such rows before, and there was an element of ritual in the argument.

Palmer-Jones phoned the University of Southampton then in an attempt to talk to Rob Earl, the young man they had met in the Windmill the weekend before. He was a postgraduate student there, but his assistant seemed surprised that anyone should expect Rob to be in the laboratory so early in the morning, and George could only leave a message.

George could understand Molly's disapproval of Rob. He was self-centred to the point of rudeness and ruthless in his determination to live his life just as he wanted. He sought new experience in a selfish, self-confident way which took no heed of his own danger or other people's inconvenience. George sometimes suspected that much of this was affectation, but could never be quite sure. He liked Rob. Before his retirement they had gone to India together on a birdwatching trip. Rob was easy company, entertaining. And he was a vivid storyteller, reliving and sharing his travels. His tales, whether of being chased by an elephant in India or delivering a baby in New Guinea, were always nearly true. He was an impulsive, intuitive birdwatcher and, when his travelling allowed, a fanatical twitcher.

Molly answered the phone. They were eating lunch, and she felt that it was typical that Rob should interrupt them. In his lazy, charming, arrogant voice he asked to speak to George and she answered abruptly. Rob liked her and enjoyed fighting her and teasing her, but he ignored her rudeness.

'It's urgent, Molly. Can I speak to him now?'

So she called her husband, secretly disappointed at being deprived of the usual banter.

'Anything about?' George asked. It came automatically, the shorthand question used by every twitcher.

'Greenish in Cornwall, at Trekewick. And six golden orioles. I was thinking of going tonight.'

'I'm surprised that you need greenish.' It was not exceptionally rare. He had been unlucky himself not to have seen it.

'I've got a lot of catching up to do after that last trip to the States, and I dipped out twice last autumn. You *are* going?'

George hardly had time to reply.

'You can give me a lift then. I might have to bring a friend.'

'I wanted to talk to you anyway.' George spoke quickly. Rob had got what he wanted and would be expecting to ring off. 'It's about Tom French.'

'I can't stop now. I've got an experiment to finish before I leave. I'll see you at about five thirty at the flat.'

He knew that they would be there and did not wait for confirmation.


They went to London first, to Queen Anne's Gate, where George had worked, and collected the report from a plump and giggling secretary. Molly was driving. She enjoyed the drama of driving through London, and her temper improved as they left the centre of the city. She drove fast and not very well.

'What is it that we're going to see?' she asked.

'Greenish warbler.'

'Is it pretty?'

'Not very, but it's a tick. It's not even very rare.'

'How can we justify driving all the way to Cornwall to see a bird that's not even pretty?'

'You enjoy it.'

It was true. She did enjoy it. She had no interest in the birds, but had become passionately enthusiastic about twitching. Each trip she became tense, excitable with panic, worried that the rarity they had travelled to see had disappeared, but then she hardly bothered to look at it. It was the chase which she enjoyed. When she was a child, the youngest in a county family, she had been taken each year

21

to Scotland where her parents and their friends shot grouse. She had hated the friends and the blood, but even then had been fascinated by the hunt.

George read the report as she drove towards Southampton. He did not discuss it and she knew better than to ask. He did not speak at all until they stopped outside the big, ugly terraced house where Rob had a flat.

Rob's friend surprised them. He had been accompanied on their trips by a number of girls, but they had been beautiful and usually silent. Tina was big, not overweight, but tall and big-boned. She had dark hair and had strong, almost masculine features. She wore tight jeans tucked into long boots, and a leather jacket and beads. She was not silent. It very soon became clear that she was an obsessive ringer. She spoke in sharp, aggressive bursts about traps, nets and rings. More than the rest of them she was, Molly felt, a hunter.

So they drove south to see greenish warbler, and there was the same tension as on every trip, the same anxiety that it might be gone; and there was the same smell, as Rob, lying on his back in the van, smoked roll-up after roll-up, and the same sound as he sang tuneless Bob Dylan. Tina crouched beside him, aware and predatory. Then there was the same conversation about other trips they had made, birds missed and birds seen. No one mentioned Tom French. In Exeter they stopped for a pint and a Chinese meal. It was nearly midnight when they started again, and when they reached Cornwall George knew that it was too late for him to sleep. He would sleep when he had seen the bird.

★

There was a derelict cottage on the edge of the shore at Trekewick where birders always stayed. Only one bedroom had been left intact, but although this had no glass in the windows, the roof and walls were sound and it was dry and comfortable. Over the years pieces of furniture appeared. There was a table, an easy chair and a couple of mattresses. Sometimes there were more or less permanent residents, but it was always the best place to stay if there was a good bird in Cornwall.

As soon as they arrived Tina unrolled her sleeping bag on one of the mattresses and slept immediately, curled up like an animal. Molly, George and Rob sat around the stained table and talked, formally. It was a strange place for a conference. The sunny weather was over and as they had driven there had been hot, heavy showers. Now it was cooler, and through the glassless windows they watched a gusting breeze blow rain clouds across the moon. When the moonlight shone through a break in the cloud and slanted onto the sea, the breaking waves were speckled with phosphorescence.

So at last they began to talk about Tom French, about the good friend he had been and the good birder, because here they could talk about him without being trivial. When they had diluted a little the horror of Tom's death with words, George said:

'Adam Anderson's father has asked me to find out if he was killed by one of us, a birder.'

'Why?' Rob was not questioning Palmer-Jones's ability to carry out Clive Anderson's request. It was the request itself which surprised him.

'He's a magistrate. He doesn't want Adam involved.'

'Did you agree?'

'I will do.'

There was a pause.

'Don't you think I should?' asked George. He had expected Rob to be enthusiastic. He had thought it the sort of project which would appeal to him, and was puzzled by the lack of response.

Rob became charming. 'Of course. If anyone can find out who did it, you can. It seems unpleasant to think that it might have been one of us. Tom was so popular.'

'I didn't know him very well. I used to see him around, in Rushy, at the marsh.' He had a picture of Tom, thin almost to the point that he looked malnourished, auburn hair, curly. He saw him walking along the shingle bank, his telescope already mounted on its tripod on his back. It had been a familiar sight. Tom belonged to Rushy.

'We started birdwatching together.' Rob spoke softly because Molly was dozing. 'We both lived in London and used to go on coach trips run by a group of old ladies teaching in our school. He didn't get any A-levels. He was hooked on birdwatching at Rushy even then, and used to sag off during the week even if there was nothing to see. He even went in winter. So he couldn't get into college and when he left school he started work in some office. I think he worked for the Social Security, but he didn't stay there for long.'

Rob interrupted his reminiscences and nodded towards the sleeping girl in the corner.

'Tina could tell you more about that time. Tom was into ringing too, then. She would have been very young but I think she was a trainee in the same ringing group. She was playing with ringing pliers when she was still in nappies. By then I'd started to do more trips abroad and I didn't see so much of him. We've been away a couple of times together. We went to Fair Isle, and to get the albatross on Hermaness in Shetland last year, and the autumn before he had a cottage on St Mary's where I stayed for a few days. I usually saw him when I went to Rushy. Sometimes he let me crash out in his room at the hotel, sometimes I stayed with Sally in Fenquay.'

'Sally?'

'His girlfriend. His first and only girlfriend, I should think. Tina was always quite keen on him. At one time she followed him everywhere, but I don't think she got anywhere. She would have scared him. Sally's quite different. She needed him. She's got a little boy called Barnaby.'

'Tom's?'

'Not as far as I know. She met a few of the twitchers when she was working on Scilly, I think. I know she's seen a few good birds. Perhaps that's why she chose to live in Norfolk. She moved to the cottage in Fenquay when Barnaby was a tiny baby. I'm not sure how Tom first met her.'

'Were they happy?'

'Before he met Sally, Tom was a typical, celibate, single-minded twitcher. His parents were elderly and he was an only child. He was really quite shy and I never saw him with another girl, except Tina, who hardly counts. He was used to living on his own in Rushy, and though Ella mothered him and treated him as family, he must have been lonely. When he met Sally you'd have thought that he was the only person ever to have fallen in love. He was ludicrous. He wanted every-thing to be perfect – all passion and romance. She couldn't live up to it. She was pretty mixed up when she moved to Fenquay. I don't know what had happened. She took an overdose about six months ago and ended up in hospital. Tom's been worried about her ever since. It became a habit. He was even worried about Barnaby the last time I saw him.'

'When was that?'

'A few days before he died. The Wednesday, I think. That was the last time I dipped out on greenish warbler. It was his night off. We had a beer, a few beers. He wouldn't be specific, and I wasn't really interested, but he was worried that Sally couldn't cope with Barnaby and asked if I thought he should tell someone.'

'What did you say?'

'To stop worrying and to come with me to see the scops owl near Basingstoke.'

'Did he go with you?'

'No, he didn't seem very interested. He said that he would tell someone called Jenny about the baby. I don't know who she is and I didn't ask. I was in no state by then to give advice.'

'Can you think of anyone who might have wanted him dead?'

The abrupt question broke through the chat, and seemed impolite. Rob inhaled on a tiny stub of cigarette and shook his head slowly.

'He seemed to get on with everyone. Even the locals in the village liked him. He used to take the kids out birding. He was still a hippie at heart, he still believed in peace and love, wanted the world to like him. That's why the business with Bernard made him so miserable.'

'Bernard?'

'Bernard Cranshaw. He's a schoolteacher. He lives in Rushy and runs the RSPB group there. He started a Young

Ornithologists club. You know, he's Mr Birdman, the local celebrity. People phone him up when the cat has fatally injured a blue tit and he gives talks to pensioners and WI groups. He loves it.'

'But he didn't love Tom.'

'It was okay at first. Tom was respectful and got Bernard to show him around. But Cranshaw's eyesight wasn't too good and Tom had a lot more experience of anything out of the ordinary, so Tom started to find most of the good stuff. When the rest of us arrived Bernard freaked out completely. He tried to throw us off the marsh one day. Said we were disturbing breeding birds. It was September! Then all his Young Ornithologists defected to Tom – they turned up at the hotel one day and asked if he would take them out. I can't imagine anything more deadly than dragging around the marsh with a bunch of kids, but he was really touched. He didn't know that they'd been going out with Bernard.'

'So how did Bernard make his displeasure known?'

'He wrote this letter to all the children's parents. I mean, it was really rambling. It said that he felt it was his duty to tell them that their children were being corrupted by a "degenerate young man with well-known immoral and anti-social tendencies." Those were the exact words. I remember Tom kept repeating them. He was incredibly upset. He didn't have a lot of confidence and he was shattered that someone should dislike him so much. The letter also said that Tom was a drug addict.'

'Was he?'

'No. He was terrified about drugs. Booze was okay, but he wouldn't touch dope.'

'How did Tom find out about the letter?'

Rob seemed preoccupied. He was looking out of the window, watching the silver sparks as the waves broke on the sand, mesmerized by the movement. There seemed to be a cold grey light and the moonlight was less powerful. George repeated his question.

'Chris, the landlord in the Blue Anchor, told him. He and Tom were friends of a sort. It was Chris and his little boy who found the body.'

Rob turned from the window and saw that George was making notes, despite the near darkness.

'Still the civil servant,' he commented gently.

'Ah, I'm getting old,' Palmer-Jones replied. 'I can't rely on memory any longer.'

He got up slowly as if he wished to emphasize his point, went to his rucksack and brought out a polythene bag with two candles and a box of matches. He lit one of the candles and stuck it onto the table. They could see that Molly was fast asleep now, her head on her arms like a child at its desk. George pulled the typewritten police report out of the large pocket in his coat and read it closely. He explained to Rob what it was, but refused to give it to him to read.

'I don't think that would be quite ethical,' he said. 'I've broken enough rules to get hold of it. Anyway it probably comes under the Official Secrets Act and I don't want to get you into trouble. I'll give you the gist.

'He was killed by a number of blows to the head, the back of the head and the neck. The weapon is described as a smooth, heavy object. Probably cylindrical. I haven't got the medical report, so I don't know why they say that.'

Rob interrupted excitedly: 'Smooth and cylindrical. That could be a telescope.' It had become something of a game.

'It's too early to say, I think. It could have been any sort of club, metal piping, even a sturdy walking stick. They don't think that Tom was killed exactly where he was found, but there are no cuts or abrasions to suggest that he was dragged along the ground.'

Rob was quite absorbed.

'If he was killed at any distance from the marsh, I don't know how the murderer could have moved the body to the pool. It's a long way from the road. I suppose that it might be possible to drive up the marsh track in a car – I've seen it done with a Land Rover. But then the body would have to be carried into the water. It sounds very risky.'

'The report doesn't mention tyre tracks at all. The police would have looked for them. There must have been dozens of people tramping up and down it all day, so that doesn't mean anything. I think that it would have been possible for two people to move him, carrying the body between them, but then, as you say, that would have been conspicuous. Of course, it was extremely foggy.

'They think that he died very early in the morning – again I've no medical evidence for that, but I think we can accept the information. The forensic experts have enormous skill and are usually frighteningly accurate. He was certainly in the water for at least ten hours. He left the hotel at five forty, so he must have been killed between then and nine a.m., but the report places the probable time of death at between five forty and seven thirty.

'The police seem to be concentrating their efforts on the hotel where he worked and are making inquiries locally. By the time they were called, many of the twitchers would have left the village. It was the day of the bimaculated lark, of course. I got the impression that a considerable number of people gave up and went elsewhere in the early afternoon, when the fog showed no sign of clearing. Any birder still in Rushy would have been in the White Lodge park. Apparently the police have started to compile a list of bird-watchers, and everyone will be questioned. Even you and I, I presume. It will be interesting to see how soon they get round to us.'

He read again to the end of the report.

'Did you know that Tom French has a conviction for possession of cannabis?'

Rob answered with absolute certainty.

'That's impossible. I told you. He was frightened of dope.'

'He appeared in court in October two years ago and received a three-year probation order. His probation officer is J. Kenning. Perhaps we've found the mysterious Jenny.'

There was no phosphorescence on the sea now. The sky and the water were separate shades of grey. George brought a flask of coffee and half a bottle of Scotch from his bag, and they drank to Tom, and to the greenish warbler they were about to see. Tina woke without fuss and dressed without modesty. When they left the cottage and went out into the cold morning, Molly was still sleeping.

They found the greenish warbler after a painstaking search of all the cover in the valley. The golden orioles had gone. George had a systematic approach to birdwatching, and Rob wandered on alone, impatient. George looked in every bush, checked the source of every moving twig or leaf. He was meticulous and wanted to savour the place. Tina followed Rob. She carried mist-net poles on her shoulder like a spear, and George did not know if she were hunting Rob or the bird. When Rob found the warbler it was so close that he could have reached out a hand to touch it.

Near the head of the valley, at the end of a lane from the village, was a tiny graveyard which must have served Trekewick and the nearby area. A high stone wall surrounded it. The wall was rough and crumbling. Rob found a foothold, lifted himself up and looked over. The bird was about four feet away in a sycamore tree. His movement disturbed it and it flew into a gorse bush. Tina had seen it in flight, but George had to wait a frustrating twenty minutes for the bird to come out of the undergrowth before he saw it well.

Tina had to catch it; it would be a ringing tick. Without explanation or asking for help, she put a single shelf net between the gorse bush and a headstone. They followed her instructions and crouched behind the wall. The bird was trapped quite quickly and she extracted it deftly from the tangle of the nylon mesh. She ringed it before letting them see it in the hand. She had very long hands, knotted and muscular like a piano player's. She let the bird go gently and reluctantly. Throughout this process she lectured on wing length and wing formula, weight and bill size. She spoke intensely, checking occasionally that they were concentrating. When the bird had been released she folded the net, took down the poles and walked off. They watched her go. Her stealthy, sure-footed tread made no noise.

George expected some comment from Rob about her, some explanation of her presence, but there was none, and he turned again to look at the warbler, which had not been frightened away by its ordeal.

They spent all morning there. They both abhorred the 'tick and run' type of twitcher. Twitching was about getting to know and appreciating new birds. Molly found the men and saw the bird. She was disappointed by its drabness and wandered off to look at plants.

Greenish warbler is not exceptionally rare, but it was a weekend, there was nothing else about and a small representative crowd began to gather. They had hoped too that the golden orioles might still be there. They were predominantly men, in groups, wearing oiled green jackets and woollen hats, despite the weather. There was the occasional resigned wife and bored, tetchy girlfriend. Rob entertained them with his story of finding the bird, a story which grew more exaggerated as the morning proceeded. Adam Anderson appeared, walking down the road to the cemetery, pushing a bicycle, and did not seem at all out of place. Palmer-Jones was curious, not surprised.

'Have you come all the way from Surrey on that?'

It seemed unlikely, but he could think of no other explanation. He would believe anything of the younger twitchers. He added:

'I'm sorry, I should have telephoned you to let you know that we were coming. We could have given you a lift.'

'That's all right.' Adam was as diffident, as shy as ever. 'The bike folds up very small. I hitch with it, and use it for the last few miles if I get stuck.'

'Well, you can always come back with us this evening. We've plenty of room.'

'Thank you very much, but I thought that I'd stay for a few days. The wind looks good.'

'This is a tick for you, is it? The greenish warbler?'

Adam blushed. He did not want to appear ungrateful, and he did not want to boast.

'Well,' he said quietly, 'I do need it for my year list.'

He set up his tripod and telescope and began earnestly to study it. George looked at the boy and wondered that his father found so much to object to. It seemed so very sad that Anderson could not see beyond his prejudices. Adam must be very lonely at home. George called over to him impulsively. The boy looked round, showing an intense look of displeasure at being disturbed, hiding it quickly when he saw who was speaking.

'When you get home, give me a ring. I'd like to see your notes on the bimaculated lark. Perhaps you could come to supper one evening.'

Adam looked very pleased, touchingly pleased.

'I'd like that,' he said, and George could tell that he meant it.

Along the coastal path, beyond the small, rocky headland, Molly and Tina were sitting together, leaning against a dry-stone wall, talking about twitchers. The sun was reflected from the water and it was hot. Molly was sketching a small plant with a tiny yellow flower and Tina was watching the fulmars – heavy, ugly seabirds, aeronautically perfect, carried over the edge of the cliff by invisible currents. She thought that if she had a fleyg net she could catch them. She returned suddenly to her conversation with Molly.

'I get lonely,' she said in her strange, aggressive way. 'That's why I come on these twitching trips. You don't know how lonely it is if you're a woman birdwatcher. I'm not really interested in the rarities. Only in ringing.'

Molly was concentrating on her drawing, but was very interested.

'Do you know Rob well?' She wanted to know exactly how things were between Tina and Rob.

'I've known him for a long time,' Tina said, 'but he's never been into ringing.' And with that statement he was dismissed. 'Tom French and I had the same trainer, and Rob went to school with Tom.'

'Was Tom your friend?'

Tina thought. At least Molly, waiting for a reply, presumed that she was thinking.

'I suppose he was a friend,' she said at last. 'He taught me a lot about birds. But he gave up ringing too.'

Tina lay back in the sun, feeling with pleasure the heat on her neck and bare arms. She was watching the fulmars and drowsing, then became suddenly and momentarily irritated because not one of them had a ring on its leg. The irritation passed but she could not return to the earlier state of relaxation. She got up and walked back along the path, enjoying the vigorous movement and the wind from the sea. Rob saw her coming, a straight, fierce figure on the horizon, and waved. He was in the shadow of the graveyard and it took a while for her eyes to adjust to it. The greenish warbler was still there, in a clump of tamarisk, about fifty feet away from the people. Rob was leaning against the wall and quite unnecessarily pointing out the bird to a group of birdwatchers. She could hear him hinting loudly that if George went to fetch Molly they could get to the pub in the village before closing time. Then, she thought partly for her benefit, he gave an exaggerated mime of disbelief as a tall, dark man in his early thirties approached them.

'Peter Littleton,' he said in a tone of stage surprise. 'I never thought to see you on the mainland again. What has happened to the bulb trade, and where is the delectable Barbara?'

Tina had reached them by now, and Rob bowed towards

her and towards the newcomer in a charade of formal introduction.

'This,' he said, 'is Peter, the friend who deserted me for
another. He had the courage, the audacity, the common sense
to marry the girl we all adored.' He was talking very loudly
and the group of birdwatchers were quickly becoming an
audience. 'Everyone who stayed on St Agnes dreamed of the
delectable Barbara, barmaid and beauty, tantalizing temptress
of the Tavern's public bar. Only Barbara relieved the tedium
of birdless, beerless afternoons, Barbara, daughter of the
largest landowner on Scilly, Barbara . . .'

The man interrupted. 'Shut up,' he said tightly. 'Have you
got a car?'

'No, but George here has.'

'Then get him to drive me to the pub.'

Molly, opportunely thinking too about the pub, wandered
vaguely up the path, still reading her plant book. George
found himself driving through the narrow, tangled lanes to
the village.

'What the hell's the matter with you?' Rob shouted from
the back of the van. 'You didn't even see the bird.'

The car was rattling over a bumpy track. Peter was crushed
in the front between Molly and George.

'The delectable Barbara has divorced me,' he shouted back.
'Besides, I've seen greenish. Many times.'

'Oh.' Rob was shocked. He considered this. 'So you're not
living on the bulb farm on St Agnes?'

'No bulb farm.'

'No rarities on your back lawn?'

'No more rarities.'

'Welcome back to the real world, mate.'

In the pub Pete told the story of the delectable Barbara and his exile from Scilly with a mixture of genuine regret and irresistible humour. George had never met him before, but had heard of him from Rob and found him larger than life, immensely appealing. Under his flippant description of his life on St Agnes and his marriage, there was an honesty and a real sadness.

'We were married about six years ago. You came to the wedding, Rob.'

Rob nodded.

'I remember it well. At least I don't remember much after the reception, but I'm sure that I enjoyed it. There was real champagne, lots of it. And a very attractive bridesmaid.'

'It was a whirlwind romance,' Peter said nostalgically, not quite seriously. 'Barbara is gorgeous to look at: dark hair and eyes, a beautiful body and a lovely bum. But my love for her got mixed up with my love for the island. I mean St Agnes is so lovely, and I'd always dreamed of being able to live there, that I think I conned myself into loving her. I didn't mean to. I didn't do it on purpose, but I knew that if I married her I'd be able to stay there.'

He grinned lecherously at Rob. 'It was real enough at the time though – midnight swims, romantic walks along Wingletang, love in the bracken.'

Rob sighed theatrically, enviously.

'In fact she was a bit dense and really boring. She had an incomprehensible passion for country and western music. Then she started to go out with the manager of the Dolphin, that dreadful new pub on St Mary's. I didn't mind. I knew that she was starting to realize that she'd had a pretty rough deal too. I wasn't very good as a farmer. It might have been easier if they'd kept animals, but I could never get enthusiastic about bulbs. They sell them before they get pretty.

'But I think we would have survived. As I said, I loved St Agnes, and I would have put up with a lot to stay there. Every Thursday she went to St Mary's to the country and western club. She told me that she was spending the night with her friend Nancy, but I knew that she was staying with the manager of the Dolphin. I always thought of him as Nancy after that. I think she was fond of him, but we stayed together. I knew that she would never leave me for him. She liked being married. Even to someone like me. It gave her some sort of prestige on the island. We'd probably still be together now if I hadn't played her at her own game.

'I was faithful for ages, honestly. It seemed a part of the bargain. But then I met a girl who was very different from Barbara. Not specially beautiful, or even clever, but she was kind and I could talk to her. And talking led to other things. She seemed to care for me. I suppose I was in love with her. Then Barbara found out and played a big scene. The girl left the island quite suddenly, before I could decide what to do. Perhaps she wasn't as serious as I'd thought. Barbara magnanimously forgave me and we settled back into married life, although it was never quite the same. Last October I was thirty. I felt that my life was slipping away in compromise so I got very drunk, hit her father on the nose, wrote "Barbara Littleton is a whore" in red paint on the outside wall of the post office and drove the new tractor into the harbour. Since then I've been sorting out the divorce. And as from today, I'm a free man.'

'So what are you going to do now?' asked George, amused and intrigued.

'I've been accepted to do a postgraduate teaching year at the University of East Anglia.'

George found it difficult to picture this apparent madman as a teacher, but Peter seemed quite serious.

'Until the course starts in the autumn, I think I'll become a twitcher,' Peter continued. He grinned. 'I'm not badly off. Barbara's family are quite wealthy and I came under a lot of financial pressure not to mention Nancy at the divorce hearing, or to spread any rumours on the island. I reluctantly allowed myself to be persuaded.

'I thought that I'd try to find somewhere to rent in Rushy. I hear it's turning up some good stuff these days. Is old Tom still up there?'

Then the humour disappeared and Rob quietly and undramatically told him what had happened. 'Tom's dead. Someone killed him.' Despite the tick they left the pub before last orders had been called.

# Chapter Three

THE PROBATION OFFICE IN Skeffingham was next to the police station, in the same tall, red-brick building, and the waiting room there, with its smell of stale cigarette smoke and sweat, reminded George of a police cell. The receptionist was surprised to see him, but not very surprised: criminals come in all classes – or perhaps, she thought, he was a product of the divorce court. A little old to be worrying about access or custody, but possibly hoping for reconciliation. She was sympathetic, automatically polite, apologetic as she showed him into the bare waiting room. As he waited George could see the plump, middle-aged receptionist watching him and wondering. She spoke on the telephone, then came out of her office, still polite, still curious.

'Miss Kenning has someone with her just now, but she says that she can see you in ten minutes if you don't mind waiting.'

He thanked her and watched her go back to her typewriter. His friends in the Home Office had helped him to trace Jennifer Kenning to the small area office in Skeffingham, and had given him a brief description of her. She was twenty-six and had been qualified for two years. Her confirmation report had said that she was 'very competent and enthusiastic, but with a tendency to over-relate to clients.' It had seemed likely that she was the Jenny in whom Tom had decided to confide.

The ten minutes of waiting turned into twenty, but George was patient. Jennifer Kenning was still talking to her client as she followed him down the stairs. She was telling him off in a friendly, exasperated sort of way. It seemed to be a continuation of the interview. The young man listened tolerantly. He had green hair and was clothed in leather and chains. He waited for her to draw breath, then made his escape, hurrying out of the door with obvious relief, turning to grin at her as she shouted after him with the date and time of the next appointment.

She still looked like a student: she had long fair hair and was wearing a flowered skirt, T-shirt and sandals. Giving him a welcoming smile and asking him to follow her, she seemed very young and somehow undaunted by her work. In contrast to the waiting room her office was bright, pretty, with posters and plants and yellow paint. She was very comfortable there, quite relaxed, and sat not behind her desk but in an easy chair beside it. She motioned him to take the other one.

'How can I help you?' she asked.

'I want to talk to you about Tom French.'

'Oh.' She was angry, but also disappointed. She had wanted to help him. 'Are you a policeman?'

'No.'

'The press.' There was even more disappointment, and contempt.

'Certainly not the press,' he said firmly.

'How did you know that I was supervising Tom French?' For the moment this was more important than to find out who he was. 'The police got my name from their records but Tom was obsessively secretive about the fact that he was on probation.'

'The Home Office put me in touch with you.'

She thought, then, that she understood:

'It's some sort of research is it, for the Home Office? The police have got all my records, but I'll help you as much as I can.'

He decided to be honest.

'It's not official research. I used to know Tom French. We shared an interest.'

'Not twitching?'

She was incredulous. She had believed all twitchers to be young, dissolute and probably unwashed. The gentleman before her was immaculate.

Palmer-Jones ignored her amusement.

'He explained it to you. Good. I used to work for the Home Office, and did some work for the police. The father of a young lad who is a twitcher too knew that. He's worried about his son's involvement in the case, and asked me to find out if Tom's death had anything to do with twitching. That's why I'm here. I really don't want to ask you to do anything unethical, just to give me some personal impressions of Tom.'

She was still uncertain.

'Adam, the lad who's causing his father concern, is very like Tom in many ways,' George said. 'He's very lonely, rather anxious. We all want to find out what happened.' He paused. 'Perhaps it would be easier if we were away from the office. Mr Anderson's generous expenses would pay for a good lunch.'

As George held the door to show Jennifer out onto the street he was aware that the receptionist was watching them, and when he turned to smile a polite goodbye, her eyes were more curious than ever. Jennifer turned too and gave her a defiant wave.

The very good lunch lasted for a long time, and George expressed some anxiety about her clients' well-being.

'I've nothing arranged, for this afternoon. There's a team meeting. I worry about my clients, but I can't get excited about team meetings. There are usually endless arguments about who leaves the tea room in a mess, and I really don't care. Especially as I'm usually the culprit. I'll tell them that there was a crisis. My clients are always having crises.'

George thought it would be rather pleasant to be helped by Jenny Kenning.

'The week before he died,' he said, 'Tom told a friend that he was worried about his girlfriend and her child, and that he was going to talk to someone called Jenny. Did he come to see you?'

'Yes. He phoned up on the Thursday morning before he died. I know because I had to check my records for the police. He was always very anxious about Sally and Barnaby; I thought that he worried unnecessarily. Sally attempted suicide once, more than six months ago. The doctors diagnosed a severe case of post-natal depression, and kept her in hospital for a couple of weeks. Besides all the chemical and physical causes, it's easy to see why she got so depressed. She lived on her own and didn't seem to know anyone. She said once that she came to Norfolk because she knew a few twitchers and had heard them talk about it, but she arrived in July and there are very few birdwatchers here in mid-summer. I got the impression that she had lived here a while as a child.

'The only cottage she could afford to rent was cold and damp. She must have been so anxious about the baby. And Barnaby was incredibly demanding when he was very small. He never seemed to sleep, and only stopped screaming when he was picked up and cuddled. She was exhausted. And even then she never took her feelings of frustration and violence out on the baby. Only on herself.

'But Tom never saw her depression as something natural which anyone else in the same circumstances would have experienced, a sort of safety valve, which at least allowed her to survive it. He saw it as a scar, an innate weakness which she'd carry around for the rest of her life. He was great when she first came out of hospital, very kind and supportive. He did a lot to make the cottage more comfortable. He played with Barnaby for hours, he even washed and changed him, to give Sally a chance to rest. He hated his work at the hotel, but carried on with it. He was trying to save so that they could get somewhere to live together, but I don't think he would have managed to save very much. He was a terrible worrier and he escaped from worry by drinking. He smoked quite heavily too, and he was very poorly paid.'

'Did you see him after he had phoned?'

'Yes, I made an appointment for him to come to the office that afternoon. He was usually free in the afternoons and he sounded very overwrought.'

'What did he want?'

'It was the same unspecific anxiety about Sally's inability to care for Barnaby. He said that she was withdrawing into herself and had refused to see him a couple of times. I tried to explain that Sally is normally a very independent person, and that she'd be feeling the need to break some of her ties with him, but he couldn't accept that. He needed to be needed. He got very angry with me when I said there was nothing that I could do. He said that Barnaby was in real danger, and should be taken away from Sally. I said that was ridiculous. He threatened to go to the NSPCC and the social services, and to tell them things which would force them to take the baby into care. I said that if he had any real illustrations of Sally's inability to care for the baby, he should tell me. He stormed out at that. It was quite unusual. He was generally a model client.'

'And do you think that he would have been able to persuade the social services to remove the child from his mother?'

She shrugged. 'It would depend what he told them, but social workers are frightened now; there's been so much publicity about abused and neglected children. They might be worried enough to take Barnaby into care, even if it were only for a short time. Sally wouldn't have been able to cope with that.

'In case there was something he hadn't told me, I went to see Sally later that afternoon. I call in to see her quite often if I'm working in Fenquay. It's a good place to get a cup of tea. She was fine and so was Barnaby. For the first time since I've known her she was making plans for the future. Tom didn't have any place in those plans, and I'm afraid it was her new independence, her new freedom from him, that had upset him.'

Jenny Kenning looked very firmly at George.

'Sally's a very strong lady, Mr Palmer-Jones. If she'd wanted to get rid of Tom she would have moved away or told him to clear off. She would not have needed to kill him.'

Palmer-Jones slowly drank the last of his coffee.

'She must have been very strong,' he said, 'very strong or very strange, to have listened to threats that her child would be taken away from her without responding.'

Jennifer got up abruptly. 'There's nothing strange about Sally,' she said very quietly. 'She may have responded to Tom's threats but she did not kill him.'

They were walking out of the hotel, a little strained together, not sure how to say goodbye. George took her arm in a small gesture of apology. 'Thank you for your help,' he said gently. 'Do get in touch if you think of anything else.'

'He would never talk about the offence.' She spoke suddenly, unexpectedly. 'He pleaded guilty at the court case. Some magistrates take a dim view of drug cases now, but it was a first offence and he got probation. But, ever since, he denied that he had ever taken drugs at all. He refused to discuss it. He didn't say that he was framed or anything like that. Just that the cannabis wasn't his.'

George watched her hurry off towards the office. She stopped once to speak briefly to a very young girl with a dirty toddler in a pushchair. He walked back to his car. Instead of taking the main road south to Norwich and London he drove west along the coast road, along the low cliffs to Rushy.

All day Bernard Cranshaw could feel his blood pressure rising. When he walked into the staffroom first thing in the morning there was a sudden silence and he knew that they had been talking about him. He hated them, hated all of them, even those who pretended to be friendly. They thought that he was inferior because he did not talk about books and plays.

But he taught woodwork and metalwork, not English litera-
ture, and he never heard them talking about his interests. He
hardly talked to them now. He had nothing in common with
them, these young graduates, with their strange hair styles
and fancy ideas. He had gone to teacher training college in
the fifties when they would take just about anybody. There
had been more like him in the school then, ordinary men
who would answer you straight, who could keep a class quiet.

His classroom was one of two in a terrapin hut. It was
meticulously, obsessively tidy. He shut the door behind him
with a feeling of relief and safety. He was teaching a second-
form class for the first period and they worked well. They
were still young enough to be excited by the tools and the
wood, and to be frightened by him. There was a soft hum
of whispered voices and the pleasant, gentle noise of scraping
and drilling. He walked around slowly, giving advice, tackling
problems, then sat at his desk to prepare a fifth-form exam
paper. Occasionally a child would come to him for help, but
generally there was an air of peace, of studied application.
He looked up sharply at a loud explosive sound which
suddenly shattered the peace of the classroom. The children
were still working quietly. The noise seemed to have come
from outside. Then there was a frenzy of sound from the
classroom next door. It seemed that all the activity of the
playground had been trapped in that room. He waited for
the noise to abate. It did so, only to reach another nerve-
jangling climax. Cranshaw strode to the adjoining door, threw
it open and yelled:

'What the hell is going on in here?'

The room was in uproar. Desks and chairs had been
piled on one side and a group of fourth-formers, barefooted,

dishevelled, were smiling aggressively in the space in the middle. Then, with embarrassment, he saw a teacher who had apparently been a part of the chaos. At least it was not a teacher, but a student teacher in her final year attached to the school. She seemed unmoved by the interruption.

'Okay kids,' she said. 'Sit down.'

They did as she said and were quiet only, he thought, because they were listening intently to the conversation between the two adults. She was wearing jeans and was barefoot too. Her toenails were pink. He stared with fascination at her toenails, trying to concentrate his eyes away from the small, firm breasts under the tight black cotton shirt.

'Sorry if we've disturbed you.' She grinned and he noticed a trace of cockney in her voice. 'It's drama workshop and I can't use the gym because they're practising Scottish dancing. Mrs Phillips said that it would be okay to use this room. It's only woodwork next door, isn't it?'

Without a word he retreated to his side of the door. She tried to keep them quiet for the rest of the period but the peace in his classroom would not return. It had been disturbed by long pink toenails, thighs in tight jeans and a low-necked black shirt. His concentration wavered and his head ached.

At lunchtime he had to queue in the supermarket for the items on the list he had made that morning before leaving home. His mother was seventy now, and although she managed to get out to the shop in the village she could not carry anything heavy. In the afternoon he had a free period, but another teacher had been timetabled to use his room. He hated using the staffroom. He sat in a corner, rigid with unfriendliness, terrified that someone would approach him to make conversation. Later he would say angrily to his mother: 'I sat there all afternoon and no one spoke a word to me.'

He left before four o'clock, hoping to avoid a meeting with the mass of joking teachers, who often met in the staffroom for coffee before they went home. They chattered like children and he despised them. Today, more especially, he hoped to avoid Mrs Phillips and her student teacher. But in the corridor he almost tripped over the headmaster, and had to walk along with him, listening to the praise of the young man who had recently been promoted as head of Cranshaw's department. Carrying the plastic bag of groceries, he felt foolish. At last he reached his car and then he had to prepare himself emotionally for his meeting with his mother.

They lived together in a small, ugly house in a street behind the Blue Anchor. They rented it and Bernard Cranshaw resented paying for major repairs, and the owner refused to, so in comparison to the rest of the street it looked shabby. He was one of a large family, but his father had died, his brothers and sisters had married and he was left at home to look after his mother. Throughout his youth he had been dependent on his mother; she had protected him from the violence – and more importantly from the sarcasm – of his father, and now she was dependent on him.

In contrast to his room at school the house was untidy, piled with papers, slides and photographs. It irritated him, but he was helpless before it. His mother left the housework to him now and once in the house he had no energy. She sucked all the energy from him, with her intense need for his attention and sympathy. Some days he tried to talk to her, to tell her about his day at school, as he would have done when he was younger, but she did not want to listen, only to be listened to.

She started to talk when he entered the house, followed him to the kitchen, touching, almost stroking his arm to ensure that she retained his attention as he cooked their meal. Usually she talked of his father. Her bitterness towards him had not ended with his death. She was a slight woman, still vain, still attempting to make herself attractive. Every month a girl came from the village to set and dye her hair. Whenever she went out and before Bernard arrived home from work she would apply make-up to her face. Despite her thinness she ate heartily and there was some relief as they took their meal in the dingy kitchen, but even as she ate she continued to talk. Real freedom came later. But tonight he would have to postpone it.

'Mother.'

She seemed surprised that he had spoken, and stared at him, her pink, glossy lips a little apart.

'Mother, I had a letter today from Kenneth Wallis. Do you remember? He used to teach with me.'

'I didn't see a letter.' She was insulted that she had not shared in this detail of his private life.

'He wrote to me at school. If you remember, he was Scots. He's teaching now in the Highlands and he's invited me to stay with him to see some of the breeding birds there.'

It was out now. He should have broached the subject more carefully, more tactfully. But then she would not have understood him.

'That was kind of him,' she said sweetly, absent-mindedly.

'Then you wouldn't mind if I went to stay with him, just for a long weekend. Mrs Simpson would come in every day to check that you were all right.'

She stared at him in horror.

'Oh no,' she said. 'Oh no, you wouldn't want to go all the way up there.'

She pouted her face to cry and two tears washed a furrow down the powder on her face, like rain on a dirty window.

'No, of course not, Mother,' he said.

As he always did, he made her a cup of tea, sat in front of the television, switched on her favourite soap opera and said:

'I'm just out to the marsh for a while, Mother. I won't be long.'

She did not seem to notice him leave the house.

Every day he went out onto the marsh after tea. As he walked away from the house he could feel that his face was flushed and sticky. The breeze from the sea made him aware of it. He forced himself to breathe slowly, to relax, to forget school and his mother. As he did so he watched a small group of waders on a pool no bigger than a puddle right at the edge of the road. Then he began to walk along the boardwalk, which he had helped to build, across the marsh to the main hide. He would just sit there a while, watching the avocets.

The avocets had only recently come to Rushy and they had young. Cranshaw had a passionate, a loving interest in them. They were his birds. He had found the nest and he had cared for them. On one occasion he had seen a group of strangers who were taking too great an interest in the birds and the nest, and had sat awake all night, hidden behind a bank of shingle, in case they had come to steal the eggs. He would have done anything to protect the eggs, to protect his birds. Now the young were paddling around the edges of the pools, feeding themselves.

The marsh was very still. At least in the middle of the
week there were few other people to disturb him. He could
hear the waves moving the shingle and the sound of the wind
over the reeds. It was then that he saw that the flap of the
hide was open. All the jarring tensions of the day returned.
Someone was in his hide, watching his birds. Did they think
that the marsh was public property, these twitchers with their
dirty habits and fancy birds? Did they think he had organized
and bullied the Conservation Trust to buy the marsh, to build
hides for them to be used as a doss-house for spiky-haired
louts with safety pins in their nostrils?

He pushed open the door of the hide.

'Don't you know you need a permit to come here?'

It was like a nightmare. The embarrassment of the drama
class was exactly duplicated. The occupant of the hide was
a well-dressed elderly man who, if he showed any reaction
at all, showed a little distaste, a little pity, and who took from
his pocket a permit which allowed him unlimited access to
the hides for the rest of the year.

George Palmer-Jones saw a man in his mid-fifties, slight,
sandy-haired, with very prominent veins on his face and neck.
The man seemed only just in control of himself; he was
balanced on the edge of hysteria. He was shaking now and
his face was very flushed. George wished that Molly was with
him. He felt awkward and did not want to be patronizing.
The man gave a terrible, nervous giggle, and with a visible
effort regained control of himself.

'Sorry about that,' he muttered. 'Should have known. But
you get all sorts here. Twitchers most of them. Got to keep
an eye on them.'

They looked in silence at the avocets. When he felt that

51

the man beside him was steady, more comfortable, Palmer-Jones said:

'I suppose you get a lot of strangers here.'

The bitterness and fury seemed to flow out of the man. He stammered as the words rushed into each other.

'They come here as if they own the place. I've lived here all my life. They wouldn't find these rarities if we hadn't put the work in. They don't know about the meetings we had, the pressure we put on the council to stop the development . . . And they contribute nothing, nothing. They're rude and dirty. They use us.'

'Some of the twitchers care enough about the place to want to live here.'

'We don't want them.' He was shouting.

'What about Tom French?' George asked. 'Didn't you want him either?'

'No,' he shouted. 'I bloody didn't. I know what you're thinking and I don't care.'

The man hid his face in his hands. George felt dirty. He knew that he had provoked the outburst, but he listened and registered every detail.

'You speak as if you hated him.'

'I did bloody hate him.'

George spoke very quietly. 'You didn't hate him enough to kill him?'

The man looked at him in astonishment, but he did not question George Palmer-Jones's right to ask. The shock of the question seemed to calm him.

'I didn't kill him,' Cranshaw said. 'I treated him like a son when he first came to stay here. I'm not married, and he never got on very well with his family. He came to see me at my house, and asked if I could show him around the marsh. He asked if there was anything he could do to help. I was pleased. No one here has ever shared my interest. Not really. No one that I could get on with. All my friends have moved away to find work. I made an effort to include him in everything I did. Most evenings he came onto the marsh with me. I thought that he cared about it. But he brought all the others, all those twitchers who came here and laughed at me. He spoiled it for me. I hated him. But I didn't kill him.'

'You wrote a letter about him, didn't you, to some of the parents in the village?'

'It was my duty.'

'In the letter you said that Tom French was a drug addict. How did you know?'

'I know things about him that you would never believe.'

'What sort of things do you know about Tom French?'

But the man was silent and empty now, staring out of bleak, fearless eyes over the marsh. The sky was grey and overcast and the wind from the sea blew into the hide. It was quite cold.

'My mother will be expecting me,' he said. 'I must go now.'

'I'd like to talk to you again,' George said quickly. 'Where do you live?'

'In the lane behind the Anchor,' said Cranshaw automatically. 'Anyone will tell you.'

George Palmer-Jones watched him walk away through the marsh. In places he was hidden by the tall reeds, so that all that could be seen was the heavy brass telescope which he carried over his shoulder.

George sat for a long time in the hide. No one disturbed him. There was no sun and no sunset, but the light seeped out of the marsh until he realized that he was staring at birds he could no longer see. Bernard Cranshaw's vulnerability had shocked him. He knew that later he would analyze the conversation, make use of the incident, but now he felt vulnerable too, as though he had been contaminated by the other man's weakness. He longed for Molly. The sounds of the marsh were unfriendly and disturbing. It was an effort to leave the hide.

As soon as he had clambered down the short wooden ladder to the boardwalk he heard voices. He thought that there were just two people, men, talking quite quietly. It seemed to him that the men had come from the small hide, nearer the road, and that now they were walking ahead of him towards the village. They were other birdwatchers perhaps, dedicated birdwatchers who had waited until there was too little light to see.

On impulse, as he passed the small hide, he walked in. The flaps had been shut and it was very dark. Suddenly, quite tangibly, he was back in Afghanistan, in Kabul, where young Europeans and Americans on the hippie trail to Kathmandu sat in cafes no Afghan used, sat with their beads and bells and guitars, smoking cannabis. In the hide the smell of cannabis, mixed and enhanced with damp wood and creosote, was unmistakable. He stood for a moment, taking it in, and as he did so other unrelated memories of a different country returned. On the same overland trip, they'd ended up in India and his mind was flooded with memories which evoked the same response as the experience had done, the same astonishment that a country could live so easily with magnificence and poverty. He was perfectly sure of his identification of the smell. Rob had smoked cannabis occasionally in the Land Rover. He supposed that twitchers had been using the hide. He was not shocked. He was, in a way, grateful.

The couple must have been walking very slowly, because he could hear them still ahead of him on the marsh. If he walked quickly he should be able to catch them before they reached the village. The use of the drug was so widespread that it would probably add little to his investigation, if he were to find out who they were, but he was interested. Besides, he needed to hurry now, to keep warm. He nearly ran the last few hundred yards, which was a firm sandy track, but when he reached the main road there was no sign of anyone. To the right the street ran straight for over half a mile to the village. There were no lights and until it reached the Blue Anchor there were no houses. There was not even a barn or a shed where a twitcher might be sleeping rough. To the left the road curved sharply, towards the White Lodge hotel. Whoever had been smoking cannabis on the marsh had headed for the hotel.

Molly was still up when he got home but she was asleep, deeply asleep in the chair in the kitchen in front of the stove. She stirred when he touched her shoulder and drank the tea he made, but did not ask what he had been doing. Only as they were preparing for bed did she remember the phone call.

'It was a girl called Sally Johnson. She said that she was a friend of Tom's, and she wants to talk to you.'

# Chapter Four

EVERY NIGHT SINCE TOM'S death Sally had been the victim of the same nightmare. She dreamed that she was trying to run across the marsh, along one of the narrow tracks through the reed bed. It was nearly dark. She could feel the wet rushes catching against her legs. She was pushing Barnaby, not in a pram but in a small, square, wooden cart. It was a great effort. She could feel the dampness of the fog on her face and in her throat and lungs. The fog was thick, tangible, with a smell and a taste. She did not know why she was there, and only wanted to get Barnaby home as soon as she could. Slowly she became aware that she was being followed and that she was frightened. She tried to run faster, but the cart was heavy and the wooden wheels were tangled with weeds and would not move round. The hunter, for this was how she thought of the person who followed her, was coming closer and was calling after her. She could not breathe. She was not sure if she was moving. The marsh and the fog seemed to be invading her body and she could not fight them off. She knew that the hunter would catch her, so she stopped to face the attacker, and stooped to lift Barnaby into her arms to comfort and protect him. But Barnaby was no longer there. Sitting in the cart like a bonfire night guy was Tom, one side of his head battered and distorted, so that he stared at her with one blank, incriminating eye. In that instant she knew that she had killed him.

She would awake, trembling. She would switch on the light, leave the safety of her bed and go to the baby's cot as if she believed that her fear was catching and he must be troubled by it. He would be lying warm and still where she had put him to sleep. She knew that she had not killed Tom French, but at the instant of waking, in the middle of the night, the image of his body and the scent of his death were so strong that she knew, too, that in some subconscious passion she could have done it, and the dream might not be dream, but memory.

The first letter had arrived the morning that Tom died. It was in a plain brown envelope with a second-class stamp and an indistinct date and place mark. Written in childish capitals it said only: 'You are a whore.'

It had worried her, that someone should dislike her so much to go to all that trouble, but she had thought that it had been sent by someone in the village. She was an unmarried mother and her boyfriend often stayed the night. She knew that her morals were the subject of discussion. And at that time she did not know that Tom had died.

The second letter was delivered by hand nine days later, while she was out at the shop, late in the afternoon. In the same writing it said: 'Nasty things happen to whores like you.'

By then she knew that Tom was dead. She sat at her kitchen table, staring at the letter, while Barnaby emptied the contents of her shopping bag onto the floor. Panic made her thinking slow and confused. Looking back she remembered the sequence of her thoughts like a slow-motion film. She should phone the police . . . Then into her mind came the faces of the policemen who had called a week before to interview her. In their eyes had been judgement and suspicion. Perhaps they would agree with the sentiment of the letters. She should phone Tom . . . Then there was the sudden sick realization that Tom was dead. She would phone Jenny Kenning . . . That had brought some relief.

She had looked away from the letter – watched detached, unable to stop him as Barnaby tipped a bag of sugar onto the floor – stepped over the mess to the phone. A friendly, polite voice on the other end of the line said that Miss Kenning was not expected back that afternoon and then would be unavailable. She would be interviewing in the office the following morning and would be at a team meeting in the afternoon. But if it was urgent, perhaps someone else could help? Sally put the phone down without replying.

In the kitchen Barnaby was earnestly tipping flour onto the sugar and looked at his mother with such pride in his creation that she laughed. She cleaned him up and fed him and survived the evening by inventing new games to entertain him. For the first time since he was a very small baby, that night she took him to bed with her. It did not stop her dreaming. As she ran across the marsh the hunter called after her: 'Whore! Whore!'

She had woken, still tense and tired, with the same feeling of guilt which always followed the dream. Barnaby was still asleep, curled up against her. The sun came through the bedroom window and made the baby's skin warm, peach-coloured. It reassured her to feel him there and she lay back, trying to rest before he woke. She listened to the early-morning sounds of birds in the garden and of cows being led from a nearby field to be milked. She and Tom had never enjoyed this early-morning time together. If he had been with her he had been restless. Dawn was the best time for bird-watching.

She thought of Barnaby's father. She could remember all that without bitterness now, the memories were a pleasant dream, an indulgence. It was sad that it had all ended so messily. When Barnaby was born things had started to go wrong. She was still convinced that it was not his birth which had caused her depression, but the sense that as her pregnancy ended, so did all contact with the man she had loved. She did not know what had made her decide to kill herself. She knew that she would not do it again. She could not remember taking the overdose. She was never sure if that forgetfulness had been caused by the drugs she had been given in the hospital. There had been so many drugs. Despite her attempts to conjure pleasant and restful memories her thoughts returned to the hospital. She had hated it. It was ugly, a collection of bleak Nissen huts, grey-painted, which only emphasized the feeling of imprisonment. Tom had brought colour with him at visiting time: flowers, posters which she hung on the wall above her bed, the wool which she had knitted into the jumper he was wearing at the time of his death. She owed Tom so much, and wasn't that just what had made her resent him?

She got out of bed and walked to the open window. The bare floor was cold to her feet. It was a sunny, gusty day, an early-spring sort of day, a day to be busy. Her movement had disturbed Barnaby. He stirred and woke. When he saw her he smiled. She carried him to the window and stood with him, looking out. She suddenly wanted to get out, to get away from the cottage and from Fenquay. She felt trapped in the cottage by the guilt which was the cause and the result of her dream, and knew that if she were to lead a normal life she would have to go out now while the impulse was still strong.

She dressed herself and Barnaby and they had a hurried picnic breakfast as she gathered together spare nappies, bib, orange juice, so that they could stay out all day. She hurried because she wanted to catch the bus to Skeffingham, and her only anxiety was that they would miss it. The postman was late. The mail arrived just as she was pulling the baby into his outdoor clothes. There was a plain brown envelope, with her name and address written in scrawled capitals. She left it on the mat where it was, carefully stepping over it, to open the door and carry Barnaby outside.

It was market day in Skeffingham and the bus was crowded. She felt very safe among the country women with their big, motherly bodies and their talk of the farm, children and home. She did not mind the stares and the whispered explanations from one woman to another behind her, that she was the girlfriend of that birdwatcher from Rushy that 'got himself killed.' Surely none of these women would send threatening letters in plain brown envelopes. The bus conductor had winked at her, and carried Barnaby's pushchair on and off the bus. She felt very safe and at home.

In Skeffingham the stalls spilled out from the market hall into the wide streets. The houses were tall, red-bricked and stately. The town was crowded. Friends from different parts of the county met and talked, and the purchase of vegetables, cloth, a cake, was less important than the gossip. Some of the stalls had been taken over by incomers, young people who sold home-made things – jewellery, basketwork, leather-work, clothes. At first Sally was suspicious of anyone who looked at her, or jostled into her, or bent to talk to Barnaby. But the market was full of pretty things. It was a kaleidoscope of colour, and her attention was caught by the bright things and she was cheered by the sense of celebration. She spoiled herself and bought an Indian silk scarf, and a pair of quilted dungarees for the baby. With a wonderful and wicked sense of extravagance, she decided to treat herself to coffee.

When Ella saw her she was sitting in the cramped tea shop in the High Street, feeding Barnaby illicit chocolate buttons to keep him quiet while she ate a toasted tea cake. So forti-fied, Sally felt able to face the older woman. Even through the window she could tell that Ella was preparing a perform-ance. As she swept into the shop towards her, Sally prepared herself to be a good audience. Ella was genuinely upset by Tom's death – before starting work at the White Lodge he had spent a lot of time in the Windmill, and had been one of her favourites – but she expressed her grief through a flamboyant mix of compassion and curiosity which in anyone else would have been offensive. She reminded Sally, loudly, of all Tom's virtues, then wiped her eyes at the thought that Barnaby would be deprived of such a wonderful father figure. In this there was an element of question which Sally refused to answer. At last the performance was over and Ella felt able to sit with Sally, slip off her shoes, drink tea and pass on all the news and gossip relevant to Tom's death.

Despite herself, Sally listened avidly. Apparently the police had interviewed the staff at the White Lodge hotel, even Mr Yates, the manager, and they had talked to all the birdwatchers who lived locally. Ella paused, and in a confidential way, as if it were a gift and bound to provide reassurance, passed to Sally the information that George Palmer-Jones had been asked to find out if any of the birdwatchers were involved in Tom's death.

In some strange way the news was reassuring. Sally had never met George Palmer-Jones, but she had heard of him. He was a vague figure in twitching mythology and, listening to Ella speaking of him with reverence, he grew even more unreal, fantastic to Sally.

For a moment there was an intense panic, when the dream again spilled over into her waking thoughts, and she believed for a while that she had something to hide, something more terrible than the secrets she had kept to herself for so long, and in that moment she knew that the omniscient Palmer-Jones would find her out. But then, more rationally, she realized how much she wanted the person who had murdered Tom to be caught, not for revenge, but because then the affair would be decently over and she would be free. She had grown wary of making important decisions on impulse, but on the bus on the way back to Fenquay she decided to contact Palmer-Jones. It would be the first constructive thing she had ever done for Tom.

On the morning after his return from Rushy George spoke to Sally on the telephone and arranged to meet her the following weekend. She was a little nervous, very friendly and only told him not to expect too much from the meeting:

'There's nothing much that I can tell you, but I thought you might like to meet me.'

Then he phoned the White Lodge to book a room for Molly and himself for the weekend. He sensed a feeling of relief, almost of gratitude in the voice that answered. He supposed that Tom's death would have had a bad effect on trade.

Sally had invited them to tea, and they drove straight to Fenquay. It was very hot, very sunny, and there was a heavy, sleepy feel to the day. The cottage was right in the middle of the village, crammed in a terrace, but it backed onto a stream, so the garden was not directly overlooked. Sally met them and took them through the two downstairs rooms to the garden. The rooms were colourful, comfortable, sparsely furnished. In one there was a big wooden box of toys, many of them home-made. On the patch of grass there was a tiny apple tree, pink with blossom. The small garden, surrounded by a high brick wall, seemed full of its scent. They sat on a patchwork blanket on the grass and drank tea and ate chocolate cake, while Barnaby showed off his new skill of walking.

George felt drowsy in the heavy atmosphere and throughout the afternoon found it hard to concentrate on what was being said. His mind wandered. He had expected to find in Sally a neurotic girl, and his first thought was that she was a woman. She was anxious and preoccupied, but still controlled and self-possessed. She must have been older than Tom and was perhaps thirty. She had wide, high cheekbones, and all her features were a little too big. Her straight fine hair was long and unstyled. The child looked at her often, uncertain in the presence of these strangers, but seemed happy and well cared for. George found himself watching her, staring as if he were invisible. She was as graceful as a ballerina. He could understand Tom's infatuation. She saw that their plates were full, gave Barnaby a plastic cup of orange juice, then sat on the grass, her legs tucked under her.

George felt that he should take the initiative in the interview, but his lethargy was such that Sally spoke first.

'I want to help you find out who killed Tom,' she said in answer to an unasked question. 'It's the only way I can come to terms with the fact that he's dead.'

'You must have cared for him very much,' said Molly gently.

'No,' Sally replied. 'Not very much at all. But he was so kind to me . . . He gave me more than I was ever able to return. If I had been able to give him some real affection, if he had been able to believe that I loved him, perhaps I wouldn't feel so dreadful now. But I wanted to be free of him and he died. It feels as if I killed him. So now I want to do something to show that I did care, in a way. Besides, I've got my own reasons for needing to know who killed him.'

She took three brown envelopes from her bag. One was still unopened. George read the two notes and, after Sally had nodded her approval, he handed them to Molly. He looked carefully at the envelopes.

'When did these arrive?' he asked.

'One on the morning that Tom died, and one on Monday. This,' she held up the unopened letter, her hand trembling, 'came the day I phoned you.'

'What are you going to do about it?'

She took a deep breath. 'I'll open it now. It's no good just pretending that this isn't happening.'

'Oh,' she said, very quietly. 'Oh, it's horrible.'

It was written in the same uneven capitals. She was blinking back the tears. She showed them.

'Because of you, Tom French is dead,' it said. 'Perhaps you will be next.'

'Have you told the police about these?'

She shook her head, still very upset.

'The police came to interview me, after Tom died. They weren't very sympathetic. I just answered their questions. A letter calling me a whore seemed pretty unimportant compared with Tom's death.'

'You'll have to tell them now.'

'I suppose I will.'

'Have you any idea who could have sent them?'

She shook her head helplessly. She was too distressed to think constructively. 'Do you think they were sent by the same person who killed Tom?'

'I don't know,' George said slowly, 'I really don't know. Have you ever heard of Bernard Cranshaw?'

'I can't remember meeting him. I've heard Tom talk about him. It always sounded to me as if he was jealous of Tom.'

'I'm sure that you're right. I'm asking because he's the only person I've met who ever expressed any antipathy towards Tom.'

Sally did not respond at all.

'Is there anything else you can tell us which might help us to find out who killed him?'

She made an effort to pull herself together, to collect her thoughts.

'No, nothing specific. But I know that something happened the week before he died. About two months ago he was offered the chance of working full time for a tour company, leading birdwatching holidays abroad. He hated working in the White Lodge and although he loved Rushy he was starting to get restless. It was the sort of thing he'd always wanted to do. The tour company was based in Bristol and he would have had to move there. He very much wanted to take the job – it was a good one and I think there'd been a lot of competition for it. I know that Rob Earl was angry. He felt that it should have been offered to him. Tom was worried about Barnaby and me.'

She gave a wry smile. 'He usually was worried about Barnaby and me. It took him a long time, but finally he decided to take the job, although I made it clear that I was not prepared to move to Bristol. I was very pleased. It gave me the chance to be independent of him, without seeming ungrateful. He knew that we had settled here. It gave him the chance to be independent of me too.

'Then, a few days before he died, suddenly he seemed to change his mind. He said that I wouldn't be able to look after Barnaby on my own. He asked me to marry him, to go to Bristol with him. When I refused he got really angry, crazy angry. I think that he'd been drinking. He said that he would get Barnaby taken into care, that he would say he was the father, and apply for custody himself. At first I was frightened. I'd never seen him like that before. He said a lot of cruel things, personal things. Then I lost my temper and told him that I never wanted to see him again. I never did.'

'Did you tell the police about your argument?'

'I didn't need to. The walls of the cottage are very thin and they interviewed the neighbours before they came to see me.'

'And nothing he said gave you any indication of what had changed his mind?'

She shook her head.

'I got the impression that it had been a very sudden change of heart though, that it wasn't something that he'd thought out clearly. The evening of the row he was late getting here. He'd been having a meal with Ella and Jack, but Ella would have been the last person to try to persuade him not to take the job. She'd understand what it meant to him.'

'Did you hear from Tom again?'

'Yes, he phoned the night before he died.'

'You spoke to him? Even though you had been so angry just a couple of days before?'

'Yes. You must understand that I had no right to be angry with him. I owed him so much. When he phoned it was as if I'd never lost my temper. There was the same concern, the same worry about me. He phoned to say that he wouldn't be coming to see me that night. He was going birdwatching early the next morning.'

'So you knew that he would be out on the marsh early on the day he died?'

'Yes, I knew.' She understood perfectly the implication of his question.

'Did you tell anyone else?'

'No, I didn't see anyone else.'

'Where were you on the Saturday morning that Tom died?'

'I was here. The police don't believe me. Someone phoned from the hotel to find out why Tom wasn't at work, and there was no reply. I heard the phone but I was bathing Barnaby. I couldn't leave him on his own in the bath, and by the time I took him out and reached the phone it had stopped ringing. I told the police but I could tell that they didn't believe me.'

Barnaby was sitting on the grass at her side, reaching forward between his bare feet, pulling the heads off daisies.

Sally pulled him closer to her, held him tight. He chortled as if it were a game, but she did not seem to be playing.

'That last letter . . . it seems to say that I had something to do with Tom's death.' She was speaking softly, without drama. 'The police have looked at Jenny Kenning's records and they know about our row, so they know all about Tom's threats to have Barnaby taken into care. When they came to see me they were very polite, but they were so suspicious.'

If that were a plea for reassurance, none came. Molly wanted to say that Sally was being silly, that of course no one could think that she had killed Tom. But George did not answer, and Molly felt that her words would be meaningless. The silence which expressed their lack of faith in Sally angered her, but George sat, still and impassive, and she dared not speak. In the village the parish bell-ringers were practising. A long way off there was the sound of a tractor. Under the apple tree the silence lingered, grew unbearable. Barnaby seemed to sense the tension and toddled away from the adults to the shady corner behind the tree and grew busy, examining dead blossoms, twigs and a cracked flower pot. It was to defend herself, to break the silence, that Sally said:

'Tom seemed very popular among the birdwatchers, but some of the younger ones resented him. He patronized them in the same way that he patronized me. He tried to tell them how to behave. He tried to show them birds they had already identified.'

'How do you know that they felt that way? Did he ever bring any of the twitchers here?'

He still spoke quietly and unassumingly, but Molly could sense Sally's hostility and her growing panic.

'I used to go out with Tom on his day off. It embarrassed me. It was like being on a royal tour. Tom expected everyone to know him. Everyone was supposed to have heard of the famous Tom French. But he hadn't found a rare bird for ages and that attitude doesn't go down well with some of the younger lads. Occasionally he brought people to stay the night here. I wouldn't have minded if it had happened more often. I enjoyed the company but Tom was afraid that it disturbed Barnaby.'

'Who did Tom bring to stay?'

'Rob Earl came most often, and there was a schoolboy who stayed a couple of times.'

'Adam Anderson?'

'I can't remember his name. He was very quiet.'

'Are there any other twitchers who were friends of yours, anyone you know at all well?'

Molly noticed a sudden tension, as if for a moment the panic had taken over. She thought that Sally would be unable to answer but the sensation passed so swiftly that Molly wondered if she had imagined it. Sally was replying calmly:

'No, just acquaintances I had met through Tom.'

'How did Tom get on with the other staff in the hotel?'

She shrugged.

'I think that they thought he was mad. But most people think that twitchers are mad. He used to go drinking with one of the chefs called Dennis. He wasn't specially friendly with any of them.'

'Do you know anything about his conviction for possession of cannabis?'

There was a slight hesitation before she shook her head.

'No, he never talked about it.'

It was obvious then that she wanted them to go. She began to talk about Barnaby's bedtime and to collect together the tea things.

George stayed, refusing to take these hints, even when Barnaby began to cry in a tired, bad-tempered way. He felt oddly dissatisfied. He knew that there was an important question still to be asked, but the essence of it eluded him. He had come close to it at one point, but his attention had wandered, so that he could not focus on it, could not form it precisely. Yet, still he could not take the decision to go. Molly finally dragged him away. He felt like a stubborn, ill-tempered child as she said goodbye to Sally. She almost seemed to be apologizing for his churlish behaviour. In the car he could sense her anger.

'What's the matter, my dear?' he asked in a voice which was meant to sound conciliatory, but sounded only tired and a little pompous.

'Why did you treat her like that? You treated her like a suspect.'

'She is a suspect.'

'But the anonymous letters . . . Surely they clear her of suspicion.'

'Do they? It seems odd that the first letter arrived on the day of Tom's death. Nobody but Sally knew that he planned to be on the marsh early. It was unusual for him to go bird-watching before work and he doesn't seem to have discussed it with anyone else. If the letter was conjured out of the same sense of hatred as the murder, then the person who committed both acts must have had the gift of second sight. I'd guess that the letter was posted on the Thursday before he died. The postmark was blurred, but it only had a second-class stamp. I doubt if Tom himself knew on Thursday that he would go out to the marsh on Saturday.'

'Are you suggesting that Sally sent the letters to herself? Because she wouldn't have known either. He didn't phone her until Friday night. Anyway, why should she draw attention to herself?'

'In the hope that people would react in just the way that you've done.'

George carefully took her hand.

'I liked her too,' he said. He paused, and for the first time that afternoon his thoughts cleared. 'Unless the letter-writer guessed that Tom would be out on the marsh early Saturday morning – and someone who knew him well and had seen the weather forecast could have guessed – the letters and the murder must be completely separate. That is possible, but it would be a very strange coincidence.'

# Chapter Five

THROUGHOUT THE AFTERNOON GEORGE Palmer-Jones had felt lethargy settle upon him like a fine dust. He felt tainted and constricted by the lack of energy. He recognized the mood and knew that it would pass, but that did not help. It had not helped him to control the interview with Sally. His refusal to give an expression of unconditional belief in her had given the wrong impression. Now she would not trust him, and it had been important to retain her trust, because he knew that she was hiding something. He was conscious too of a deeper sense of failure that had nothing to do with the investigation. She was a beautiful woman, and he had not impressed her at all. He felt old and boring. She could not believe in him, and his pride was hurt. He was taunted by the certainty that he had missed an essential point; there had been some word or inflection or insinuation which should have been followed up. He had handled the whole meeting with abysmal incompetence.

He did not speak as he drove from Fenquay, through Rushy village, past the track which led to the marsh, to the

White Lodge hotel. Molly knew better than to try to speak to him.

The hotel was set well back from the road in several acres of well-kept park, with cropped grass and some mature oaks. It had once been a pleasant country house, white and solid, a country gentleman's house with stables, dogs and a well-stocked working garden. Now it was clean, bland, a replica of many other hotels owned by the same large company. There was the same expensive lack of comfort, the same absence of staff. They almost had the place to themselves. Only one other couple sat in the restaurant for dinner.

The food was indifferent – the garden had been superseded by the freezer – it was badly served and George's mood deepened, and turned to rage. Molly made no attempt to intrude. She had already forgiven his lack of tact with Sally. She too recognized his mood. They finished a tiny cup of lukewarm coffee and in a futile gesture of anger he got noisily to his feet. With more purpose than he had shown all day, he made for the bar. Molly stopped him:

'Not yet.'

He looked at her. She became, briefly, the focus of his temper.

'It's too early to start drinking yet. Especially in that mood. I want to go to see Ella and Jack. You know that they'll be offended if they hear that we've been staying in Rushy and haven't called.'

Passive still, he allowed himself to be led to the bedroom to change back into his old, comfortable, birdwatching clothes. They left the hotel by a double door at the end of the reception area. This was a square room, furnished with low, impractical chairs in an unpleasant shade of orange. Another double door led to the dining room and bar. By the side of the receptionist's desk was a door marked 'Staff Only' which appeared to lead from the main building to an annex presumably housing the kitchens and staff accommodation. A bored, middle-aged woman sat behind the desk and discreetly read a magazine. She smiled brightly and dutifully as they walked past.

'Tom French must have left this way the morning he was killed,' Molly said as she walked out onto the gravelled drive. They both knew that she was trying to stimulate his interest, to shift his lethargy. 'According to your report the last person to see him alive was the night porter, and surely he would be sitting at the reception desk. Which way would he have gone from here?'

George considered, involved despite himself. 'Towards the marsh, I should think. Most birders usually start at the marsh. So he would go straight along the drive to the road, and then left towards the village.'

'Where do you think that he was killed?'

'I just don't know. I don't think that the police know. Just that the body had been shifted into the marsh. It's a very large area for them to search properly. It was so foggy that he could have been murdered right by the side of the road without too much risk. I'm more interested in the problem of moving the body to the marsh. I wonder why it was moved. Perhaps because it was in a place where it would be immediately seen once the fog lifted.'

They had already left the hotel behind them. They took the path which Tom must have taken, along the drive with its avenue of trees, towards the road. It was still hot but the heat was oppressive and over the sea there was a mountain of thunder clouds.

'Mister. Hey, Mister.'

Even from the call they knew that the man who followed them was not quite normal. It was a wild voice, childishly excited. They turned to see a tall, uncoordinated man of indeterminate age, who was running. His feet scattered the gravel on the path, his loose jacket flapped open. As he reached them he grinned intimately. His teeth were grey and badly spaced.

'Hello, I'm Terry.' He held out a large hand to them, then dropped it uncertainly when there was no immediate response.

'Hello Terry,' said Molly kindly. He rewarded her with another grin.

'Nice lady,' he said. He patted her arm, then turned to George and asked automatically:

'Are you my friend?'

'I don't think that I know you well enough to be your friend.' George was irritable. He felt that the situation was ridiculous and that he needed to assert his control.

'Don't be so pompous, George. Of course he's your friend, Terry.'

Molly smiled again at the man, who had turned hurt from George, understanding the tone if not the words.

'I haven't got no friends here any more. Not since they killed Tommy.'

'Terry,' George said quickly before the man could walk away, 'was Tommy your friend?' He spoke kindly, as he would have done to a child.

The man nodded and shuffled uncomfortably. In his transparent face they saw grief, but they only had time to see and to respond to this before it disappeared and his mood changed.

75

'Have you got any fags?' he asked hopefully, then, with a leer at Molly: 'Are you going to buy me a present?'

'Did Tommy buy you presents?' George asked.

Terry shook his head in disappointment. 'He never bought Terry presents. He never took me out neither. He used to go to the bar with Dennis, but they never asked me. And I was Tom's friend.'

'Was Dennis a friend of Tom's?'

Terry made a movement with his head as if he did not understand.

'We were Tommy's friends too, Terry,' George said carefully. He did not want to frighten the man into a change of mood. 'If you talk to me about Tommy we'll buy you a present. We'll give you lots of cigarettes.'

'What do you want to know?' Terry was suspicious, but overeager to give the right information, to tell the man what he wanted to hear. As he waited for the reply, George realized that it was almost dark. The trees were black silhouettes against a colourless sky. Then, like a child who knows the answer to a test, Terry waved his arm excitedly. He turned his face towards them, and even in the fading light they could see that it glowed with pride and achievement.

'I know,' he said. 'I know. You want me to tell you about seeing him dead that morning.'

'That's right, Terry,' said Molly very gently. 'That's just what we want to know. How clever of you to guess. Will you tell us about it?'

'About seeing Tom going down the marsh track?'

'No, Terry.' Molly could sense George's impatience, and put her hand on his arm to stop him interrupting. 'About seeing Tom dead.'

'That's right,' said the man, nodding his head vigorously. 'Dead. Going down the marsh track. In the fog.'

'Why don't you tell me all about it, Terry? Start from the beginning. Where did you first see him? Was anybody with him?'

They could see that he wanted to tell them. He was fighting to form the words to tell his story, frustrated because he was so inarticulate. He nodded his head in answer to the last question. Then a car drove along the road and swung into the drive of the hotel. Terry was caught in the beam of the headlight, like an actor in a spotlight. The light had startled him, as an animal or a very small baby is frightened by a sudden noise. Before they realized what he was going to do he had run away, across the lawn and into the darkness. They called after him, but he did not seem to hear them.

George helplessly watched him go, confused by his story, but relieved that at last they had found someone who claimed to know a little about Tom's death. He felt old and tired and knew that he wouldn't have the energy to follow the man now.

'I presume that he works in the hotel,' he said, 'so we'll have the opportunity to speak to him tomorrow. Do you think he knew something, or was he just making it up to please us?'

Molly considered, trying to compare Terry with former clients with the same degree of disability.

'He was certainly trying to please us, but I think that there must have been at least some basis of truth.'

'Why do you think that he hasn't said before that he saw the body? The police interviewed everyone in the hotel.'

'Perhaps they only asked very specific questions and didn't

give him the chance to tell them. Or perhaps they confused him and didn't understand him. I wonder where he lives.'

'Ella will know.'

They walked in silence to the village. Ella's cottage was the first house they came to, opposite the Blue Anchor. It was a short walk. There was a moon, but the hot weather had turned to thunder, and it was covered quite often by heavy storm clouds. The wind seemed to blow the dark shadows and the moonlight across the marsh. The strange light and their encounter with Terry gave the evening a dream-like quality, which heightened the imagination. Molly found herself conjuring a thick fog and a dead man moving, ghostly and magical, towards the shingle. George was attempting to visualize in a more rational way what Terry could have seen.

Ella was in the kitchen. The curtains were not drawn and they could see her from the road. She was asleep in front of the Aga, her legs stretched in front of her, one strand of her long, dark hair falling across her forehead. Jack was standing at the table, his back to them. He was skinning a rabbit, deftly moving the sharp knife between skin and flesh. Beside him, leaning against the heavy dresser, was a gun. He turned to take the jointed rabbit and the mess of skin and guts into the scullery, and saw them. He smiled a welcome, and beckoned them to open the door to enter, while he went to wash his hands.

The door opened straight into the kitchen. The warmth and the light dazed them, and the smell of dogs and apples and strong tobacco. The noise of their entry wakened Ella. She stood up quickly, wondering how long they had been there, hurriedly tidying her dress and her hair, using the uncurtained window as a mirror. She sat them in the two comfortable chairs, apologizing because there was no fire in the lounge, and after putting the kettle on the range, she perched on a little wooden stool. Jack came back from the scullery with tumblers and a bottle of whisky. He was a tall, thin, angular man. He was still a little in awe of his wife, proud of her beauty, and he was content to let her do most of the talking.

She was talking now, amusing them with a story of a young twitcher who had offended her by questioning the validity of a piece of information she had passed to him. Silently Jack poured out large drinks, passed them round. He caught George's eye and smiled.

'Well now, Ella,' he said slowly. 'Why don't you shut up and let George ask you some questions.'

Shut up she did, without taking offence. She turned to George, smiling expectantly, full of curiosity.

'I thought this was a social visit. I didn't know you wanted to ask questions. I thought all that would be secret.'

'It is a social visit, but you know everyone in Rushy so well that I thought you might be able to help. You're friendly with the birders and the locals, and so, I suppose, was Tom.'

'Well,' she breathed, leaning forward, her elbows on her strong, shapely knees, her eyes gleaming with excitement, 'what do you want to know?'

'We've just met a rather strange individual in the hotel grounds. He says that his name is Terry. Do you know him?'

'Of course,' she said. She was a little disappointed. She had been expecting some dramatic revelation. 'But he's harmless, you know. He can't be the one you're looking for.'

'Oh?'

This was all she needed to provide them with a full life history.

'He came from the big hospital over towards Skeffingham. That must have been about ten years ago. The Lodge was a different place then, I can tell you. The major and his wife still ran it, and we had a lovely class of guest. I used to go in sometimes as a chambermaid if they were busy. They only had local staff then. The hospital asked the hotel to give Terry a job. The major took him on a month's trial to do the dirty work in the kitchen, then said that he could stay. But he wouldn't let Terry live in. He felt that he couldn't take the responsibility with all the elderly guests, so the hospital looked for lodgings in the village.

'They asked Mrs Black if he could stay with her. They explained that he'd be working long hours, so she wouldn't see a lot of him. She wasn't at all sure what to do. She needed the money because her husband Billy had just run away with the barmaid from the Dragon at Fenquay. We talked about it and agreed that she ought to take him in. She's never regretted it. I think she's fond of him now, though she wouldn't want to admit it, because folks would laugh. We've never had any trouble with Terry. The village is used to him now.'

'Has he ever been violent?'

'No.' She laughed sadly. 'The village lads used to bully him and tease him. He's bigger than any of them but he never had the guts to fight back.'

'Does he tell the truth? Can you rely on what he tells you, or does he make things up?'

'No,' she answered uncertainly. 'He doesn't exactly tell stories, but sometimes he gets a bit confused.' She looked at George anxiously. 'He wouldn't have hurt Tom. Tom was the only person in that hotel who was kind to him.'

George cupped the glass of whisky in his hands, before

looking directly at Ella. 'As I understand it,' he said, 'everyone seems to have liked Tom. Except perhaps Bernard Cranshaw.'

'Ah.' She seemed slightly embarrassed. 'You'll have heard about the letter, then.'

George nodded. 'Was it common knowledge in the village?'

'Oh yes. There were six or seven children who went to Tom and asked him to take them birdwatching. The parents of all those kids got letters from Bernard about Tom.'

'How did the parents react?'

'It made me so cross.'

She relived her anger at the memory of battles fought on Tom's behalf with neighbours and customers.

'A lot of them believed it and stopped their kids from going out on the marsh with Tom. You see, Bernard was born and brought up in the village and Tom was an incomer . . .'

'With long hair and a girlfriend who was an unmarried mother,' George finished. 'Yes, I see.'

'He couldn't have killed him.' Jack spoke suddenly. He was apologetic because he had interrupted. He almost blushed. They stared at him, surprised at his outburst. 'Cranshaw couldn't have killed Tom. Not early on that Saturday morning.'

'And how do you know that?' Ella asked, curious, a little offended at having to admit her ignorance.

'His mother had fallen again. Don't you remember? I did tell you.' He looked at her wistfully, hoping that she would be able to relieve him of the burden of telling his story. As she looked blank, he continued.

'I was on my way to dig bait on the shore at the bottom of Anchor Lane. It was early – well before six, I'd guess. I'd just parked my car on that bit of grass at the end of the lane when Bernard came out of the house. There was a real thick fog, but I could tell that he was agitated. He must have seen me but he didn't say anything. He was in an awful state. I went up to him and asked if I could help and he almost broke down. He was worried about his mother who'd had a fall. He said she'd got out of bed to go to the bathroom, then must have tripped, because he'd found her at the bottom of the stairs. They're not on the phone. I'd done a bit of first aid so I went in to have a look at her. She didn't seem too bad, only shaken and a bit bruised, but she was making a terrible fuss. I could tell that Bernard was worried so I said that I'd go and fetch Dr Jamieson. I drove round to his house. I was there for some time.' He looked at Ella. 'You know what the doctor's like.'

Ella snorted, expressing her disapproval of the elderly doctor who was notorious for his lack of urgency and absent-mindedness.

'It took him a long time to get dressed and ready, so it was nearly seven thirty by the time we reached Bernard's house.'

'So you waited for the doctor,' George said. 'You didn't drive straight back to Anchor Lane.'

'No, I waited. The doctor was worried about driving in the fog so I took him in my car.'

'Did you notice anything unusual on the road? Did you see anyone?'

'I can't remember. It was hard work just to keep the car on the road. I've never known a fog like that one.'

'So Bernard Cranshaw was alone for over an hour while you were fetching the doctor?'

'Well, he wasn't alone. His mother was with him.'

'He wouldn't have left his mother to go out on the marsh,'

said Ella, eager to contribute. 'He's very close to his mother, isn't he, Jack?'

Jack nodded.

'Was Bernard dressed when he came out of the house to tell you about his mother's fall?' George asked.

Jack nodded again. 'He said that he'd got up early to go out birdwatching.'

'When you came back with the doctor was there any sign that he'd been out at all?'

'I got the impression that he'd stayed with his mother, but it never occurred to me that he might have gone out.'

'Has Bernard ever been married?' asked Molly, trying to form a picture of the strange man whom George had described to her.

'No,' Ella replied. 'There was some talk about it a few years back when he was seeing a lot of a nurse in Skeffingham, but his mother was very ill again, and nothing came of it.'

'How long did the doctor stay at the Cranshaws' house?' George found the whole incident of Cranshaw's mother frustrating. He could not quite believe it.

'Oh, only a matter of minutes I think. There was nothing seriously wrong with Mrs Cranshaw. I waited and took the doctor home. Then I went back to Anchor Lane to start baitdigging. Bernard was still there then.'

'Did he say anything to you?'

'No, I didn't even see him. I could hear him and his mother talking. They'd left the window open.'

'You must be right then,' said George reluctantly. 'He didn't kill Tom French. I suppose that he might have gone out in the hour when you were fetching the doctor, but it wouldn't have given him much time, especially as the murderer moved the body. He had no way of knowing that you'd take so long. The forensic report said that it was possible, although unlikely, that he was killed after seven thirty. He was certainly dead by nine. What time did you get back to Anchor Lane after taking the doctor home?'

'It must have been about eight fifteen, but Bernard didn't leave the house before nine. I was working at that end of the beach and I could hear them talking. You know how sound carries in the fog.'

'In that case I think that we can discount Bernard Cranshaw.'

In the silence that followed, Jack refilled the glasses and Ella made tea. When she was settled on her stool once more, George turned to her.

'Tom came to have a meal with you a few days before he died. How did he seem? Can you remember what you were talking about?'

'The police asked me that,' she said, 'so I've been thinking about it. He didn't seem very different. He was a bit quiet, but he'd been working all day and I thought that he was tired.'

'And can you remember what you were talking about?'

'Yes,' she said. 'I'd had a letter from Peter Littleton. It was a shame his marriage didn't work out, but what a letter it was! It made me laugh out loud when I read it and I had Sandra in fits when I told her some of the things he'd written. I thought it might cheer Tom up a bit so I read it to him.'

'Did it cheer him up?'

'No. He didn't seem to find it funny at all.'

They left Ella and Jack's warm kitchen reluctantly. George was more eager to go than Molly, who was enjoying the conversation. She always felt at home and relaxed there. George felt restless, uncertain. All the information he had gained during the day led in circles. The frustration and helplessness were returning. It was his fault. He should have asked different questions of different people. The only person to claim to see the body couldn't be trusted to give a reliable account of events and they had allowed him to run away!

But now, at least, he had some information. He had something to work on. He knew that he would sleep badly. Even in sleep his mind would be working, sorting through the information. He could feel already the tension of insomnia.

It was to put off the moment when he would have to attempt to sleep that he went into the hotel bar. It was very near to closing time. The bar had been unpleasantly modernized and there was a lot of noise. George regretted the restlessness which had made him leave Ella's kitchen. A large young man, with long greasy hair tied back in a ponytail, still wearing the check trousers which identified him as a member of the kitchen staff, was sitting at the bar. He seemed to be telling a rude, unfunny joke to the barman. The barman, who had seen George enter and seemed inclined to serve him, motioned to the big man to stop.

'Now now, Den. Tell me later.'

George looked with renewed interest at the other customer. Dennis. The chef who had gone drinking with Tom. He ordered a drink for himself, then with an exaggerated politeness asked if he could buy one for Dennis. The young man expressed surprise at his good fortune rather than thanks, but allowed himself to be taken to a corner where they would not be overheard.

'I'm interested in finding out how Tom French died,' George said. He was in no mood for subtlety. 'I understand that you were a friend of his.'

'Well, I don't know about a friend. We used to have a few drinks together after work.' The man had a West-Country accent. He was very suspicious.

'I was talking to Terry this evening. He seemed to imply that you and Tom were friends.' George was at his most pompous.

'Terry!' Dennis's derision was directed not only at Terry, but at George for being so gullible. 'You don't want to listen to him.'

George was goaded into direct attack.

'Someone working at this hotel smokes cannabis. Is it you?'

Dennis was frightened.

'Don't you talk like that. If anyone hears you I could lose my job.'

'So you admit that you do?'

'No, of course I don't.'

'Where did you get it from? From Tom French?'

'Tom? Tom never smoked.' The astonishment in that reply at least seemed genuine to George.

Dennis had answered the questions despite himself, but after his last outburst he seemed to realize what he was doing. He stood up, levering his huge body off the chair by leaning on the table. He thrust his face towards George.

'You leave me alone,' he said. 'You hear. You don't know what you're messing with.'

With a swagger, he left the room.

The next day Molly went to find Terry. She waited until the receptionist was answering the telephone before going through the door marked 'Staff Only'. The corridor was dirty and untidy, cluttered with furniture awaiting repair, tools, overalls.

Terry was alone in the kitchen. He was leaning over a huge sink. His hair was long in the front, and he was peering through it, concentrating hard on the pan he was cleaning. He heard Molly close the door behind her.

'You get out of here,' he said. 'You're not allowed in here. Dennis, he'll have a fit if he sees you in here.'

'You promised to tell me all about Tom. Look, I've brought you some cigarettes.'

She held the packet towards him. But he was very nervous because she was in the kitchen, and it was forbidden to let anyone in the kitchen.

'Dennis is my friend,' he said, taking the cigarettes, as if that fact had been disputed. 'Dennis says that if I talk to you he'll make them send me back to the hospital.'

'That doesn't sound very friendly.'

Terry, after many years' practice, was sensitive to mockery. He peered at her suspiciously, hurt. He looked sulky and betrayed and stood fidgeting, waiting for her to go.

'You said you were my friend.'

'Terry, I am your friend.'

She could only see the bottom half of his face because of the long, untidy fringe. He almost seemed to hide behind it. Molly watched him and waited for some reaction. His clothes were patched and ill-fitting, but they were clean and so was he. Mrs Black looked after him well. His face was blank, and he faced her, sullen and unresponsive.

'Terry,' she said in desperation, 'if I buy you a present, any present you like, will you tell me about Tommy?'

'What I told you about Tommy, it wasn't the truth.' He spoke flatly, not trying to sound convincing, not caring. He peered through his hair, squinting up to look at her defiantly.

'Why did you lie about Tommy?'

'Because I'm batty.' He laughed, bending double in a mirth-less parody of laughter. 'Batty Terry.'

She left the kitchen, knowing further persuasion to be pointless. George had frightened Dennis so much that the chef had threatened Terry. She was worried that George would blame himself, and that the self-doubt would return. But when she found him he hardly seemed to listen to what she had to say. Ella had phoned him. There was a penduline tit at Scardrift Flat, near Scarsea. He had packed and wanted to leave immediately.

# Chapter Six

EVERYONE OF ANY CONSEQUENCE was at Scardrift that afternoon. Every section of birdwatching society was represented. There were ringers, staying at the observatory, who affected to ignore the chaos and walked round the traps as usual, returning to the hut with a handful of bird bags. They appeared to show as much interest in the common birds they had caught, conscientiously ageing and sexing them, then attaching the dainty metal ring to one leg, as the twitchers outside did in the penduline tit. They tried to ignore Tina, who watched them, giving the occasional blunt word of advice. She wore denim shorts and a skimpy, washed-out, sleeveless shirt. It was plain that she wore nothing else.

There were the unemployed, full-time twitchers who had hitched north up the motorways. They stood with dirty, studied nonchalance and discussed their winter's work at the oil terminal at Sullom Voe on Shetland or a proposed trip to Thailand.

Two respectable twitchers in their thirties, who had arrived in a smart company car, left their wives and children with a picnic on the beach and began to circulate among the crowd. As members of the British Birds Rarities Committee, they took the final decision about whether a bird was what it had been claimed to be. They were recognized, asked endless questions about records submitted and rejected.

Locals, beginners, looked with envy and excitement at the expensive binoculars and telescopes, listened to the talk of birding exploits, understanding only half the jargon, as strangers talked of 'stringers', 'dipping out', being 'gripped off'. They pointed out to each other the well-known bird-watchers, whose names they had read in *British Birds*.

So there were twitchers and dudes, RSPB members and photographers, children and old men who had been twitchers before anyone knew what that word meant.

In the centre of the crowd Rob Earl and Pete Littleton were being loud, silly, telling obscene jokes about Vera, the notorious female twitcher who hunted birds and men with the same determination. They had spent three hours at lunch-time in the pub at Scarsea. Adam Anderson sat apart from them and carefully, shyly cleaned the lenses of his binoculars.

Of the hundreds of people there, only six had seen the bird. It had been caught by a keen schoolboy staying at the observatory, who had done a trap round at dawn. It had been shown to observatory members, ringed and released. The warden had wanted to keep news of the bird secret. He resented the invasion, the noise, the lack of privacy which always followed the discovery of a rarity. Scardrift was his place and these outsiders did not appreciate it. But the schoolboy was on the grapevine. Every weekend he phoned a person whom he had never met, who lived in Manchester, to find out 'what was about'. If there was anything good within cycling or public transport distance he would go to see it. He could not resist the temptation to give information rather than to receive it. He could not resist the glory. The warden would never know how the news had escaped. The boy phoned from a call box in Scarsea to his friend in Manchester, and by the time the majority of Ella's customers were arriving at the Windmill for a late breakfast, the news was there, waiting for them. By lunchtime it had reached Bristol, Tyneside and South Wales.

It seemed inconceivable that the bird would have moved during the day. If it was there at dawn, if it were still alive, it would still be there at three o'clock in the afternoon. A rumour spread that the warden had taken it in his car and released it some miles away along the Yorkshire coast. This was denied by observatory members who had seen the bird released.

Scardrift Flat is a thin crescent of land curling down into the North Sea. It seems that the sandy land is held together only by the mass of vegetation, the bramble and the buckthorn that cover it. Somewhere in those acres of tangled undergrowth the bird must be resting and feeding. On the beach the wives sat in the sun watching the children build sandcastles, too accustomed to their husbands' obsession to wonder again at the madness of it. They were only grateful that the sun was shining and that the bird had not arrived in the industrial wastes of Merseyside or Tyneside, where there would be nowhere for the children to play. The birdwatchers moved about the area slowly, in small depressed groups, waiting for something to happen. Many drifted back to their cars to return to Norfolk and the Windmill, and reliable information from other parts of the country.

There had been many false alarms. Anyone staring intently at one spot, or pulling his telescope out of his case, would attract an immediate crowd. So when one of the locals, a middle-aged man with Boots binoculars, nervously called to a teenager with long hair and a long list, that he had 'summat a bit funny' in the middle of a thicket of buckthorn the boy sauntered over to look. He knew immediately that the bird had been found, and one raised hand was enough to bring all the birdwatchers in the area to see. The thicket was at the mainland end of the point, but the news spread to the tip without a word being spoken. There was a sound of running footsteps, which attracted people from hidden clumps of undergrowth, from the beach, onto the one track which led up the flat. Soon the watchers were organized into a wide semi-circle surrounding the bushes. Tripods were set up and binoculars focused, and after a few minutes of complete silence, when the bird was stared at and appreciated, tiny details of its plumage and behaviour were discussed and notes were taken.

Adam Anderson pushed to the front of the crowd with quiet, polite determination. He was sure that he had been looking in that area just before the bird was found, and was angry with himself because he had failed to see it. He stared intently, his concentration so great that he could have been alone, as he made notes of the tail size and shape, leg colour, all the features which made the bird a penduline tit.

Pete Littleton watched the bird with a real sense of joy. He could feel the sun and a slight breeze on his bare arms. The bird was lovely, so small, unique and beautiful as it moved – as if it were arrogantly unaware of the people staring at it – in the bush with its fresh, green foliage. He was free now, his divorce and his move from the Scilly islands complete. It was spring and he had the energy and the will to start again.

Rob Earl lay on his back, his battered telescope leaning against his leg. He focused automatically on the bird and tried to concentrate on it. But he was thinking of the letter he had received that morning, offering him the opportunity of working for a travel company leading birdwatching tours to South America, Africa and even twice a year to Siberia and Mongolia. His research would be completed by the summer. He desperately wanted the job. But now he felt uneasy, a little frightened of accepting. For perhaps the first time in his life he wondered if he should do just what he wanted to do.

With an envy that approached hatred Tina looked at the metal ring on the bird's leg.


George Palmer-Jones had not expected to see the bird. He was ashamed of his flight from the hotel, from the frustration and claustrophobia of his investigation. He did not deserve to see the bird. Nothing else was going right for him. But having made the decision to go for it, he would play the game according to the rules. He would pretend that he had a chance of seeing it. And all the time he knew that he was deceiving himself, playing double bluff with fate, because only if he convinced himself that he would not see it would he have any chance at all of its still being there. Yet, with a certainty that was not only self-justification, he felt that the answer to all his questions about Tom, and why he died, was not at the White Lodge, but where birdwatchers were. He drove as fast as the Morris Minor would go through the Lincolnshire flatness, over the magic, apparently endless Humber Bridge, through city docklands, to the open windy land beyond. That part of the country had the feel of an island to him. The area had a definite boundary, the locals knew everyone who lived there and there was a lot of sky. He was very tense now. His mind was concentrated on pushing away any speculation that he might see the bird, on preparing himself for the inevitable disappointment.

Even when they arrived, after having paid the extortionate parking fee to the assistant warden, who leapt out of the observatory to stop them, and had driven up the sandy track and parked the car, he would not let himself believe that the bird was still there. Even when he saw the organized crowd of people, they were so relaxed, so apparently indifferent about the bird they studied, that his disappointment was real, not manufactured. And then he was standing with them, and somebody was pointing out the bird, and the tension suddenly left him.

The hunter had found his prey. It was the most wonderful feeling, the elation that followed the sight of a new bird, especially a bird as good as this. How much greater the satisfaction, he thought, to have found it. If I had found a bird like that I would be high as a kite for days, I would be crazy with the pleasure of it. I would be insane.

These words which he had allowed to eddy around his mind in drunken anticipation suddenly shocked him. He had always considered his obsession for birds to be relatively harmless, but now his own experience showed that it could alter mood, sense, even personality, like a drug. Did it also have the power to make a person dangerous enough to commit murder? Twitching was a desire for possession and that was always wrong. Was it possible, as Clive Anderson suggested, that for one individual at least the overwhelming passion for rare birds had become so addictive that in comparison human life became unimportant?

He looked around him at the crowd which now had the atmosphere of a picnic or a carnival. Rob Earl and Pete were clowning still to entertain a group of small children. With their jeans rolled up to their knees they were paddling in the shallow water, pretending to splash each other and the children. Pete Littleton lifted a little boy onto his shoulders, and yelled in simulated agony as the boy caught hold of his hair in an attempt to hold on. The intensity, the fanaticism in the faces had disappeared. Cameras were pointed at wives, girl-friends, the sea, as often as at birds. Adam Anderson had set aside his binoculars with some reluctance, and had been persuaded to join in a game of football. Tina was playing too, for the opposite team, and was more skilful and quick-footed than he was. She tackled him, they tripped and fell laughing together onto the sand. The fantasy of a sinister, mad birdwatcher, so obsessed with the need to see rare birds that he became a dangerous killer, dissolved with the laughter and the sunshine and the teasing children's voices. Palmer-Jones realized that the image was ridiculous.

There was, after all, no connection between any of the birdwatchers and Tom's murder, nothing that could be considered a motive. It seemed that twitchers had felt nothing but admiration and friendship for Tom French. If his attitude to the younger birders had been a little arrogant, perhaps that was only to be expected from a man of so much experience, who resented having little time to spend in the field.

Nor could Rob Earl's anger that a job he had wanted had been given to Tom be considered sufficient motive to kill. In any event he only had Sally's opinion of these facts, and she herself was under graver suspicion.

Perhaps Anderson had been quite mistaken, and it had been an area of Tom's life which had nothing to do with twitchers or twitching that had led to his death. Although he had always claimed his innocence, he had been convicted of a drug offence. It seemed probable that Dennis smoked cannabis; he had certainly successfully prevented Terry from giving away his story of the morning of Tom's death. But could Terry be relied upon to give accurate information, and if he had seen Tom that morning why had he not spoken to anyone else? Then there was Bernard Cranshaw. Was it really sensible to suppose that he had killed Tom French, just because the younger man was considered the better bird-watcher? At least George felt that away from Rushy he had some sense of perspective.

But then, as the penduline tit came into clear view, he knew that again he was deluding himself and that his only reason for coming to Scardrift was to see the bird. It was hanging on to a thin branch of stubby sycamore. The sun caught the warm red of the colour on its back and throat. Despite its size – it was smaller, George realized, than a blue tit – all the details of its plumage were bright and clear. He was about to turn to see if anyone else was looking at the bird, waiting to share his pleasure in it, when it flew. He was thrilled to get a good view of it in flight and he even heard it call, a soft, plaintive call, like a robin. Then it was gone. It flew high, into the sun, so that he could not follow it. It was never seen again.

With the bird went his elation. Usually he enjoyed this

time in a twitching trip, when the bird had been seen, and when it had gone or there was no light left to look at it. People could talk, drink, play darts, with a clear conscience. Then you began to know the birdwatchers as real people, who could talk not only about birds, but about politics, work, families, women. He enjoyed the gossip, was stimulated by contact with young men whose opinions he might have dismissed had they not been such good birders. It made him feel tolerant, broad-minded to sit in a pub with a group of scruffily dressed youths, and to be accepted by them, although he never would have admitted that to himself. Today he knew that he had to talk to Rob Earl and he resented the intrusion of awkwardness when he should have been celebrating.

Now that the bird had gone, people were drifting away to the pub in Scarsea, Norfolk, home. There was a queue of cars on the sandy track, with the drivers waiting good-naturedly. Rob was asleep, lying against a sand dune, his binoculars still around his neck. The hands which were folded across them were strong. Even in sleep, there was an arrogance in his expression – he slept because he chose to, not because he needed to.

George spoke his name, and he woke. He rolled lazily onto one side, so that he was propped up on an elbow, and he grinned his satisfied grin.

'That was one of the best birds I've seen in Britain.'

George agreed, then asked: 'What are you doing tonight?'

'Pete Littleton is renting a place in Rushy. I'm staying with him, and going back to Southampton tomorrow night.'

'Why didn't you tell me that both you and Tom French had applied for the same tour leader's job in Bristol?'

'I don't know. I knew that I ought to tell you. But I couldn't admit that he had won. I was shattered when I found out that they'd offered him the job. It really hurt my pride. Even after he died.'

'Did you try to persuade Tom not to take the job?'

'Of course not. It wasn't the job that was so important, although I would have been brilliant, much better than Tom.' He was only half joking. 'I just don't like losing. They've written to me offering me the post now, but I'm not sure if I'm going to take it.'

'Why not?'

'I don't like being second best.'

He looked straight at George.

'Aren't you going to ask me what I was doing on the morning Tom died?'

'Is there any need to ask?'

'You're playing detective, aren't you? I must be a suspect.'

'As you say, you must be a suspect. Have you spoken to the police?'

'They spoke to me. But they, apparently, don't have your source of information. They don't know about the job. They just asked me where I was on that Saturday morning.'

'So where were you?'

'I was on the marsh,' he said slowly. 'All morning I was on the marsh. Mostly in the hides waiting for the fog to lift. I could just see the avocets and I was sketching them.'

He grinned and the tension between them was relieved.

'I can show you the notebook if you like, but I suppose that could hardly count as evidence.'

'Did you see anyone else?'

'People were coming in and out of the hide all morning, mostly in groups of two or three.'

'Did you go down the marsh track?'

'Only later, at about eleven. I went to the village to buy some tobacco. Then I went to the Windmill for a blow-out greasy breakfast.'

'You should take that job,' George said. 'You'd be good.'

Molly had seen the penduline tit and had thought it pretty. She liked small, pale, delicate birds, but enjoyed them only for the time she could see them. If she was shown the same bird on the following day she would not recognize it. She went birdwatching with George for the excitement of the chase, the new places they visited, and because the people they met at each rare bird fascinated her.

She had not expected to feel as bereft at retirement as she had done. She had always been involved in so many activities outside work, perhaps too many activities, so that the family life, her time with the children, had always seemed muddled and frenetic. She had thought that she would enjoy a time of quiet, enjoy having the time to do things well. But she had missed work desperately. It was not just that she missed feeling useful, although that was important. It was that she missed meeting people who were different, unusual, unconventional. The people she met at work usually had problems, and it was the problems which set them apart, but Molly's focus had been not on the problem, but the person. It was this curiosity, this fascination with people which had remained with her after retirement, and which she found difficult to satisfy. Norton's Cross gossip sustained her interest for a while, but its residents turned out to be tediously sane and unadventurous. Her introduction to the twitching world had brought her into contact with dozens of new people of different ages, from different backgrounds, most of whom were friendly, most of whom enjoyed talking about themselves, even if only in terms of the birds they had seen and the trips they planned. Many people recognized her, but did not know who she was. She did not talk a lot, but she listened. A trip to see a rarity was as much an adventure for her as it was for her husband.

So while George had been studying the bird in detail she had sought out old friends among the crowd, listening first to the anxieties of an undergraduate who was trying to combine the stresses of twitching with working for finals, and was being distracted from both by a girl in the first year at his university. Vera, mocked and teased by the men – more, Molly thought, because she frightened and attracted them than because they found her genuinely amusing – wanted to talk about her divorce and her affair with an American birder ten years her junior. Vera was very alive. Everything about her – her femininity, her clothes, her aggression – was overstated to the point of caricature. Despite her noise, Molly found her very restful. Vera always did all the talking. Molly had only met Pete Littleton once before, at Trekewick, but she had found him entertaining, and she was flattered when he recognized her and came to talk to her. He, of all the people with whom she had spoken that afternoon, seemed unequivocally happy.

'I know that I'll get bored by the freedom very soon,' he said. 'So I intend to enjoy every minute of it before I do.'

'Was it really so bad being married to Barbara and living on St Agnes?'

'Oh, it wasn't only Barbara,' he replied vaguely. 'There were other worries. But they're all cleared up now. So today I've seen a new bird, the sun's shining, and I refuse to talk about anything unpleasant.'

And he had charmed her with his description of his return to Rushy, Ella's reaction to him, the cottage he had rented there and his views of the teaching profession and his aim to reform it.

'Rushy is so special,' he said, 'because most of the locals are happy to have birders around. They think we're a bit mad, but they treat us like human beings. On Scilly the islanders barricade themselves in for the autumn. They hate the birdwatchers. I suppose there are so many birders on Scilly in October that there's bound to be some damage. There is one bloke, though, in Rushy who doesn't seem very friendly towards us. I was out on the marsh early one morning last week and someone started to fire an airgun at me. I don't suppose it could have done me any real damage, but it was pretty frightening. He wasn't a kid either. It was a middle-aged man.'

'Was it Bernard Cranshaw?'

'I don't know. It's so long since I've been in Rushy that I don't know many of the locals by name. He was really wild, shouting at me and shaking his fist. I was just out on the reserve watching the avocet chicks.'

Pete shook his head, wondering at the odd behaviour of the man on the marsh, but not really worried by it. He looked at his watch, remarked that the pub would be open and walked away to find Rob.

The beach was nearly empty now and, with the people, the light was draining away from the flat. The sea was quite calm and the sand where Molly sat was still warm. Soon only two figures remained. They lay on the soft, dry sand, quite near to her, but oblivious of her. They were two young people, lying on their stomachs, close together but not touching. They were deep in conversation, running their fingers through the sand. She recognized them: Adam and Tina, long dark hair next to long fair hair. She watched them tenderly and with, she told herself, an old woman's romantic spirit, she hoped that they were falling in love.

The pub was crowded with celebrating birdwatchers. The path to the bar was an obstacle race of tripods and telescopes, cross-legged teenagers and pints of beer. In a cramped corner a darts match was being played between the Scarsea team and the best of the twitchers. An ancient jukebox played muffled Rolling Stones.

George and Molly sat in the window seat, separated from the rest of the room by the noise and the smoke. They could not have been overheard.

'So Bernard Cranshaw has been taking pot shots at Pete Littleton?'

'I suppose it was him. The description sounds right.'

'I've still not worked out how Bernard knew that Tom had a conviction for a drug offence. Tom seems to have made every effort to keep it quiet. I wouldn't have thought that Bernard would have been friendly with the types at the White Lodge. I should have mentioned his name to Dennis.'

Molly looked out at the crowded room, picking up odd phrases of shouted conversation. Involved as she was in her discussion with George she was still interested in what was going on around her.

George was talking again, and she had to concentrate to hear what he was saying.

'So you talked to Rob Earl about the Bristol job.' She

repeated his words to confirm that she had heard him correctly.

George was impatient. 'Yes, I did. He said that the only reason he didn't mention it was that his pride was hurt.'

'That certainly sounds like Rob.'

'I suppose so. But it was pretty silly not to tell me before.'

They sat in silence, drinking. George seemed deep in thought and Molly's attention was once more drawn to the birdwatchers. A group of teenagers sat in a tight circle on the floor. From the scraps of conversation she knew that they were talking about birds.

'But how did you know that it was bimaculated lark, Adam?' asked a dark-haired boy with a painfully thin moustache. 'Did it hit you straight away?'

Molly closely studied the boy who replied. On the beach she had been aware of him, but she had not looked at him. This was Anderson's boy, whose distress at Tom's death had caused the investigation to take place. George had said that he was lonely, loveless. Tina would be good for him. She would bully him into happiness. Certainly he seemed animated enough as he answered.

'It was obvious really. It either had to be bimaculated or calandra, and once I got a good view of it . . .' and there followed a list of intricate plumage details. Molly lost interest and turned her attention elsewhere, thinking fleetingly that at least birdwatching compensated a little for any problems at home.

George was wishing that he could relax as he usually did on an occasion such as this. It had always been like this when he was working. There had always been the irritation, the tension and the constructive bad temper, but even in the middle of an investigation he had been able to relax by bird-watching. Now he was denied even that. With a sudden childish anger at his discomfort, because he was not experiencing his usual high after a tick, he wondered whether he should give it all up: not only the investigation into Tom's death, but birdwatching, twitching. It was an obsession. The depth of his feeling as they had driven to Scardrift had upset him. He was too mature to lose control in that way. He was vainly trying to contemplate a life in which birdwatching had no place when he saw Adam Anderson diffidently pushing through the crowd towards him. He had been to the bar and was carrying a drink each for Molly and George. He blushed as he set the drinks on the table for them, obviously uncertain whether his gesture of generosity would be regarded as impertinence.

Molly was immediately and suitably appreciative. The boy relaxed.

'I hope you don't mind my asking, but at Trekewick you said that you'd like to see my notes on the bimaculated lark. If you're free one night next week, perhaps I could bring them round to show you,' he mumbled shyly.

George felt touched and guilty. At Trekewick he had made a vague, offhand invitation. Adam had been looking forward to the visit, had been waiting for a definite invitation which had never arrived.

'I do want to see those notes very much,' he said with some sincerity. 'Come tomorrow evening for supper, at about seven. That's convenient for you, Molly, isn't it?'

Molly nodded. She found Adam an interesting young man, and she was curious to see if he would mention Tina.

An enthusiastic discussion between George and Adam

followed about the diagnostic features of penduline tit. By the end of the evening George was playing darts for the twitchers' B team, and all thought of retirement was forgotten.

# Chapter Seven

TERRY COULD NOT SETTLE to work after talking to Molly. He felt restless and uncomfortable. She was a nice lady and he had upset her. She would have been his friend. Now she would not like him. He brushed his hair back from his face and rubbed his eyes with the back of a red, wet hand. In the sink the water was cold and the pan was still dirty. Then he remembered the cigarettes and immediately all thoughts of Molly disappeared. But he was not allowed to smoke in the kitchen. It was better to leave work early than to smoke in the kitchen. He filled the pan with clean water and started to scrape the remnants of burnt food from the sides, but the thought of the cigarettes distracted him. He left the pan in the sink, wiped his hands on a greasy tea towel, and went out of the hotel quietly, by his own secret way, so that no one would see him.

He did not go home. Mrs Black would be cross because he had left work early, and she did not like him to smoke. It was very hot, very sunny, and he walked through the village feeling brave because he ought to be at work.

Then he decided to run away. Dennis did not make him

decide. Dennis shouted a lot, but he was used to Dennis. He was walking past the bookshop, staring in at the window at the posters and shiny covers on the books. Inside there was a birdwatcher, elderly and innocent, browsing, binoculars around his neck. Terry had never seen him before. But it was then that he decided to run away, because there were always birdwatchers in Rushy. The binoculars reminded him of the person he had seen on the marsh track with Tom. Sooner or later that person would come to Rushy again, and would see Terry and would kill him too.

Terry had run away before. Not from Mrs Black. He liked her and would be sad to leave her. He had run away from children's homes when he was a boy, and once from the hospital. He had been good at it and it always took them a long time to catch him.

He was excited about running away, and wished that he could tell someone, but it was Sunday and everywhere was quiet. Only the tourist shops were open and they were mostly empty. As he walked past the village hall a group of children spilled out of their Sunday school class and began racing and fighting. They hardly noticed him, and when a few, through habit, called after him: 'Batty Terry, Batty Terry,' there was no malice in it. He waved to them and watched them chase away home to their Sunday lunches.

With the disappearance of the children the village seemed to grow even hotter, more sleepy. He walked aimlessly, not making any plans. He had forgotten why he was going, but a memory of his fear, though vague, kept him moving through the village towards the shore. Through open windows came the smell of cooking and lunchtime sounds and the voices of babies. He smoked one of his cigarettes, enjoying it thoroughly, and turned into Anchor Lane.

The door of the Anchor was open and he was nearly distracted. He had been paid the day before and had some money left after paying Mrs Black for his keep. Inside the pub two men stood at the bar. It looked cool and brown in there and he had enough money to buy them a drink. They would talk to him then. Then he saw a young couple sitting in the shadow, in a corner. The girl looked up. When she saw him standing there, hesitating, she smiled at him. Around her neck she wore binoculars, and on the wooden table between her and the boy there was an open book, with pictures of birds. The fear came back and with a sudden awkward movement he turned and ran away, leaving the girl bewildered.

He ran on down the road, his strange, flat-footed gait carrying him quickly past the villas. Where the road turned into a grassy footpath at the edge of the marsh, he slowed down. Cows grazed there and he was frightened of cows. He had to walk slowly so they would not notice him. He could not run on the shingle. There, he stopped and took off the raincoat which he had been wearing despite the sunshine. He dropped it where he was, then went back for it, realizing that he might need it later. He took off his shoes and socks and carried them, walking painfully across the shingle bank to the sea edge, where there was a little sand. His feet made soft, wet imprints on the sand, and he laughed with delight when the waves reached his feet. He walked east along the edge of the shore towards Skeffingham, along the straight, endless beach interrupted only by wet wooden breakwaters and scattered families, the people small and unreal in the distance. He knew now where he was going.

★

Adam lay on the bed. It was late afternoon, but he had drawn the curtains and it was nearly dark. On the bed beside him lay an old copy of *British Birds* magazine – the edition of the previous November, which listed the year's rarities and the people who had found them. He liked to see his name in print. He had not found any of the birds listed, but on two occasions had been the second observer. Because of his initials, his name came first. Next year the bimaculated lark would be there, and his first place would be justified.

He went over in his mind the details of the weekend. The penduline tit was a good bird to get. He saw it as he had seen it in the field, and regretted again that he had not been the person to find it. He remembered Tina, strong and alive, playing football on the sand, and the thrill of touch as they fell together, and the companionship of their shared conversation. He wished that he had made a definite arrangement to see her again. He wondered when they would next meet. He let himself imagine what it would be like to kiss her.

Yet, underneath these normal, teenage dreams, he was frightened. Important as Tina was, the fear dismissed any pleasure in the thought of her. There was no one to tell. No one would believe him. He had thought, for a moment, that he might tell Tina, but realized almost immediately that she was the last person to tell, and that she must not be involved.

He had always hidden in his room. It had been his room since he had been a baby. Once, in some gesture of paternal affection, his father had had a new room furnished and decorated for him, a big room in the attic. There had been a table with a huge and sophisticated model train set, already laid out on the green baize. He had come home from school at the beginning of the Christmas holiday to be greeted by the new room. He had not been able to face it and had refused to move. There had been a confrontation, but he had won. It was one of the few times he had won. In his small dark room, which he kept very tidy, but which had a slightly musty human smell, he felt safe. His father thought that he had been too young to remember his mother, but he remembered a sense of her, a scent which had become associated in his mind with the scent of his room.

He remembered too, very clearly, a number of incidents connected with her. He was sure that they had happened, but he had never discussed them with his father, so this had never been confirmed. He did not know where his mother was now. He knew that she had remarried, twice. He supposed that she was still alive.

Adam wondered sometimes if it was his mother who had caused the distance, the coldness between his father and himself. She still seemed to stand between them. A relative had once told Adam that he looked very like his mother. When he was a child he had tried to please his father, but had always felt that he was a disappointment. He had lived for years with his father's mockery.

He remembered, still with embarrassment, the evening he had brought Tom French home to stay. Tom had been at his peak then, a celebrity, and he had given time, experience, even an old pair of binoculars to Adam. They had been together, to see a rarity, quite near to the village where the Andersons lived. For some reason Tom had not been able to get home, so Adam had invited him to stay at his house, proud to do something in return. His father, unusually, had been in, and although finally he had allowed Tom to stay, he had been offensive, rude, as if there had been some intense personal animosity between them. Tom had been understanding, of course, but Adam had felt awkward about the incident for a long time afterwards. His father's obvious dislike of Tom made the man's concern now, his attempt to find out how the twitcher died, a little hard to accept. Adam tended to see it only as a desire to meddle, but did not give the matter much thought. He had long ago given up trying to understand his father.

He began to prepare himself to go out. He always found it difficult to leave his room, and tonight was going to be important. He wanted Mr and Mrs Palmer-Jones to like him. He was just pulling a clean sweater over his head when he heard the noise of the front door. His father was home.

He knew that his father had tried to get closer to him since Tom had died. The new attempt at friendship disturbed him. It was too late. Still angry at the memory of his father's rudeness to Tom, he did not know how to respond to the clumsy gestures of sympathy. It confused Adam. It was easier to hate his father. Yet the habit of detached and insincere politeness remained and helped him to survive. Since early childhood, after scenes and tantrums had been punished or ignored, Adam had found cold politeness to be his most effective weapon. It gave nothing away. It gave his father no excuse to seek contact.

'Adam,' his father shouted up the stairs. 'Adam, are you at home?'

Adam looked in the mirror, composed himself and opened the bedroom door.

'Yes, Father,' he said flatly. 'I'm here.'

His father was waiting for him at the bottom of the stairs, his round face, tilted upwards, was strangely unfamiliar. His lack of height, his attitude as he waited for his son, made him almost human.

'Are you going out?' Clive Anderson asked. He tried to sound interested, but he had asked the question so many times before, with disapproval, as Adam set out with rucksack and binoculars, that it was almost ritual.

'Yes, Father. Mr and Mrs Palmer-Jones have invited me to supper.'

Forgetting his rule not to give away more information than was necessary, he added: 'They want to see my notes on a bird I found in Norfolk.'

'Ah, I see.'

Adam knew suddenly that his father was jealous of George Palmer-Jones, jealous of the confidence that his son placed in him. Adam wanted to say to his father: 'Can I show them to you? Would you like to see them?' He wanted to say: 'I think I'm in trouble. I may need your help. Please help me,' but that would have been weakness and his father would have despised him.

Mr Anderson approached his son cautiously, placed a hand on his shoulder.

'Well, have a good time.'

Adam shrank away from the touch. He said, very politely: 'Thank you, Father.'

Clive Anderson, an old man, watched the boy go, and the hatred of Tom French returned, hatred of the man who had turned Adam against him, of the man who had corrupted his son.

Molly Palmer-Jones had to remind her husband that Adam had been invited to supper. He was preoccupied with the details, the mechanics of Tom's death. He sat at the kitchen table, as she prepared the meal, and he wrote innumerable lists, and a chart that was a precise timetable of events. She disliked cooking in front of him. She was a good cook, but clumsy, perhaps a little unhygienic, and he was critical of her untidiness. Finally, exasperated by his concentration and the tiny, precise writing which she could not read from the end of the table where she stood rolling pastry, she sent him to the garden to cut a lettuce for the salad.

From the kitchen window Molly could see Adam approaching the house. On his face was an expression of profound concentration. He looked at his watch and, apparently nervous that he might be too early, he waited at the gate. He could not see Molly, but he stooped, pretending to tie the lace of his shoe.

*Why is it so important for him to get things right?* she thought. *Does he want to please us specially, or is he nervous before meeting anybody?*

He opened the gate, fumbling with the catch which had never properly worked. Molly saw the boy blush and realized that George must be walking towards him from the vegetable garden. She felt the colour come to her own cheeks as she remembered with a vivid pain her own, shy teenage days.

She could not hear what was being said and like a mime the scene unfolded in front of the window. George, a lettuce in one hand, held the other palm upwards to show that it was dirty: an explanation that he could not shake hands. Adam, awkward, not sure how to react to this formality, looked at his feet, twitched the hair from his eyes, then, glad at last of something to do, followed George towards the house. She saw that in one hand he clutched a battered oilskin notebook. As they reached the back door she began to hear their conversation, and the enthusiasm of the words distracted her attention from Adam's nervous mannerisms. Perhaps, she thought, they have just become a habit, and to watch him without hearing him gives a misleading impression. Or perhaps verbally he is very good at covering up how scared he is of meeting people.

George came into the kitchen and went to the sink with the lettuce, but Adam hovered at the door, looking in uncertainly. At home the kitchen was clinically clean. Mrs Pargeter, the housekeeper, had insisted on machines to wash, beat and blend, a freezer and a split-level cooker. Her kitchen was a workplace, like a laboratory. This was a place to savour, a collage of colour and smell. One wall was covered by wooden shelves. On them were tall jars of preserved fruit, bottles of home-brewed beer, books and dust. On the floor stood pottery jars of flour and sugar, on the walls were pans hanging from nails and rusty ancient pieces of kitchen gadgetry. It was all stacked layer on layer, glass and wood on the stone wall, pot and earthenware against red-tile floor, each overlaid by the smell of fruit and spice and cooking food.

'Come on in.' George had noticed the hesitation with surprise. 'Molly doesn't mind us in here, do you?' He put his arm round his wife and squeezed her in a joking, tender way. The show of affection hurt Adam.

'I suppose not, if you sit there out of the way.' She was a short, spry woman and she was laughing at them. She pointed to the far end of the kitchen table, the only end uncluttered. All her movements were vigorous and spontaneous.

'Her bark is worse than her bite. The rudeness is directed at me, not you.' George felt a need to reassure the boy.

They sat together at the table, sharing a bottle of beer,

poring over the notebook Adam had brought. Molly watched as she chopped onion and carrot and mint for the salad in a smooth wooden bowl. She was glad that George was being kind. She thought that something was upsetting the thin, white lad, who now discussed so intensely the plumage details of bimaculated and calandra lark.

Molly bullied them into clearing a space on the kitchen table so that they could eat. Adam felt himself relax. The beer was strong and he was not used to drinking. At first he fought against the sense of well-being, but the two people who sat with him were so kind and caring that he could not believe that they would do him any harm. The food was delicious and as they ate, George poured more beer. Afterwards there was sloe gin, sweet, strong and scented. They went into another room to drink it, a small sitting room with deep, comfortable armchairs and a fire.

Adam found that he was talking too much, about birds, birders, Scilly and Shetland. George listened, gave gentle, considered replies. Adam fell silent, disconcerted because he found it so easy to talk. In the silence Molly's deep breathing turned into a snore. She was sleeping. George grinned at Adam, totally unembarrassed. Then, seriously, he said:

'I'd like to talk about Tom. Do you mind?'

Adam shook his head.

'How well did you know him?'

'Well. He was the first twitcher I met. He introduced me to it.'

'Were you close to him?'

Adam hesitated. 'Not exactly close. He was quite a bit older than me. But he taught me all I know about birds. That made him very important.'

'Can you tell me where you were on that Saturday morning, what you did and who you saw?'

'I got to Rushy late on Friday night. You know that the weather map looked good, so I wanted to make an early start on Saturday. I dossed in the shed by the coastguard store. You know, next to the Windmill.'

George did know. It was a popular place for the twitchers to sleep.

'Was anyone else there?'

'There was someone I didn't know, an older man. He said he'd come from Cheshire for the weekend. He sounded a bit of a stringer. And Rob Earl was there.'

'Did you see the Cheshire stringer again during the day?'

'He was at the lark I think and in Ella's afterwards, but I didn't see him in the morning. He was still asleep when we left.'

'What about Rob?'

'We went to the hides together, but it was too foggy to see anything much. I thought it might be better inland, so I went through the village to the copse. Rob stayed on the marsh.'

'Which way did you go to the village? Down the wide marsh track and onto the road?'

'I suppose so. I usually go that way.'

'Did you see anyone?'

'No, a couple of times I thought I heard someone, but it was probably my imagination. I've never been out in a fog that thick before and it was really weird. But what's so important about the marsh track? I thought that Tom was killed by the pool.'

The question was asked politely, diffidently.

'His body was found by the pool. But someone who was walking down the road from the village saw him dead at the marsh track. I'm sure that you'll understand that I can't tell you who that witness is. You didn't see anything?'

Adam shook his head.

'What time were you walking that way?'

'I should think it was about seven.'

'That would probably be too early to have seen anything. What did Rob do when you went off towards the village?'

'I don't know. I left him in one of the hides.'

'And what did you do for the rest of the day? Until you found the lark?'

'I stayed out. I did the copse thoroughly and I'd been round the White Lodge several times before I found the bird. I was positive that there must be something good among all that stuff, I just knew it.'

'Were you on your own?'

'Yes, I don't like birding in a crowd. I met people in the copse and the Lodge park, but only to ask them if anything had been seen.'

George lay back in his chair, forming his words carefully.

'You know the younger birders better than I do. Has anyone noticed anything odd?'

Adam seemed pleased to be consulted.

'No, nobody's said anything to me and I haven't heard anything on the grapevine. No rumours.'

He seemed uncertain about whether he should continue. George said nothing.

'There is one point . . . I wasn't sure if I should say anything . . . Do you remember I met you at Trekewick, at the greenish?'

George nodded.

'There was a friend of Rob Earl's at the bird. I'd never

seen him before. His name's Pete Littleton. He gave the impression that he'd just got to the mainland from Scilly and that it was his first trip into the field since he'd got here.'

'Yes, that's right.'

'Well, it wasn't his first trip into the field. I'm sure that he was at Rushy on that Saturday afternoon, the day Tom died. I saw him at the Lodge park and he asked me if I'd seen anything. I wondered who he was. He seemed to know what he was talking about.'

Adam stopped, knowing that again he was talking too much, too loudly. He looked at George, whose face showed no surprise, no reaction at all.

Another connection, George was thinking. Too many connections. Tom's mood had changed when Ella told him that Pete was moving back to the mainland, and Adam saw Pete on the afternoon of the day Tom died. But what real connection was there between Pete Littleton and Tom French?

He said: 'Is there anything else you think I should know about Tom?'

'He'd been in court,' Adam answered quickly. 'But I expect you'll have found out about that. He'd been in court for smoking dope.'

'So you know about that? Did Tom tell you?'

'Only because he had to. I was at Sally's cottage with him one afternoon when his probation officer turned up. They were all really embarrassed. It was awful. He just told me that he'd been done for possession of cannabis. That's all.'

'Did you tell anyone about it?'

'Of course not.' But he was blushing, and there was the nervous twitch to flick the hair from his eyes.

'Someone gave Bernard Cranshaw the idea that Tom was a drug addict. That was mentioned in the letter which he wrote to the parents of the children Tom was taking bird-watching. You don't know anything about it?'

Adam shook his head to emphasize his denial.

'Do you use cannabis yourself?' There was real interest and no judgement in the question.

'Only occasionally.' He paused. 'You won't tell my father.' It was a statement not a question, and no response was necessary.

'What sort of 'scope do you use?' asked George, acknowledging nothing odd in the sudden change of topic.

'One of the new Optylons.'

'That's one of the short, stocky models?'

Adam agreed.

'The description of the murder weapon could fit a telescope. Have any of the twitchers changed their 'scope recently? Or have you noticed one that's out of alignment, damaged in any way?'

'No.'

'Do you have one of the old, heavy, brass telescopes?'

Adam answered without hesitation. 'Yes, it was my first 'scope. I don't use it now.'

'Where is it?'

'In my room at home.'

George gave no other explanation for the series of questions. He got up to go to the kitchen to fetch the bottle of sloe gin. As if by magic, Molly woke. Adam suspected that perhaps she had not been so deeply asleep after all. To finish the evening they talked about pleasant things, favourite birds, and birds which they most wanted to see, and favourite places.

'St Agnes,' Adam said, 'and not just because of the birds. I like going in the spring when there aren't too many bird-watchers and the islanders are more friendly. Everything's on a small scale – little fields and pretty cottages. It's safe there. I love the Scillies.'

'Fair Isle,' said George. 'Magnificent cliffs, all the seabird colonies, and a comfortable bird observatory with a licence. And a good many ticks.'

'Bardsey,' said Molly. 'Because it's totally remote. No telephone, no newspapers, no television. And because the mountain is so dramatic, and because of the choughs.'

'Isn't it strange,' said Adam, pleased that they had something in common, 'that we all like islands?'

He left then. Despite the alcohol and the warmth, he felt strangely clear-headed. He concentrated on leaving slowly, politely, on giving no impression of panic. George walked with him down the garden path to the gate. As with his father, Adam felt the impulse to ask for protection. But when, at the gate, George waited as if he expected some confidence, fear overcame the boy. It was too late for confidence. He walked away.

George and Molly sat in the kitchen in the midst of the dirty plates and pans, and drank from big, round cups of tea.

'I'm worried about that child,' said Molly, and George was surprised because she seemed so anxious and so serious. 'You realize that he's frightened.'

'Social workers don't have a monopoly on perception.'

'Do you think that he killed Tom French?'

'Ah, so that occurred to you.'

'Will you answer my question?'

'I think that it's possible. He's certainly very worried. He had the opportunity. He admits that he was alone on the morning of the murder, and he owns two telescopes, either of which could have been the weapon. But he's very slight and thin, and he doesn't own a car, so I can't imagine how he would have moved the body. And why would he have wanted to murder Tom? They were friends.'

Molly seemed only a little reassured. 'What are you going to do about him?'

'Keep an eye on him, try to get to know him better, gain his trust and find out why he's so scared. And talk again to the other people who were at Rushy that day to see if we can build up an alibi for him.'

'All evening I was expecting him to say something important,' Molly said, 'some dramatic revelation. Maybe we're overreacting, and we're just not used to teenagers any more.' She lapsed into nostalgia for the time when her children were teenagers, gawky and rebellious and still dependent.

She felt tired and uneasy, but knew George would not leave the matter alone. The only occasions of real ill feeling within their family had occurred because of his insistence on getting to the root of problems. The children, as adolescents, had deeply resented the intrusion, the endless inquests, their father's flawless and irritating reason.

She watched her husband and felt a deep and overwhelming tenderness as he shuffled his notes on the table before him. He could have been an undergraduate again, revising mindlessly for finals, reading texts he knew already by memory. The demands were his own and she knew that she could not share the responsibility, but she knew too, by experience, that she could help him.

'What conclusions have you reached?' she asked, dragging his attention away from the abstract words on the pages.

'None,' he said angrily. 'I'm incompetent. They were right to retire me.'

'Tell me how far you've got.'

He knew quite well what she was doing, that she could sense his panic, the fruitless activity. She was trying to soothe him. But she was not patronizing; she did want to know.

'I've written down the sequence of events on the morning of the murder, a kind of timetable for everyone who might have been involved. That's quite straightforward. It's the connection between all the people which has been obsessing me. Of course, most of them are birdwatchers, but I have a feeling that there's more to it than that. There's some emotional connection. I can see a tension between them. They're more aware of each other than they're pretending . . .'

He hesitated. 'Do you think that we can persuade Terry to talk to us again?'

There was an edge of desperation in his voice.

'He might talk to someone he trusts,' Molly said.

'There's Mrs Black, his landlady. He might be prepared to talk to her.'

'We must find out what he knows. He's in danger himself. The murderer might have seen him.'

'Make a note to speak to Mrs Black.' She spoke softly, but it was enough to stem the rising anxiety. She continued quickly:

'Which of those people had any reason to kill Tom French?'

'I don't know. I just don't know. At first I thought that there could be no convincing motive. I didn't know him very well, but he came across as being the last person in the world to be a murder victim. He was gentle, very softly spoken – as Rob said, he seemed to be a hippie out of his time. Now, almost too many people seem to have disliked him or to have been afraid of him. That just doesn't make sense. It's not in keeping with the man I knew. And does dislike provide an adequate motive for murder? Bernard Cranshaw disliked him because Tom usurped his position as local expert. Sally was afraid of him because he threatened to have her baby taken into care. The fact that Dennis put pressure on Terry not to talk to us indicates that he may have some motive. Rob Earl saw him as a rival for the job in Bristol. And Adam and Pete Littleton are involved because they both knew him, and because they were both there. And because somehow I sense that they're involved.

'At the moment the conviction for possession of cannabis seems to be the only factor which links them all together. I'm certain that Dennis uses drugs. It seems that he and Tom used to drink together, but I find it hard to believe that they were particularly friendly. Sally knows more about Tom's court appearance than she's told us. Adam wanted to make sure that I knew that Tom had been in court and Cranshaw used it in his fight to stop Tom taking the children onto the marsh.'

He was talking very quickly, it seemed almost at random, but he was talking with enthusiasm and interest. The sense of panic and helplessness had passed. With a sudden burst of energy George stood up and made a token attempt to tidy the plates for washing up – his ritual rebuke to Molly.

She did not respond with anger or sarcasm as she usually did. She caught his eye and smiled, relieved. Now that the crisis had passed, she relaxed and allowed her thoughts to return to Adam Anderson. She would try to find an opportunity to speak to him again. She was quite confident that she could persuade him to confide in her.

# Chapter Eight

THE NEXT DAY ADAM Anderson disappeared. He was in his room all night, because when his father knocked on his door to say goodbye at eight in the morning his son replied. Clive Anderson presumed that he was still in bed. But when Mrs Pargeter came out of the kitchen at eight thirty to pick up the mail, she noticed that the front door was not properly closed. She had not heard Adam come down the stairs, and it did not occur to her then that he had left the house. Perhaps the door was not tightly shut because Adam had been afraid that it would make a noise and that then the housekeeper would come out and ask where he was going. When Mrs Pargeter went to make the beds and realized that Adam was not in, she was not worried. Adam was sometimes away for days, for weeks at a time without letting anyone know. She was not paid to concern herself with her employer's son's manners. As usual the bed was already made and the room was tidy.

When Clive Anderson came home from work to discover that his son was not there, he seemed to experience a little guilty relief. He told himself that it had been a hard day at work and that Adam's presence always added to the stress. His son's unprepossessing appearance, his apparent inability to communicate, always reminded him that, as a father, he was a failure. Tonight there would be no forced conversation over dinner, he would not have to pretend interest in what his son had been doing. After the meal he allowed himself a brandy to celebrate the luxury of being alone.

It was ten o'clock when Mrs Pargeter pointed out that Adam's binoculars, telescope and tripod were on the table in the hall. He always left them there and she always complained about it. Adam never went out for more than a few hours without his optical equipment. Mr Anderson tried to think of other, reasonable explanations for his son's absence, but realized that there were none. His only friends were bird-watchers and he would not be out all day without his binoculars. Mrs Pargeter was surprised by her employer's anxiety. Anderson dialled George Palmer-Jones's number and let the telephone ring and ring, long after it was reasonable to expect a reply.

A windmill stood in the cafe car park and Ella had named her snack bar after it. It was not a real mill. It was, if anything, a wind pump, but the locals called it the windmill and it had become a landmark on the marshes. There was nothing at-tractive about Ella's windmill: it was a rotten, wooden frame held together with enormous rusting bolts and pieces of scrap metal. It had been built twenty years previously by a group of undergraduates who wished to prove the potential of wind power. They had chosen the site because of its exposure to the north-easterly winds and because it contained an old, freshwater well, the only relic perhaps of an ancient village, long since eroded by the sea. They decided that they would harness the wind to pump fresh water to the surface. This seemed to give the experiment some validity and did have a practical application because the cottage near to the site had no mains water. Later the coastguard service bought the cottage and converted it to house their staff. The students' experiment had failed. The water in the well had been brackish, the structure poorly designed. The students went on to other projects.

No one from the university came to remove the windmill, and when Ella bought the site for the snack bar it was still there, ugly as a gallows, with tatters of canvas hanging from the sails. She had always meant to have it taken down, but when the workmen came to build the cafe they seemed to forget it and now she was used to it. It was the tallest object on the marsh, and it broke the clean line of the shingle bank against the sky, but usually she never noticed that it was there.

However, that day, the day of Adam's disappearance, the dilapidated silhouette irritated her. It represented her laziness, her lack of care for the place. She should have seen to it. It was a scarecrow of a thing, a monstrosity. She focused her anger on Jack – he should have seen to it. It was his respon-sibility too. It would give the wrong impression. She could transform the restaurant with flowers and decorations but how could she hide that pile of scrap metal? She considered stringing it with fairy lights, then wondered for a crazy moment if she could have it removed in a day. She was, for a while, distracted by this possibility, but when she had concluded that too many problems were involved, the irritation had passed.

Nothing held Ella's attention for very long and she had too much energy to sulk. She had other, more important, more pleasant things to consider.

She was having a party and it would be the most magnificent party ever given in Rushy. It was to be a celebration of Rushy and the marsh. The spring before, the village had been the base for an RSPB film crew, who had made a documentary film about the natural history of the area. For a while the village had pretended to ignore the film crew's presence, but in private the strangers had been the subject of great interest and speculation. There had been real excitement when a television personality, who was to act as narrator, stayed at the White Lodge and drank in the pub. Ella, immediately, had made it her business to become indispensable to the cameramen. She made sandwiches for them, and flasks of tea. The film appealed to her theatrical nature. Through her the village learnt all about the details of filming, and Rushy became quite possessive about their film.

It was already very successful. It had won awards and was soon to appear on television. There had been a premiere in London and members of the royal family had attended. The second public showing was to be in Rushy, as a tribute to the village. Ella, whose party would follow the show, felt that somehow, through association, the influence of royalty should be felt. She had taken over the small buffet supper planned by the local RSPB group and transformed it into something more suitable. She had been planning the party, brooding about it, dreaming about it for months. It was to be a spectacle. The Windmill was closed for the day so that she and Sandra could lay out the tables, prepare the food. The freezer was already filled with pies and flans, other committee members were making the sweets, providing the wine. She wanted everything to be perfect and very grand. As she ran over the details of the meal in her mind, her anxiety eased. She was wonderfully confident that everything would go smoothly, and she prepared to enjoy the power of organization.

That morning Pete Littleton woke early. On Scilly he had resented the early mornings, the busy grey dawns, the earnest discussions at six in the morning about bulb prices and disease. If he had been able to contribute any skill or opinion to the operation, perhaps he would have enjoyed it more. But it had been made clear to him that he was only there to learn, that he served no useful purpose. Now, to get up early was a choice which he exercised more and more frequently, even if he did not intend to go out. After years of being attached to an extended family, even as an outsider, he found the privacy of the cottage intoxicating. The means of obtaining the privacy had been distasteful, but he knew that the unpleasantness had been worthwhile.

He had rented his cottage from a middle-aged woman who lived and worked in London, and who used Rushy as a refuge for herself and her cats. The extreme simplicity of the decoration and furnishing seemed to indicate a need for an antidote to London. It suited Peter's mood. He liked the secretive aspect of the cottage, the way it was hidden behind a jumbled screen of red roofs and flint. The entrance was from a cobbled lane through an arched door in a high wall into a flagged yard. From the lane the house was invisible. The door from the yard led straight into a large kitchen, stone-floored, cold, with an enamel sink, a tap and a Calor Gas stove. The small living room was carpeted. There was one easy chair and cupboards on each side of the fireplace which were filled with books and maps. Upstairs there was one large bedroom.

Peter washed at the sink in the kitchen and dressed. He fried bacon and eggs in a large, heavy pan. The day seemed damp and miserable and he was in no hurry to go out. As he ate his breakfast he planned his day meticulously. Tonight he would dress up and go to the film show and Ella's party. But first, in the afternoon, he had an appointment.


In the cottage next door, Mrs Black was tense and tired. She seemed not to have slept for two nights. Terry had not come home for two nights. He had stayed out before, occasionally, and it always worried her. She had become so fond of him. Once he had gone to a dance at the hospital in Skeffingham where he had lived for so many years. The hospital invited him back quite often for socials and parties and always arranged transport for him. On that occasion, however, he had decided that he wanted to walk, had become tired on the way and slept rough in a ditch. She had phoned the police then, and felt so foolish when he turned up the next morning, hungry and affectionate, not realizing at all that she might be concerned. She reminded herself of this incident as she waited for him and worried.

On Sunday evening she had expected him home for tea, but was not surprised when he did not turn up. It was not unusual for him to work overtime. At eleven she had phoned the White Lodge, preparing to be angry on Terry's behalf because he had been kept so late. A rude receptionist told her that Terry had left work before lunch without telling anyone that he was going. That too had happened occasionally before.

On Monday, throughout the day, she tried to find him. She phoned the hospital and asked carefully and discreetly in the village if anyone had seen him. She did it so well, she was so cheerful and casual, that no one seemed to realize that Terry was missing or to sense that she was worried. All evening she set herself deadlines which passed. If he's not here by nine o'clock, she thought, I'll phone the police. Then it was ten o'clock, then eleven. Still she did nothing. It was not a fear of looking foolish which prevented her from telephoning the police now. She was frightened that they would think that Terry had run away because he had killed Tom French. She had known that they suspected Terry when they had questioned him. They had confused him with their complicated questions. This would be the excuse which they needed to arrest him. She felt helpless, very frightened. At midnight she went to bed. She had not phoned the police.

On Tuesday morning she prepared breakfast for herself, thinking that it would be unlucky to cook for him too, but hoping, praying, that he would walk in. At eight she telephoned the police station. She had not eaten her breakfast. The voice at the end of the telephone was bland, but she imagined that there was satisfaction in it, imagined almost that it was gloating. She was frightened that they would never find Terry, that he had had an accident, that he would never come home, but she was more frightened about what would happen if they did find him.

She had planned to watch the film in the village hall. She had thought that Terry would enjoy it. Instead she stayed in, waiting for something to happen.

Rob Earl woke that morning with a sense of energy and decision, but lay back on the untidy bed, wishing that he still shared the room with the girlfriend who had usually been persuaded to get up first to make the tea. He missed her about the place and she had been obliging about cooking breakfast and making tea, a good-natured young woman. It had been a convenient arrangement but in some respects it was perhaps just as well that she had left. She had started to resent the birdwatching and to grow tedious on the subject of other friends who were getting married and having babies. At times like this, though, he missed her.

It had been her room first, and he had not changed it when she went. The plants had died and been thrown away eventually, but the arty prints on the walls, the big bowl of dried flowers and grasses standing in the empty fireplace, even some of the books and records had belonged to her. He had imposed a smell of tobacco, but little else. She had left, quite suddenly, on a foggy autumn morning, without giving an explanation. He had thought her devoted and had been, for a while, bereft. Not only his pride had been hurt. It was not until later, when he met her again, that he had understood why she walked out in that way.

The doorbell rang and he went downstairs, still dressed only in underpants, to open it. Tina stood there and walked into the shabby hall unmoved, but unamused by his lack of clothes.

'I didn't think you'd be ready,' she said sternly. She was dressed in a university sweatshirt and tight jeans tucked into long, black leather boots. She was carrying a sleeping bag, but had no other luggage.

He had forgotten that she would be coming and that at a bird club meeting the night before he had suggested that they go together to Rushy. She had not been invited specifically to Ella's party, but knew that Ella would ask her if she was at the film. He knew from experience that it was much easier to hitchhike if he had a girl with him, and he needed to get to Rushy quickly.

Since her trip to Scarsea, Tina had not been able to settle. She wanted to see Adam again. They had not made a definite arrangement to meet at Rushy, but she thought it possible that he would be there. It had become urgent that she should see him again.

Rob followed her up the stairs to his room. The lino was gritty under his bare feet. He wondered why she always wore such dramatic clothes.

'You can't go to Ella's party like that. Everyone will be very smart. Even me. Ella won't invite you if you're not wearing a dress.'

For the first time since he had known her, she lost her self-possession.

'I didn't know what to wear,' she said. 'I haven't got anything. Nothing suitable. Perhaps I'd better not come.'

He felt quite sorry for her – quite paternal, he thought mockingly. 'I think my girlfriend left some things here when she went,' he said. 'You must be about the same size.'

They rummaged in a big wardrobe and found a dress, in a peasant style which would go with her boots. It was made of dark green velvet, with a flowered yoke. She tried it on secretly in the kitchen, while he dressed, then folded it carefully, lovingly into a carrier bag.

They got a lift almost immediately and Rob congratulated himself that he had thought to invite Tina to accompany him. They did not speak as they travelled. Both were preoccupied with Rushy, the evening ahead, and what could be achieved there.

Sally had been invited by Ella to the film show and party. Ella had been forceful and Sally had accepted, intending to find an excuse not to go later. She had not seriously considered that she would attend. Then Ella arranged a babysitter for her, and asked her to help to serve food and wash up, so that she could not refuse to go without appearing to mind helping. Ella asked the Palmer-Joneses to drive Sally from Fenquay to the church hall and it was impossible then for her to stay away.

Once it became inevitable that she would go to the film, Sally was surprised to realize that she might enjoy the evening. She had woken up excited, because there was something different to look forward to. She had not dreamed about the letters. There had been no more of them and she had begun to dismiss them, to believe again that they had been sent by some crank in the village. She had still not reported the letters to the police. That afternoon, while Barnaby was sleeping, she prepared for the evening. She washed her hair and ironed her prettiest summer dress. She acted almost as if she had someone to dress up for.

★

All day Bernard Cranshaw looked forward to the film with nervous anticipation. It was, in a special way, his film. Of all the villagers he had been most involved, and he felt that the film was a celebration of his work on the marsh. It proved that the RSPB recognized the importance of his work there, but he felt that the help he had given in making the film would not be appreciated, that other people would take the credit. He was not worried that the film would be badly received but was desperately anxious that he would not be acknowledged as the moving force behind the project. He had brooded about it, and believed that other people were conspiring to take the glory due to him.

It even seemed that fate was against him, because the day before he had sprained his wrist in a silly accident at work. The incident had infuriated him. He had slipped down the short flight of steps outside the staffroom and had fallen almost at the feet of two giggling fourth-form girls, making, he knew, a ludicrous spectacle. It had been lunchtime and the playground full of children. The other staff had made a great drama of the event and the nurse had insisted that he wear a sling. The sling presented few practical difficulties – although writing was impossible – but he felt in a strange way that it indicated that he was incompetent. In his battle for recognition as the true champion of Rushy Marsh, it was a psychological handicap. He was the director of the North Norfolk Natural History Society which, with the local RSPB group, was presenting the film. The chairman of the RSPB members' group was a solicitor, a fat, toad-like, conceited man who would want to take charge of the proceedings, run the show, and Cranshaw felt that the sling would give the man the excuse.

Cranshaw knew that he had been indispensable to the film

crew. He had helped to set up many of the shots, had carried heavy equipment to the hides while the fat solicitor sat in his warm car and muttered about a heart complaint. But he knew too that he could not match the solicitor's ability to organize events and words.

He left school early so that he could dress and be at the hall before anyone else arrived. He wanted to make his presence felt and to be there to welcome the important guests. He had planned to leave soup and sandwiches for his mother's supper, and to do without a meal himself. He had thought that she would be happy to watch the television until he returned, but his mother had other plans. He had not realized that she was aware of anything unusual, but she wanted to go with him. When he arrived home she was dressed in her best clothes, her face was a mask of make-up, and the smell of her perfume sickened him as he approached her to impress on her that she could not go with him.

It took an hour of persuasion and considerable energy to resist her whining and her tears. She had set her mind on it. He said that she was not well enough, that the hall would be cold, that he would be worried about her. He forced himself to appear concerned and solicitous and at last she responded and allowed herself to be settled on the sofa with tea and chocolates. When he finally left the house alone he was exhausted, but he still found time to go to the Windmill to check the arrangements for the party. Nothing could be left to chance.


Tina and Rob met Peter Littleton on the marsh in the middle of the afternoon as they had arranged. It was a still, damp day, grey and colourless. There was no movement.

Even the birds appeared part of a black and white photo-graph and the marsh seemed deserted of people. They sat in one of the hides talking for a while, then separated. Tina wanted to be alone to look for Adam and went off towards the shingle bank and the Windmill. Rob said that he wanted a long walk, and that he would go right along the beach towards Skeffingham. He did not ask Peter to go with him and walked away very quickly with long, easy strides, and Peter saw his silhouette on the bank after an almost un-believably short space of time. Peter felt quite relaxed and contented, and sat dreaming for a while in the hide. He had a leisurely stroll around the marsh, just for appearances' sake, then returned to the cottage for tea and hot buttered toast.

When Tina returned to the cottage to prepare for the party Peter found her sullen and uncommunicative. She changed into the velvet dress, but seemed to have little interest in her appearance. She could not upset Peter's good humour and he opened a bottle of wine and gave her a glass, and they waited silently for Rob.

Rob was late, wet and irritable. As he changed he gave his excuses and drank Peter's wine.

'I saw a funny gull on the sea. It was too far away to identify properly, but there was something odd about it. Something about the head shape. I set up the 'scope and waited for ages, hoping that it would fly, but the sea was dead calm and it didn't move. The light got worse and worse and it started to drizzle, so I had to come away in the end.'

'What do you think it might have been?' Peter asked. Tina was not listening.

Rob was oddly vague about the bird and refused to put a

name to it. He changed the subject and suggested that they had time for a quick drink in the Anchor before the start of the film.

The hall was next to the church on a small incline to the south of the village. It was a square, stone building surrounded by trees. When Bernard Cranshaw arrived he noted with irritation that a number of large, expensive cars were already parked outside. He was too late, and someone else would have taken charge. His presence would not even be noticed. Aggressively he pushed his way inside.

The hall filled quickly. Ella watched with excitement, recognizing not only friends and neighbours from the village, but a carload from one of the inland market towns and a family of wealthy landowners who lived in the biggest house in the district. She laid her coat across the seats next to hers to save them for Sally, Molly and George. When they arrived she waved and beckoned to them. Her excitement and enjoyment were infectious, and Sally felt like a child on Christmas Eve as the lights dimmed ready for the film to begin.

When Peter Littleton, Rob Earl and Tina arrived, breathless after running from the Anchor, the hall was full and the film was about to start. They perched on trestle tables at the back. There the wild boys and girls of the village already sat, defiantly wearing their leather jackets, chewing gum and whispering to each other obscurely obscene jokes.

The film was delicate and haunting, capturing the sense of space on the marsh and its strange, clear beauty. There were close-up shots of waders and wildfowl. It provided an intimate picture of the birds' lives. Villagers who had come to the film just because it provided them with the chance of a night out were fascinated by the insight into the wild creatures' behaviour, by the detailed view of a bird they thought they knew well, but which they had only seen at a distance.

Afterwards there were speeches made by the producer who thanked the people of Rushy for their cooperation in the making of the film, by the regional officer of the RSPB thanking the film crew and everyone who had paid to be there that night, and by Bernard Cranshaw who, in a long and tortuous way, said exactly the same as the previous speakers. At last he finished and the audience began to leave. There was the sound of motorbikes as the leather-clad young people rode away in search of some other diversion, and the sound of soft Norfolk voices in gossip.

Only the favoured few remained, those who had been invited to the Windmill for supper. Rob obtained the necessary invitation for Tina. The only thing that the guests had in common was their interest in birds and that Ella thought them worth inviting. Many she did not know personally – their names had been given by the organizations presenting the show – but she had made inquiries about them and was satisfied as to their birdwatching competence. There was an elderly wildlife artist whose paintings fetched huge prices in London galleries, a young biologist who presented a BBC wildlife programme, the television comedian who had introduced the show, national officers of the RSPB and their wives, and local committee members. Then there were Ella's special friends, whom she had invited on her own account: George and Molly Palmer-Jones, Peter Littleton and Rob Earl with Tina. Sally had left before the speeches to help Sandra with last-minute preparations for the meal.

The Windmill had been transformed for the occasion. There were stiff white cloths on the tables, bowls of flowers, the best silver and glass in the village begged and borrowed from its owners. Ella, magnificent in crimson silk, looking more impressive than ever, black curls swept back from her forehead and allowed to fall down her back, waited at the door to greet all her guests. The cars arrived in procession from the village hall. She stood like an opera singer preparing to sing. It was nearly dark – before the party finished there would be more rain – and the silhouette of the windmill could only just be seen against the sky. It looked, not untidy, but dramatic, and she was glad that it was still there, a suitable backdrop to the evening's entertainment. She welcomed her guests with a theatrical dignity, so that attention was diverted from the prefabricated hut, the shabby little snack bar, and was concentrated instead on the sense of occasion, the sense of celebration. It was a real party. Already the bottles of wine were being opened, and heavy china plates, disguised by napkins and covered with food, were being carried from the kitchen.

Molly studied with interest the reaction of the guests to Ella. No one, not even the suburban RSPB wives, had found the performance ridiculous or embarrassing. Most men seemed spellbound by her physical magnificence. The elderly artist took her hand and kissed it. Bernard Cranshaw seemed not to notice that she was there, but walked straight past her, took a glass of wine from a tray, and drank it in loud, unpleasant gulps. Rob Earl caricatured her formality as he introduced her again to Tina, and Peter gave her a big kiss on both cheeks.

George Palmer-Jones had watched Bernard Cranshaw's

arrival with interest and walked, apparently without purpose, towards the man who now held a second glass in his left hand.

'How is your mother now?' George asked politely. 'I understand that she had a fall a couple of weeks ago.'

'Yes.' Bernard spoke abruptly, strangely, as if he were thinking of something else. George could not tell whether or not the man recognized him. 'Yes, she did. She's better now though, I think.'

'How did she fall?'

'She was going to the bathroom and fell down the stairs.'

'When did it happen?'

'Oh, early one Saturday morning. She gets confused in the mornings. She's very good for her age, but a bit unsteady early in the day.'

'Must have been unpleasant for her. Inconvenient for you too. You usually go out on the marsh at weekends, don't you? I suppose her accident kept you in.'

'What?' He still seemed preoccupied. 'No, after the doctor came, she seemed to be comfortable. I always go out on Saturday mornings.'

'What time would that have been?'

There was no suggestion that this was an interrogation. It was polite and courteous interest.

'I can't remember that. How should I know?' the man replied sharply.

'Did you go out as soon as the doctor left?'

'Eh?' He had gone too far. Cranshaw's attention was jerked back to the present. Only now did he seem to realize what they were talking about.

'I don't know. What the hell's this about anyway?'

Luckily he seemed not to expect an answer, and when George began to talk about the film he joined in, explaining in quite an interesting way how some of the shots had been taken. He left soon after, and Molly heard him say to Ella that his mother would be expecting him home. He seemed genuinely sorry that he had to leave early.

Rob and Peter were getting cheerfully drunk. Rob Earl had decided to accept the tour leader's job in Bristol and he was talking about the places he would be visiting through work. He seemed to have thrown off his earlier irritation, but there was something forced about his laughter. Peter was giggling gently. Tina drank little, but appeared unoffended by the men's behaviour. Molly felt that her instinct about Tina and Adam had been right and experienced a maternal sympathy for the girl, who seemed lost and lonely.

Molly watched her husband skilfully separate Peter from the others and move with him out of earshot of Rob and Tina. Peter did not notice what was happening.

George made no attempt to conceal the purpose of the conversation.

'I understand that you were in Rushy the weekend that Tom died. Is that true?'

He appeared to talk quite naturally, but his voice was pitched so low that no one else could hear what he was saying.

Peter had been pulling faces at two of Sandra's children who were confined to the kitchen, but who had been peeping round the door, their curiosity stronger than their fear of their mother. He stopped. Palmer-Jones's voice demanded full attention and a serious answer.

'I was in London for most of the weekend. I just came to Rushy for the day. I didn't know that Tom was dead until I met you at Trekewick. I must have left Rushy before they found his body. I didn't think that the fog would clear and I left at about four.'

'When we saw you at Trekewick you gave the impression that you had only recently left St Agnes. Certainly you didn't get in touch with any of your friends. Why was that?'

Peter said nothing. George thought for a while that he was going to refuse to answer, but he seemed to be making a real effort to be accurate.

'I needed time to sort myself out. I was in quite a state. I might not have seemed upset about what happened on Scilly, but I felt – damaged. I wasn't ready to talk to anyone about it. That's why I didn't go into the Windmill that Saturday. I didn't want to see anyone I knew.'

'How did you get to Rushy? What time did you arrive?'

'I'd hired a car for the whole weekend. I arrived at about nine and parked on the other side of the village. I don't know why I came, really. I felt silly creeping about in the fog trying to avoid people. But the weather forecast was so good that I couldn't stay away. How did you know I was there?'

'A young birder saw you. Why have you never told anyone that you were here that day?'

'It just seemed easier. I couldn't face having to explain what I'd been doing. And I hadn't seen anything so what was the point?'

He turned away, but smiled to show that he was not angry, took another glass of wine and went back to Tina and Rob.

Sally had been intimidated by the first crowd of guests and had hidden in the kitchen, refilling empty plates, cutting warm sausage rolls into what Ella had described as a size fit for sophisticated mouths. With a feeling of envy at other people's self-confidence, she listened to the guests beyond the open door, to the conversation and the laughter. She could hear Ella, already a little loud with wine and the triumph of her success. And then she heard another voice, a voice she recognized. The words which she heard contained a certain, a specific meaning for her and she felt certain she knew who had killed Tom French.

George took Sally home. Ella had found her in the kitchen looking pale and shaken. Sally claimed to have been sick. She certainly looked ill, George thought, as they drove towards Fenquay, but her defensive explanation of the illness, the almost hysterical insistence that she leave the Windmill by the back door, seemed to suggest a different reason for her desire to leave the party. When asked, gently, if she had received any further anonymous letters, she answered in an offhand way, as if she had forgotten all about them. Then she refused to talk to him, and when he dropped her outside her cottage she did not invite him in. He offered to see her safely inside, but she ignored him and was out of the car before he had finished speaking. There was nothing to do but to drive back to Rushy.

The smell of her terror seemed to linger in the car. It accused him, telling him that he had been too detached, not committed, not strong enough in his search for the killer. Her fear had been wild and irrational. So was murder. He would not find his answers through reason and intellect. This was no crossword to be solved by a gentleman in an armchair. Murder was mad and unreasonable and gentlemen had no part in it.

He parked his car as usual next to the windmill in the car park. It had started to rain, a soft, sea-mist drizzle, but there was no wind. When he first heard the noise he thought that a sudden gust must have caused the wood in the windmill to twist and creak, but there had been no wind. Again there was a faint call like a cat or a gull. He almost ignored it, put it down to his imagination and went on in to join the party, which had become louder since his absence. There was music now and the sound had, perhaps, been part of a record. The lights and the music were very attractive.

But he heard the noise again and it seemed to come from below him. It was a sound of pain. In his car was a torch and, as he shone it around the windmill, he noticed first a mark on the soft, damp wood of one of the uprights, as if it had been cut horizontally, then saw that the rotten planks covering the well had split and shattered. With concentrated panic, he tore the splintered planks away and shone the torch down the well. A long way down he saw a white face, the eyes huge in the sudden light. Adam Anderson was crouched like a hunted animal on a metal grille which only half covered the black, stinking water.

# Chapter Nine

As THEY PULLED HIM out through the wooden supports of the windmill he could have been ten years younger. His fear had shrivelled him, so that he looked smaller. George almost expected him to cry, but he was dry-eyed and white, shivering, as frightened and wary of his rescuers as he was of the well. It had taken little time to get him out of the shaft. Tina had run to the coastguard cottage. The men there were still awake, they had ropes and knew about climbing. George shouted reassurance down to him and explained what was happening, but Adam did not say a word. In the glare of car headlights the coastguards worked efficiently and light-heartedly, including Adam in their jokes. He did not reply.

Ella had tried to clear the place of anyone who could be of no use, but people were reluctant to go until Adam was safely out of the well. They gathered in small groups, watching, wanting to be a part of the rescue. Yet the rain grew more persistent and the coastguards' attitude dispelled any sense of drama. Common sense overcame curiosity. They had a good story to tell at parties and did not need to be present

145

at the actual outcome. Car engines were started, there were subdued calls of farewell and the place emptied. Ella, Rob and Peter went inside to begin to clear up; Molly was talking on the telephone to Clive Anderson.

When Adam was pulled free only George Palmer-Jones and Tina were there to see. Tina had mud on the hem of her dress and on her face. She said nothing to Adam, but waited and watched him, apparently hoping that he would turn to her for comfort. When he did not respond she bent to help the men to clear their equipment, to coil their ropes, and allowed herself a few tears of relief and disappointment.

They all left George to deal with Adam. They stood quite close together. It was as though they were alone.

'I'd better call an ambulance,' George said, 'to make sure that nothing's broken.'

Adam spoke for the first time.

'No.' The sudden sound was explosive, startling. 'No fuss. I don't need an ambulance.'

'Who pushed you?' George asked.

'I don't know.' Then with sudden panic: 'No one. No one pushed me. I fell in. It was all my fault. I wanted to see how deep it was and I fell in.'

'You must tell me. And tell the police. Tell them what really happened. They'll send somebody to look after you. They'll make sure that it doesn't happen again.'

Then the boy did begin to cry. With frightened and hysterical sobs, he begged George to believe that it was an accident, not to tell the police. George put his arm round Adam, held him very tight, tried to calm him. Tina watched the intimacy with pain, turned away and walked into the building.

George felt that the physical contact gave him some of

the status of fatherhood. He felt privileged and responsible.

'You must tell me,' he repeated. 'You know that you can trust me. You must let me help you.'

But the white face turned up to him, beseeching him not to ask any more. George was helpless and angry, but could not direct his anger towards the boy.

They walked together towards the Windmill kitchen where there was hot strong tea and whisky. Tina sat next to him and tried to take his hand, but Adam still ignored her. There were no more questions. Ella presided over the teapot and made concerned and comforting noises. The others sat quietly, shocked and sympathetic.

Slowly, with great control, Adam told his story. He had been out on the marsh. He had seen very little and, not knowing that the Windmill had closed for the day, went there to see if anything had been seen elsewhere in the district. When he found it was shut he had waited, hoping to see other birders. He had heard stories about the well and had tried to lift the planks covering the shaft to see how deep it was. He had lost his balance and slipped. He was sorry to have caused so much trouble. He seemed very tired, and spoke as if he were making a great effort.

Molly too had accepted responsibility for Adam. She had told Mr Anderson that they would find him a bed for the night and that they would take care of him. Finally, it was Ella who looked after him. When she saw that he was exhausted she wrapped him in a blanket, sat him in her car and drove him back to the cottage. She did not ask him questions or expect him to tell her what had happened. The room she gave him was small and safe, like his room at home, and he slept without dreaming.

George had told Ella that he would lock up. He was not tired. They sat in the kitchen surrounded by the debris of the party. Molly made another pot of tea. They had finished the Scotch.

'Did anyone see Adam today?'

There had been lazy, companionable gossip at the table. They were enjoying the safe outcome of the drama. The question broke through the gentle conversation with a rudeness and authority which Rob resented immediately.

'Why? Should we have wiped his nose, taken his hand and told him to find somewhere safer to play?'

'No. But you might have seen who pushed him.'

'But he said that he fell by accident.'

'Yes. He said that he fell.'

'But you think that he was pushed.'

Tina interrupted aggressively:

'Who do you think pushed him? What makes you think that it wasn't an accident?'

George was irritated by their questions. There was no time for polite explanation.

'Just accept that I need to know if anyone saw him. Perhaps you could all tell me what you were doing this afternoon.'

But they had no sense of urgency and began to speculate about Adam's story and the possibility that he was telling the truth.

'He could have fallen,' Peter said. 'Those planks were really rotten.'

'Why does he say that he fell if he was pushed?' Tina asked.

Molly answered before George had a chance to speak:

'Because he's frightened. He's so frightened that he can't think clearly, and he can't trust anyone enough to tell them what really happened.' She saw that she had hurt Tina and went on quickly, 'He's the sort of person who can't confide easily. It doesn't mean that he doesn't want to.'

Peter was continuing his own line of thought.

'It seemed strange that he was so vague about the time he fell,' he said. 'I know that he didn't have a watch, but I would have thought he could have made a rough guess.'

'He did say that he had been in the well for some time when the cars arrived for the party,' Rob reminded him. 'He says that he shouted but no one heard him. That's not surprising. Everyone arrived at the same time and there was a lot of noise.'

'It must have been horrible,' Tina said. 'To be there in the dark, to know that people were so close to you, and not to be able to make them hear.'

Peter was still trying to fix the time of the incident.

'If he was telling the truth about hearing the cars at the party, he fell or was pushed some time in the late afternoon or early evening. I was here at about four o'clock.' After this announcement he went on to answer George's question, smiling as if to apologize that it had taken so long to come to the point.

'I stayed in the cottage all morning, then met Rob as I'd arranged in the hide, at about two thirty. Tina was with him. Tina and Rob went off on their own, Tina first. They both headed for the Windmill, but I saw Rob on the shingle bank soon after. I went for a walk on the marsh, then did the coastguard garden and came back past the Windmill. I didn't go in. I thought that Ella might rope me in to make sandwiches. I went straight back to the cottage and it was half past four when I arrived home.'

'Did you see anyone on the marsh?'

'No one at all. I didn't even see Ella. I just presumed that she was there.'

There was a short silence and then Tina started to speak. She talked abruptly, defensively, and Molly thought that she was blushing.

'If you must know, I was looking for Adam. We'd been talking at Scarsea. He asked me to look out for a copy of the *Handbook* for him. Someone at the university bird club has one for sale. I wanted to let him know.'

'What made you think that he would be at Rushy today?'

She shrugged. 'He always seems to be here. And I thought he might be at the film.'

'Where did you look for him?'

'I went past the Windmill onto the shingle bank. I didn't see him or anyone else. If he'd been on the marsh I would have seen him from there. Then I went to look at that patch of cover between the Windmill and the coastguards. We've been thinking of building a Heligoland trap over it and I wanted to work out how much wood and wire netting we'd need.'

'What did you do then?'

'I went back to Peter's cottage to get ready for the party. I got back soon after five, I should think.'

Rob repeated his movements of the afternoon.

'So you walked straight along the beach towards Skeffingham. Did you see anyone?'

'A few fishermen and bait diggers.'

'Which way did you come home?'

'I walked straight back along the track past the Windmill.'

'What time did you get back?'

'About six o'clock.'

'Have we got any idea what Adam was doing earlier in the day?' Peter asked.

George looked with a question at Molly. She shook her head.

'He left home quite early, just after the postman had been, his father says. But no one knows where he went. That's not unusual apparently, but his father says that he hadn't gone birdwatching – he'd left his binoculars and telescope at home.'

'No,' Rob said definitely. 'That can't be right. He wouldn't have come to Rushy without his optical gear. If his father's telling the truth, he can't have planned to come to Rushy.'

'If he left home soon after the postman had called at the house, could he have had a letter,' Tina asked tentatively, 'arranging to meet him?'

'That wouldn't have stopped him bringing his binoculars.'

There was no more tea and they were starting to feel cold. George drove them all back to the cottage. There Peter gave up his room for George and Molly, and placed his sleeping bag next to Rob and Tina on the living-room floor. George did not go to bed, and was astonished that Molly could lie in the big, shapeless bed in an undisturbed slumber. The sense that the person who had inspired such terror in Adam and in Sally was beyond logic, beyond reason, remained with him. The routine of arranging the details of time and place seemed futile, irrelevant. He felt that he was hiding his weakness behind a pretence of efficiency. But still he was compelled to do it, to ignore his urge for some kind of unspecific, irrational action. He could not sleep.

Once more he read through his notes, intending to add to them the details of the information gained that evening. As he sat at the small table in Peter's bedroom he could hear the young people talking in the room below him and realized that they too would go without sleep. He read the cramped, precise writing of the notes, looked at the plans he had made, then set the paper aside with dissatisfaction. All the facts were important, but he felt, now, that he knew them by heart. He was sure that he was missing something vital, some connection, something which would give a new perspective on the major characters involved. Because he was sure now that he had met all the major characters. He had talked to the murderer.

He was sure that the person who had killed Tom and who had tried to kill Adam was someone he knew. But the details of time and place and opportunity had not helped. All the people he was considering as possible suspects had the opportunity of attacking Adam, and all except Cranshaw could have killed Tom French. Even the exclusion of Cranshaw depended only on Jack's inconclusive evidence. He took a fresh sheet of paper and made a list of the people he meant to see the next day. He must see Terry. If Terry persisted with his story that he had seen nothing, George must talk to his landlady in the hope that she could get the truth from him. It was ludicrous that they had an eye witness but no information. He must talk to Bernard Cranshaw, whose instability was obvious, and who knew, George thought, more than he was telling. That evening, at the Windmill, George had felt that Cranshaw was hiding something. He would talk to Ella, to anyone who might have been out on the marsh, who might have seen Adam. And he would talk to Adam himself. He dreaded that interview and did not expect much from it. By now the boy would have had time to perfect his story.

It was light and he was very cold when he climbed into the big, soft bed next to Molly. Although he was cold he did not hold her. He was afraid of waking her. He lay straight, on his back, and slept only lightly, allowing his mind to continue its work. So when he woke he knew where Peter Littleton fitted into it all. He had made the vital connection.

The door was opened to them as soon as they knocked. Mrs Black was a large woman. She wore a flowered apron over her dark clothes.

'You've come about Terry,' she said flatly.

'That's right,' said George. He wasn't surprised. The whole village must know about his inquiries by now.

'You'd better come in then.'

He was surprised by her lack of hospitality, at the resentment in her voice. She showed them into a spotless, cramped living room.

'Well,' she said. 'Have you found him?'

When they did not reply she asked:

'You *are* from the police?'

'No, Mrs Black. My name's Palmer-Jones. I wanted to talk to Terry. What has happened to him?'

She looked exhausted.

'I don't know. The police think that he's run away because he killed Tom French. They're looking for him.'

Because they were not the police, she motioned them to sit down, and sat herself, large and proud, in an upright chair, fierce despite her tiredness and depression.

'But that's not true, Mr Palmer-Jones. He's a kind, good-natured boy. I wouldn't be afraid to think of him as my son.

153

He has never hurt anyone in his life and I can't believe that he would hurt Tommy, his friend. He always called Tommy his friend. He's been with me for a long time, Mr Palmer-Jones, and I know more about him than a policeman who's never met him.'

Molly went over to the stiff, controlled woman and took her hand. Mrs Black, with her dark clothes and her tense, mindless grief, reminded Molly of a person recently bereaved.

'We don't think that Terry killed anyone, Mrs Black. When did he go missing?'

'Sunday. He left work early. Before lunch.'

Molly was still holding the woman's hand. She looked quickly at her husband.

'That must have been soon after I spoke to him.'

Then she said very gently:

'Mrs Black, do you have any idea where Terry went?'

She shook her head. Silent tears ran down her cheeks.

'I phoned the hospital,' she said. 'If he was worried or upset why didn't he talk to me? I would have helped him.'

'The hospital?' Molly asked, ignoring her impulse to comfort and reassure the woman.

'Since he was a boy until he came to stay with me, he lived in a big hospital just outside Skeffingham. It was the only place I could think where he would go.'

'Do you know where he lived before he was sent to the hospital?'

'He never talked about it. He didn't have much of a memory. I think it was with his grandfather, but even the staff at the hospital didn't seem to know. It was twenty-five years ago.'

'Did anyone in the village see him after he left the hotel?'

'Yes. The landlord of the Blue Anchor saw him. He looked in at the pub, but he didn't stop.'

'Did he have any money with him?'

'Not much. They didn't pay him much.'

The big woman seemed at last to realize what was happening and to think rationally.

'Why do you think he ran away?' she asked. 'If he didn't kill Tom, why did he run away?'

'I talked to Terry on Saturday,' Molly said, 'and again on Sunday. We think that he saw someone else on the morning of Tom's death. Someone frightened Terry, so that he wouldn't tell us exactly what he saw. Perhaps he was so frightened that he ran away.'

'Or perhaps whoever killed Tommy killed Terry so that he wouldn't talk.'

Mrs Black's panic had dissolved her control.

'That's always a possibility, Mrs Black,' said George, stiff, formal. 'But I don't think so. We need to find Terry. He's the only person who can help us. If you can think of anywhere he may be hiding, any friend he may have gone to, will you telephone us? Then we can clear him of suspicion.'

His authority and formality reassured her. She believed him, believed implicitly that Terry was alive. She smiled and wiped the tears from her eyes.

'I've been a silly old woman,' she said. 'Find him and bring him home.'


When they left Mrs Black, George went to the Cranshaws' house and Molly went to the Windmill to ask discreetly if anyone had seen Adam on the previous day.

George did not expect Bernard Cranshaw to be there – he would surely be at work in Skeffingham – but he could speak to Mrs Cranshaw about the day when she tripped down the stairs, the day Tom French died. Perhaps she would remember if Bernard went out at all while they were waiting for the doctor. Bernard had told George that he was on the marsh on the morning of Tom's death. But what time did he go? Jack had heard voices in the Cranshaw house when he returned to the marsh to dig bait. If Bernard was still there then, and if Terry had seen the murderer on his way to work, it would have been impossible for Bernard to have killed Tom. He hoped that Mrs Cranshaw could bring a little more certainty to the situation.

He found the place quite easily. The road behind the Blue Anchor was more modern than most in the village. The houses had been built in the thirties. They were suburban, villa-style houses which looked quite incongruous by the side of the marsh. It was a grey, damp day and George was aware of a faint, unpleasant smell, which the westerly winds carried from a chemical plant many miles inland. He stood for a while outside the house which was furthest from the village, nearest to the sea. The effect of the salt wind could be seen on the paint, which was peeling away from the wooden door and window frames. In the garden a row of winter vegetables, sprouting and gone to seed, had been burnt black by salt spray. He knocked at the door and had to wait several minutes before there was any reply.

Inside, Mrs Cranshaw was taking off her apron, arranging her hair, putting on lipstick, unable to face any visitor in her natural state. She was excited. She did not have many visitors. George Palmer-Jones saw a little, elderly lady with a thin face, who, but for the badly applied make-up and dyed, permed hair, would have been beautiful. The hair was so fine and the curls so tight that pink bald areas of scalp showed through the perm. As he stood on the doorstep, George looked down on the strange pink and black head. As he watched, the head tipped back and Margaret Cranshaw smiled up at him.

She asked him in before he had a chance to say who he was or what he wanted. As she led him into the dusty, cluttered lounge she talked without stopping about the weather. There must have been more than a dozen photographs in the room. There were out-of-focus shots of the marsh and of birds in the hand, pictures of her children and grandchildren, family groups, but in the most prominent position one of herself as a young girl, with a shy, provocative smile. She formed the same smile as she asked her visitor to sit down. He moved a pile of women's magazines from a chair and sat uncomfortably.

'I'm a friend of your son, Bernard,' George said. He had to interrupt a string of excuses for the untidiness of the room to speak. 'I'm a birdwatcher too.'

She smiled a vacant, benevolent smile, said, 'That's nice,' and carried on the train of her conversation.

George tried again.

'I saw a rare bird on the marsh, one morning a couple of weeks back. It was on a Saturday, and I wondered if perhaps he'd seen it. It was the day when I understand you had an accident. I thought perhaps you could tell me if he was out on the marsh that day.'

It never occurred to her to wonder how he knew about her accident or why he had not been in touch with Bernard before. She enjoyed talking about the accident. The whole story seemed very exaggerated. She answered George's questions quite promptly. It seemed that she could carry on a sensible conversation if the subject was herself.

'It was lucky that Jack Benn was just outside when you needed help,' George said. 'I believe he went to get the doctor for you. I suppose that Bernard stayed with you while you waited for the doctor to arrive.'

'Oh yes!' she said. 'He couldn't leave me. I was in agony, in terrible pain. And I was feeling a wee bit peckish by then, so he made us both some breakfast. I think he was cross because he wanted to be out on the marsh. Birdwatching seems to be such a silly habit for a grown man.'

She gasped in mock horror, put her hand to her mouth and giggled coquettishly.

'Oh naughty me,' she simpered. 'I'd forgotten that you were a birdwatcher too. What must you think of me!'

He ignored this and asked:

'What happened when the doctor came?'

She looked sulky. She obviously did not like the doctor.

'He's such a rude man. He hardly stayed any time at all, and he wouldn't give me anything for the terrible pain except aspirin. And then Bernard went out and left me all by myself, and I didn't see anyone else until lunchtime when Mrs Simpson popped in. At times Bernard can be so thoughtless. He's changed so much since he was a boy.'

'Do you know what time Bernard went out?' George asked.

'Yes,' she said, 'because I was very upset, and I called after him to stay with me, but he didn't take any notice. He went out as soon as Jack Benn had driven off with the doctor.'

'And do you know what time that was?'

'I was just going to tell you. It was eight o'clock; because I heard it on the radio. I had the radio on the local station for the news.'

The radio. So the voices – which Jack had heard later in the morning, when he parked his car outside the Cranshaws', could have come from the radio. But eight o'clock was too late. If Terry had been at work on time that Saturday, and had been telling the truth about seeing Tom, he had been dead before eight o'clock.

George stood up, grateful that he had extracted the information he needed and that now he could escape.

'I'm sorry to have missed Bernard,' he said. 'I'll have to call round to see him again.'

'He'll want you to get in touch if it's about a bird,' she said. 'He gets cross if I don't pass on messages about birds.' She was suddenly efficient. 'I've got the name and address of his school, with the telephone number. He wrote it down in case I needed him urgently. I'll get it for you.'

It was tucked behind the big photograph of Margaret as a young girl. She held it out to him with one of her smiles.

'You keep it,' she said. 'Bernard can write it out again for me tonight.'

He did not look at the paper until he was out of the house. The smell of the damp marsh and the chemical factory seemed healthy compared with the atmosphere inside. The name, address and phone number of Skeffingham Comprehensive School were written in sprawling capitals, which George had seen before. He knew now why Sally Johnson had received no more anonymous letters. He had thought that the writing in the letters had been disguised, but it was the normal, if unconventional, writing of Bernard Cranshaw – who had sprained his wrist, was wearing a sling and could not write.

When George and Molly had started out into the village that morning the three young people had still been asleep, lying like big, blue slugs in their sleeping bags. George almost decided to go to Peter's cottage as he walked to the village. He was impatient to confirm his theory about the young man who had recently returned from Scilly. But the list which he had made the night before still controlled his movements. He had a compulsive belief in lists. And Peter would sleep for hours.

He had arranged to meet Molly at Ella's home, and when he arrived, all three – Molly, Ella and Adam – were sitting at the kitchen table, eating a lunch of bread, cheese and salad. Adam still looked very tired and white. The weight of his long hair seemed to drag the skin tight across his forehead and around his eyes, so that the eyes themselves seemed very prominent, like clear glass marbles. Ella was still being solicitous and protective. George sat with them at the table, but shook his head when Ella offered him a plate.

'Why did you come to Rushy yesterday?' he said to Adam.

Ella looked angry, as if she were preparing to protest at this treatment of the boy, but she said nothing.

George's voice was cold, and Adam seemed perplexed, a little hurt.

'To go birding,' he said firmly. 'The weather looked good.'

'Without your binoculars.'

'I was hitching. I didn't want to bring all the gear. I thought I could borrow some.'

'That's ridiculous and you know it.'

Adam shrugged his shoulders, indicating that he was prepared to say nothing more. Although he still looked frail, George sensed that any attempt to make him talk was futile. But, feeling that he had to try, he asked with heavy sarcasm:

'While you were "birding" on the marsh, did you meet anyone you knew? Did you see Bernard Cranshaw for instance?'

'Bernard Cranshaw?' The boy seemed genuinely puzzled. 'No, why?'

'What about Tina or Peter Littleton or Rob Earl? They were out on the marsh all afternoon.'

'I might have seen them about.' He refused to say more.

George watched in silence as the boy gathered the plates together and defiantly left the room. They could hear the sounds of washing up in the scullery.

'Has he said anything to you?' George asked Ella.

'I haven't asked him,' she answered pointedly. 'He's only a boy. He's been through enough.'

'Has he had any visitors? Has anyone been here asking about him?'

'That Tina came in to see him not long ago. She seems a nice girl, though she wears those funny clothes. I left them alone together, but I don't think she got any more out of him than you did. I reckon she was upset when she went.'

'Don't let him go out by himself this afternoon, and don't let him see anyone else on his own.'

She did not understand. George explained:

'Whatever he says, someone tried to kill him. I don't want that person to have the opportunity to try again.'

Her imagination was captured by the situation. She became

the heroine of countless television spy films. She lowered her voice to a whisper.

'Just leave it to me,' she said. 'You can trust me to look after him.'

Despite himself, George smiled. He asked:

'Did you see Adam yesterday?'

She shook her head, disappointed that she could contribute nothing more.

'Did you see Bernard Cranshaw around the Windmill yesterday afternoon?'

'I'd arranged to meet him there at quarter to five.' Her voice rose angrily. 'And what he wanted to see me about I don't know. I waited until quarter past and then I went.'

'Was the Windmill locked up all afternoon?'

'No. Sandra went home at dinnertime and Jack and I were out in the van picking up china and glass from the village, but we came back a couple of times to deliver the wine and the puddings.'

Molly and George started back to Peter's cottage. George was walking very fast.

'I was able to talk to quite a few of the twitchers in the cafe,' Molly said. 'Most of them were here yesterday morning, but they all went off to Fenquay for the tide in the afternoon. It seems rather odd. No one saw Adam at all. But Adam won't tell me in any detail what he was doing in the morning, or even what time he got here, so it's difficult to check.'

'I'm worried about that boy. Can we trust Ella to keep an eye on him?'

'I think so, now she understands it's important. Did you get anything useful from Mrs Cranshaw?'

George explained what had happened.

'So Bernard wrote the letters,' he said. 'I don't know what to do about it. I suppose that I should go to the police, but I don't think that Sally has reported the letters to them. I want to talk to Cranshaw first in any event. I want to find out who told him about Tom's conviction for possession of cannabis.'

'You don't talk as if he killed Tom.'

'I don't think that he did, though I'm not sure why. There's the timing. Even if he left his house at eight o'clock, he can't have got to the track before twenty past. But it's not just that. I can accept that he might have hit out at Tom in a crazy fit of anger, but whoever pushed Adam down the well planned it. Adam was coming to meet someone – otherwise he would have brought his binoculars and telescope. I'm not ruling Cranshaw out entirely, but I'm not convinced.'

'So knowing who wrote the letters doesn't help find out who killed Tom.'

'I'm not sure. It may just be a horrible coincidence. Or perhaps not quite a coincidence. I've an idea that Tom provoked the same response in Cranshaw and the murderer. He made people angry. I'm sure that Bernard originally wrote to Sally as a means of hurting Tom.'

'But everyone says that Tom was a kind person, a gentle person.'

'Perhaps he was. But kind and gentle people can be intensely irritating. Sally knows that.'

Molly was breaking into a run, in an attempt to keep up with George. Now that he had fulfilled all the obligations of the list, he was desperately impatient to talk to Peter. Peter was the one person to link all the strands of the mystery surrounding Tom. George arrived at the cottage several paces before Molly. She wondered why he did not go in, then realized that the door was locked. A note had been pinned to it.

*Key next door. Help yourselves to anything you need.*
*Phone call from Dave W. Black stork near Perth.*
*Sorry we couldn't take you, but we already have a full car.*
*See you in a few days.*

*Peter, Rob and Tina*

'I don't believe it,' George said bitterly. 'First Terry and now Peter. It's like a conspiracy.'

He turned to Molly and shouted, 'Come on! We'll have to get the car. We're going to Fenquay to see Sally.'

# Chapter Ten

SALLY WAS SURPRISED TO see them, a little wary, although she tried to be friendly. The greyness and the rain had been blown away by a strong wind from the sea and she was hanging nappies on the line. Her blonde hair was swept back from her face, and her long skirt was tangled between her legs. She walked back into the house in front of them, the washing basket held on one hip, her back very straight, her body swaying slightly as she walked. She made coffee for them while they played with Barnaby, piling bricks in a tower for him to knock down. He laughed, reaching out to the tower before it was properly completed, laughing deeply with the whole of his small body. Sally came from the kitchen to sit with them, pleased by Barnaby's happiness despite her anxiety. She sat very still, waiting for George to speak. First he drank his coffee, and still she waited, without a word, while he emptied the mug and placed it on a shelf out of Barnaby's reach. She allowed herself one nervous gesture during this time, twisting a silver ring which she wore on her middle finger.

'I think I may have some good news for you about the letters,' he said. 'I know who wrote them.'

Molly, who seemed to have been forgotten by both adults, watched and was puzzled by Sally's reaction. *She thinks she knows who wrote them,* she thought. *She's afraid she knows who wrote them, and she doesn't want anyone else to know.*

'Is it anyone I know?' Sally asked.

She waited for an answer, Molly thought, like a child waiting for an exam result.

'I don't think so,' George said. 'It was Bernard Cranshaw. He never liked Tom.'

Her relief was controlled but very obvious to Molly, who was watching for it. Sally relaxed and, perhaps in an attempt to hide her relief, bent to build Barnaby's tower once more.

When she said nothing, George continued talking.

'I don't know what to do with the information. It's your decision. I'm convinced that Cranshaw wrote the letters to you. I feel that I should tell the police about it, but if I do that, they'll want to talk to you; and if Cranshaw doesn't plead guilty you'll probably have to appear in court as a witness. On the other hand I could talk to him, and only call in the police if the letters start again. As I said, it's your decision.'

'But won't you have to tell the police? Doesn't that mean that he killed Tom?' There was something hopeful, almost pleading in her voice.

'I don't think so,' George said. 'I think the letters were a coincidence. The later letters mention Tom's death. But the first, which arrived on the day he was killed, says nothing about it. I can't see how Tom's death could have been planned far enough in advance to allow the first letter to reach you on the Saturday morning, even if it was posted on the morning before. Bernard Cranshaw may have killed your boyfriend, but unless the police have more information than I do, in which case they would already have charged him, they won't be able to prove it.'

Now the subject of the letters seemed hardly to interest her. 'Don't tell the police then,' she said. 'I don't think I could face any more questions.'

There was another silence, broken only by Barnaby's noisy attempt to climb onto Molly's knee. Sally suddenly seemed to become aware again of her duty as hostess and said politely, making conversation:

'Thank you for giving me a lift home last night. I hope that you didn't miss too much of the party.'

'Not at all,' George said. 'Are you feeling better?'

'Oh, I'm fine now. I feel very guilty about having dragged you away.'

'In the circumstances, perhaps it's as well that you did.'

'In the circumstances?' The routine politeness had disappeared. She sensed from his tone that something had happened at the party in her absence and she was frightened.

'I'm sure that you know that under the wooden experimental windmill in the car park at Ella's, there's an old disused well. When I returned to the party after bringing you home, I heard a noise from the well. One of the younger twitchers, Adam Anderson, was trapped in the well shaft, on a metal grille which half covers the water at the bottom, he had been there for some hours and, of course, he was very frightened. He says that he fell. Molly and I had received the impression that Adam knew something about Tom's death, something he was too frightened to talk about. I don't suppose you know

167

anything about it? You seemed very anxious to leave the party in a hurry last night.'

She ignored the last remark and simply shook her head in answer to the question. Unless she was a very good actress, she had not known about Adam. But she was not totally surprised. She had expected to hear something.

'I think that I saw him yesterday,' she said. 'Adam Anderson, I mean. He was here in Fenquay.'

George felt that she was trying to divert his attention, but he had to follow this up:

'What time did you see him?'

'It was late morning, perhaps midday. He was in that smart coffee shop on the quay. I was walking past. He was sitting in a corner and the light's not very good in there, but I'm sure that it was him. He looked straight at me, but he didn't wave or anything.'

'Was he on his own?'

'There was another person sitting at his table, but the coffee shop was busy. I don't know if they were together.'

'Was it a man or a woman?'

'Man, I think, but I didn't see his face. I didn't take much notice.'

She was, George thought, prepared for the next question.

'Do you know Peter Littleton?'

She looked at him, looked straight into his eyes.

'No,' she said. She was clever. There was a question and a lack of concern in her voice.

'He's a birdwatcher,' George said easily. 'Did you never hear Tom talk about him? He knew Tom well.' She shook her head.

'Why?' she asked carelessly, matching his tone. 'Do you think that he killed Tom?'

He did not reply directly. 'I need to know a little more about him.'

Then, as if it were quite unconnected, he said: 'Where did you meet Tom?'

'Here,' she said quickly. 'In Rushy. It was last July, when I moved into the cottage. He used to come birdwatching to Fenquay occasionally. I'd bought a chair from a junk shop in the village and I was trying to carry it home, balanced on the baby's pram. He saw me and helped me. I knew a bit about birds, so we had something in common.'

George did not comment and she continued in explanation: 'I came to Fenquay because I lived here once, when I was about six. I had foster parents here. I even went to the village school for a term. I was so happy. My foster father used to take me to see all the animals on the farm. He was a farm worker and we lived in a cottage just outside the village. They were very calm people – nothing seemed to upset them. Although I was only with them for six months, I was more settled than I've ever been. Then my mother decided that she wanted me back and I had to move with her to London. I never saw my foster parents again. They don't live here any more, but I suppose that I wanted Barnaby to grow up in a place where I'd been happy. He was just three months old when I moved in.'

George asked, ruthlessly Molly thought:

'You said that you knew a little about ornithology. When did you become interested in birds?'

'When I left school, I did hotel work. I worked in Scotland and in mid-Wales. I met some birdwatchers near Tregaron.'

'Have you ever been to the Isles of Scilly?'

'Yes,' she said uncertainly. 'I worked for a season in a hotel on Tresco.'

'When?'

'Two summers ago.'

'Did you meet any birdwatchers there?'

'Yes,' she said.

'But not Tom.'

'No,' she said definitely. 'Not Tom.'

'And not Peter Littleton?'

'I don't know anyone called Peter Littleton.' She was so desperate to convince them, she was nearly shouting.

Barnaby looked up from his bricks, and in his child's nonsense language gave a perfect imitation of the tone and inflection of her last sentence. It was a piece of pure clowning and he looked around him, expecting applause. When, in the embarrassed silence, none came, he clapped himself and laughed, and only then did the adults join in.

They drove back to Ella's cottage then. They had promised Adam a lift home. Ella seemed to have taken George's instructions seriously. Sandra was coping at the Windmill on her own, and Ella had stayed at home to protect the boy. She was sitting at the window waiting for them. But when they walked into the kitchen, she was nearly in tears.

'He's gone,' she said. 'You told me not to leave him on his own with anyone. I didn't. I really didn't. But they were getting on so well, and he seemed to be cheering up . . .'

'Ella,' George said. 'Do calm down and tell us just what happened.'

'Just after you left they turned up.'

'Who turned up?'

'Tina, Rob and Peter. You said not to leave Adam alone with anyone. Well, there were three of them, so I thought that he would be safe. I hadn't made the beds even, so I went upstairs. I was only gone for ten minutes. When I came down they'd all gone . . . He left a note.'

She held out a piece of paper to George. It was a near replica of that pinned to Peter's door.

'Thanks for everything. I've gone to Perth with the others to see a black stork. Don't worry.'

'Silly young fool,' George said quietly to himself. 'Silly young fool.'

Ella was working herself into a state of hysteria. George tried to reassure her.

'Now don't you worry, my dear. You couldn't have stopped Adam going with the others even if you'd been here. They'll be back as soon as they've seen the bird. He surely wouldn't have gone with them if he hadn't felt safe, although I must admit that I'm surprised.' He realized that he was being anything but reassuring and added briskly: 'We must accept that he knows what he's doing . . . I need to make an urgent phone call now, Ella. Can I use your telephone?'

He made a phone call to Jenny Kenning. The polite, curious voice of the receptionist replied immediately and there was only a short pause before he was put through to the probation officer.

'Hello,' she said, busy, friendly, detached. 'How are things going?'

He did not know how to answer that.

'I need your help again,' he said. 'Could you tell me where Tom French was convicted and sentenced, and where the offence actually took place?'

On this occasion Jenny Kenning did not hesitate about whether she should give him the information.

'Just hang on,' she said, 'I'll look in the file. I know that the order wasn't made in a local court.'

There was a short delay.

'I've found the original social inquiry report,' she said. 'Tom appeared in Penzance Magistrates' Court. The offence occurred while he was on holiday on St Mary's in the Isles of Scilly. Is that any help?'

'That's just what I wanted to know. You're wonderful.'

'Put in a good word for me when I get the sack for skipping team meetings.'

He laughed and was about to replace the phone when she stopped him.

'You might be interested to know that one of Tom's friends is up in court soon – for possession of cannabis and assaulting the police. He's on remand.'

'One of Tom's friends?'

He was surprised. He thought of the twitchers he knew and wondered why he had not heard about any arrest.

'Dennis Shawcroft,' she said. 'He's a chef at the White Lodge.'

Somehow he had never thought of Tom and Dennis as friends.

'Were they friends?' he asked.

'They used to drink together. Tom liked to think of everyone as his friend. He mentioned Dennis occasionally.'

'Do you know when Dennis was taken into custody?'

'No, not without checking. But it was one day last week, because one of my colleagues visited him in the remand centre on Monday.'

So Dennis had not been involved in Adam's accident. If he was in the remand centre he could not have pushed the boy down the well. George wondered if the police suspected Dennis of Tom's death – a charge of assaulting the police was serious enough to warrant remand in custody, but it was also an easy charge to fabricate. Perhaps the police wanted time to collect further information. Perhaps they knew something which he didn't.

'When is his case due to be heard?'

'Not for a fortnight. I must go. I'm wanted in the divorce court. Come and take me out to lunch again some time.'

'I will,' he said. 'Thank you so much. You've been a tremendous help.'

He stood for a while by the phone. Tom's probation order was made in October, two years previously. That summer Sally had been on Tresco, Peter on St Agnes and Tom on St Mary's, all Scilly islands, and all the young people had been interested in birds. It was impossible to suppose that they had never met. Peter admitted knowing Tom, claimed that they had been friends – surely he would have invited Tom to visit him on St Agnes. Peter would know if there had been any connection between Sally and Tom then. And if Sally had worked on Tresco for a whole season, she must at least have recognized the name of the son-in-law of one of the biggest landowners on Scilly. Why was she suddenly taken ill on the night of Ella's party? To avoid seeing Peter, because he knew something of her relationship with Tom? Because she knew something about Adam's 'accident'?

There was a sudden intense frustration that now he knew the right questions he had no one to answer them. Tom was dead. Sally refused to speak and Peter was in Perth, watching a black stork. Even Rob, who had spent a 'few days' with Tom on St Mary's that autumn, was not available. But he had to know. Before he could make use of his information about Bernard Cranshaw, before he could come to any conclusion about Dennis, he had to know. The desire for sudden and dramatic action returned, and now it was irresistible. He had talked and listened for long enough, and he had achieved nothing. Now, perhaps, action was appropriate. There was nothing further he could do to protect Adam until he returned from Scotland. He would go that night. He opened the door into Ella's kitchen.

'I'll take you home,' he said to Molly. 'I'm going to Scilly. I'll go on my own.'


In the evenings Terry sat in his den and remembered his grandfather. He had never known his parents, but he could remember his grandfather well and all the things the old man had taught him. His grandfather had been good at running away – from fanners and keepers and the policeman in the village. He hadn't mixed with the people in the village, although he had been born there. Terry knew that he had moved around a lot – he'd been to Canada and had hooked up with the travelling people, picking fruit and vegetables. Grandfather had told him stories about the travellers. When Terry had lived with him, his home had still been a caravan, hidden from the road and the village by a small thicket and from the nearest farm by an enormous forest of bramble and gorse. The farmer, a drunken Welshman, had been mourning the death of a wife who had left him just enough money to allow him to grieve, and to let the farm grow derelict. Perhaps, at some time, he had given Terry's grandfather permission to live in the rusty, filthy caravan, but he took no notice of his tenant.

Terry could remember his years with his grandfather more clearly than all his time in hospital. Sometimes they had done casual work for local farmers – his grandfather never sent him to school and Terry always worked with him. Some days his grandfather had stayed in bed until the afternoon. Terry was quite often left alone. He had learnt how to make snares and to cook rabbits, and the best farms and fields and gardens to steal from. The village children had laughed at him and the grown-ups had shouted at him. Sometimes he was hungry and quite often he was very cold.

His grandfather had frightened him with the stories of the Welfare Man. When the Welfare Man finally turned up, Terry was surprised because he was friendly. Terry liked him rather more than Grandfather and went with him quite happily. The children's homes and the foster parents had been different, and he ran away from them.

Now, sitting in the evening sun, the farm seemed not much different. The caravan had gone and the house had been done up, but the thicket and the brambles and the gorse still made it a good place to hide. Terry was proud that he had found it again. He had walked from Skeffingham, and it had been evening when he had arrived. For a while the absence of the caravan had confused him; he expected everything to be the same. Then he had remembered the dens he made as a child and in the warm, still evening he had built a secret home, by tunnelling through the brambles, cutting out branches until he had cleared a space long and wide enough for him to lie in and just high enough for him to sit up.

Now, three days later, it was as if Mrs Black and the White Lodge hotel had never existed. He never thought about them. He lived just as he had as a child. Since leaving Skeffingham he had seen nobody. The farmhouse was empty – perhaps it had been turned into a holiday home. As he had grown more adventurous he had explored first the outbuildings of the farm, then the house itself, breaking in through the kitchen window. Its pantry had been filled with tinned food and now he added tinned meat, cold baked beans and soup to his diet of stolen vegetables. He improved his home by making a roof from a sheet of corrugated iron taken from an outhouse, and by laying an empty fertilizer sack on the floor. He never thought about why he had run away or why he was there.

By the time they reached the place carefully marked on their map, it was too late for there to be any hope of seeing black stork. They had driven Peter's hire car through a small, grey village, crossed a low bridge over a grey, shallow river and parked. It was not quite dark, but there was little colour left in the landscape. Gentle wooded hills rose out of a wide river valley. Even at the bridge at the base of the valley there was a sense of being high above sea level, a smell of peat and a cold wind. Following the detailed instructions given to Rob, they walked along the shingle track which was all that remained of the railway line that had once followed the course of the river. All around it was very quiet – there were no cars on the road from the village – and the sound of their feet on the shingle filled the dusk, allowing no opportunity for speech. They had been told that there was a place to sleep and they found it, an old signal box, stripped now of its brass fittings and levers, but still sound and dry, its steps solid. Like a hide, its big window looked out across the woods and flood meadows. They made tea on a Primus, and fried bacon and talked about twitching.

Despite himself Adam was content, carried along by the spirit of the trip. He had been surprised when the others had asked him to go with them and was too eager to get away from Rushy to consider the risk. He knew that he had offended Tina. She had come to Ella's on her own at first, had tried to be friendly, but had asked too many questions. He had been surprised when she had returned with the others and the news of the black stork. She seemed to realize now that he had nothing to say. Perhaps, when it was all forgotten, they could be friendly again. He sat cross-legged on his sleeping bag and listened to the others, wishing occasionally that he had the confidence to join in.

Tina had been injured by Adam's attitude to her. Her pride had been hurt. She had come to Rushy because she hoped to see him. She had even dressed up for him. She was determined now not to show that she had cared for him, and directed her conversation towards Rob and Peter. She no longer cared whether Adam thought he had slipped down the well or whether he thought that he had been pushed. He was a silly young boy who had no interest in ringing. She was arguing with Rob and Peter about the relative merits of ringing and twitching.

'At least ringing has some scientific value,' she said. 'There's some purpose to it. We know far more about migration and population patterns because of the ringing scheme. Twitching is just a game.'

'You're quite right,' Rob Earl said. 'It's all just a game.'

'Why don't you cheat?' she asked. 'If you were out on your own you could claim to have seen anything and nobody would know.'

'I would know,' Peter said. 'Twitching is very competitive,

especially if you're going for a year list, but it's still seeing the thing that counts, enjoying it for yourself, not describing it to somebody else.'

'What's so special about a year list?'

'There's something exciting about seeing how many birds you can see in Britain in one year. It's a challenge.'

Rob stretched. 'I only believe in a world list. Nothing else is the same.'

'But don't people cheat?' Tina persisted. 'What about stringers?'

'Stringers aren't usually cheats. They don't purposely fabricate. They're just bad birders. They're too optimistic. If they see a bird which might be a rarity, they claim it anyway. It doesn't do them any good. Once you get a reputation as a stringer no one believes anything you see.'

Rob Earl was lying on his back on the floor, his rucksack under his head, a roll-up between his lips. *Did he try to look like that?* Adam wondered. *Did he cultivate that Bob Dylan image with his beard, dark eyes and strange clothes?* Rob lit a match by striking it against his thumbnail, and Adam decided that he did. Adam sat forward and prepared to speak, but Rob continued:

'It's all a matter of ethics,' he said. 'Twitchers' ethics. Tom was a great believer in twitchers' ethics, wasn't he? We were always taking the piss. He had a rule for every occasion and no one ever took any notice.'

'I didn't know Tom very well once he gave up ringing,' Tina said. 'He was a good ringer. He always handled the birds so carefully. What sort of a twitcher was he?'

'He had too many principles,' Rob said. 'When he lived up to them he was boring and when he didn't he was guilty.'

'That's very cruel,' she said. 'Didn't you like him?'

'Yes, I liked him. But I never felt relaxed with him. He was too kind, too generous. It was as if he had such a low opinion of himself that he had to buy your friendship. He was never rude or bad-tempered.'

Peter was sitting by the window. There was no moon, but the stars were sharp and bright.

'The last time I saw Tom,' he said, 'was at a party on St Mary's, the autumn before last. He'd rented a whole cottage for himself and he had a party. As you say, he liked to make big, generous gestures. But I don't think that he was buying friendship, he genuinely wanted people to have a good time. Like lots of twitchers, he didn't have any social life outside birding. It was one of those magic evenings when everyone you meet is interesting or beautiful and they make you feel the same, and you drink enough but not too much, and the music is good. I had to leave before everyone else to get back to St Agnes, Barbara and the milking. I looked for Tom to say goodbye, but I couldn't find him.'

He stared, unseeing, through the window and remembered the girl who had made the party magic. She had been possessed by a wild gaiety that night, which had been quite unusual, although she had drunk nothing. She had danced with him. They had never danced together before. He had said goodbye to her, not knowing that it would be for the last time. He wondered if he had been right to leave St Agnes, and if it had all been worthwhile.

Rob was thinking about Tom French. He had told Tina that he had liked him. That, of course, was untrue. Tom had been pompous. He had told Rob once about a rare bird he had found on some private land. Rob put it out on the

179

grapevine, and Tom had been furious. There had not been much damage – a hedge had been a little dented in places – but Tom had lectured him about ethics and responsibility, and the image of the birdwatcher in the community. It had made him sick. He wondered if Tina would have understood if he had told her the truth. She was a strange girl. He had thought that she had been close to Tom at one time, but she seemed quite detached now. Perhaps she was just very honest. Not a hypocrite like most other people, like him. He wondered how many people were really sorry that Tom was dead.

Adam quietly said goodnight to the others and climbed into his sleeping bag. He wished he could be more like them, more relaxed, more extrovert. He hoped desperately that he was not spoiling the trip for them. He slept fitfully, troubled occasionally by a nightmare of water and claustrophobia.

Tina did not lie near to Adam, but she slept lightly and when he cried out in his sleep she woke up. She began to devise a weird and complicated trap to catch a black stork and soon drifted back towards sleep. After all, she thought as she dozed, men were only a distraction. Since meeting Adam at Scardrift Flat she had not been able to concentrate on her ringing. Neither had she been able to give full attention to her university work and that was important. She wanted to be a professional ornithologist, not to play at it like these twitchers. She should have realized that it would not work with Adam, should be grateful that she had come to her senses so quickly. She should have learnt her lesson from Tom. She had been infatuated with him when she was sitting O-levels and she hadn't got the grades she had hoped for. She hadn't resented it. Not then. Not until Tom gave up ringing, gave up serious birdwatching and became a twitcher.

Twitching was a distraction too. She should never have come on this trip. She was missing an important lecture, but she had wanted to see the bird. She hoped that they would see the stork early the next day, so that she could return to Southampton to her work and the ringing group. She slept again and dreamed happily of cannon-netting thousands of waders, many with foreign rings.

Peter sat all night, by the window.

Only Rob slept soundly.

George caught the overnight train to Penzance. Watching the lights of Bridgewater station flash past, he tried to convince himself that the journey was necessary. The train was warm and comfortable and nearly empty. He wanted to sleep. Only guilt kept him awake, the sense that he was playing truant, and an overwhelming anxiety for Adam's safety. He began to read his notes and lists, a ritual gesture in an attempt to relieve his guilt, but he could not concentrate, and fell asleep, still holding his briefcase on his knee.

Alone, in her bed, Sally cried herself to sleep.

# Chapter Eleven

In Scilly it was already high summer, too late for flowers, too late to avoid holidaymakers. The helicopter was crowded, there was no pleasure in the flight, none of the usual anticipation at the first sight of the islands. George was in a hurry. He wanted to complete his inquiries in a day, knowing his haste to be as illogical as his journey, and he found in the packed streets, the lingering, scantily dressed people, a target for his anger and frustration. As he reached the harbour a tripper boat was just about to leave for Tresco and he took it, although he had planned to visit St Agnes first. He could not contemplate waiting. It was hot, even on the water, and the flat, open boat seemed alive with pink-fleshed teenage girls, as a bait box is with maggots.

He had never liked Tresco. There was something obscene about its fertility; there were too many green shiny plants, too much green altogether. The abundance of its vegetation was reflected by the affluence of its residents. It was the rich person's island and perhaps it was this rather than the geography of Tresco which coloured his attitude to it. The cloying smell of exotic shrubs and the expensive scent of the women drinking gin in the lounge bar of the pub had become confused in his mind, and he did not know which he disliked the most.

George had already telephoned the hotel, and one of the under-managers was expecting him. The man's obsequious distaste did nothing to improve his temper.

'As I explained, I want to speak to one of your staff who knew Sally Johnson. You employed her here two seasons ago.'

'Yes, sir, and your reason for wanting to know?' He never asked a question directly, as if it were more delicate to seek information only by inflection, by a gentle wheedling. 'I don't think you said you were a policeman?'

'It's a Home Office matter,' Palmer-Jones said, and thought: *If he wants to know any more let him ask me directly.* But the man seemed satisfied. Perhaps he didn't want to show his ignorance about the sphere of influence of the Home Office.

'There is one lady who may be able to help – our head waitress, Annie. Your young lady worked under her in the dining room. We have so many casual staff that I'm sure you won't expect me to remember. But Annie will be able to help you. Please don't keep her away from her duties for too long. We're rather busy and it will soon be lunchtime. If you'd like to use my office, I'll send her to you.'

Annie cheered him immediately. She was an energetic, middle-aged woman with short grey hair who had the competent, efficient air of a nurse. Making sure that the manager had gone, she sat down and stretched her tired feet in front of her, grateful for the unexpected rest. She spoke with a north-country accent.

'Sally was a quiet girl, hard-working. She'd come with good references from a big hotel in Scotland, but she had no airs and graces. The residents didn't take to her, you know, as they did to some of the girls, because she didn't push herself forward, she didn't make any effort to be friendly to them. But she was a good worker. We missed her when she left.'

'Did she have any boyfriends? Perhaps among the guests. Did she talk about anyone special?'

'No. I'd never seen her with a boy. That's why I was so surprised when she left like that. We didn't have any idea. She always went away from the island on her days off, but she said that she was exploring. Walking, you know. She was that type of girl. Quiet, reserved. That's why we were all so shocked.'

'Shocked?'

'Aye. When we realized she was expecting. She started to be late coming down in the mornings, and one of the other girls found her being sick. I think she was hoping, you know, that it wasn't true, but she had to believe it in the end. It's happening all the time here, though you'd think these days they'd have more sense. But I never would have expected it of Sal.'

'And did she never mention anybody who could have been the father? Anybody at all?'

'I remember, the day just before she left – she went quite suddenly without telling anybody. He—' she pointed to the desk where George sat – 'he was furious. Well the day before, she went to a party on St Mary's. She worked herself into a terrible state about it because she was supposed to be working that night, and none of the girls would swap with her. She was so upset that I let her go in the end. She'd have been no use at work. I suppose it was expecting that was making her so depressed. One of the girls asked her about the party. You know how malicious these girls can be. They were teasing her about some man they'd seen her with, and to stop them Sally told them about the party. It wasn't an islander who was giving it, it was a birdwatcher. You know, they all come to the islands in the autumn.'

'Do you know his name?'

She shook her head regretfully. 'I remember that she stayed out all night. I was worried about her because she'd been so depressed. She got the first boat back the next morning. Then she must have packed up all her stuff. She left that day. I never saw her again.'

'And she never got in touch? You didn't know what had happened to her?'

Annie shook her head. 'No, though the police were here looking for her later that week. They scared me at first. I wondered what had happened. I thought she might have had an accident. But they said they just wanted to take a statement from her. They'd raided that party she went to, and they'd found drugs there. They wanted her to be a witness. I never would have thought that she'd be mixed up in anything like that.'

'Do you remember any details of the case? Who was being charged?'

'No. The police didn't mention anything like that.'

George prepared to leave then, and Annie, regretfully, got up to go back to work.

'Did you know Peter Littleton?' George asked suddenly.

'The one that married that lass on St Agnes? Aye, of course I know the name and I knew him by sight. He used to bring

185

his wife here for dinner, sometimes, when they were first married, but I haven't seen him for a couple of years. He's left her now, you know.'

'Did Sally Johnson know him?'

'I don't think she would have known him, but she would have known of him, that's for certain. He was a character. Everyone on Scilly knew of him.'

George held the door for her and followed her out. It was cool and quiet in the hotel. Outside, the heat and the humidity overpowered him. Even on the sea, in the crowded, noisy boat, it seemed unnaturally airless. When he arrived at St Mary's he was told that there were no tripper boats that day to St Agnes, so he chartered one himself, taking a momentary pleasure in asking for a receipt so that he could charge the expense to Clive Anderson. As soon as he had enjoyed the thought, it seemed in poor taste.

Because there were no day trippers, St Agnes was quiet. It was midday and the pub near the quay was open but, despite tremendous temptation, he walked past. He had been to St Agnes often enough for some of the locals to recognize him, but he did not feel ready yet to answer questions. St Agnes was his favourite Scilly isle. As he walked up the track, between the drystone walls, the familiar and peaceful sights and smells relaxed him. He felt at home.

He was walking past the Gugh, the sandy peninsula on the east of the island, when somebody called his name. Before he turned he recognized the voice. Charlotte Cavanagh had been schoolmistress on St Agnes for thirty years. She had come to the island as a young widow straight after the war. When she retired she moved from the schoolhouse to a tiny cottage on the shore, but little else had changed. The islanders had admired her, and been afraid of her when she first arrived, brave and outspoken and a little wild. She still kept herself apart. She was Mrs Cavanagh to most of them, and she rarely mixed socially with any of the island families. She was passionately interested in the islands, in their history, natural history and archaeology. She painted them and wrote about them, but she still did not belong.

She was very tall, and was dressed as dramatically and eccentrically as usual, in bright orange corduroy trousers, a fisherman's smock and sandals. Her grey hair was short and her face was long and bony, very forceful and expressive. She was carrying a sketch pad and pencils.

'Darling boy,' she said. 'You knew I was bored and you've come to see me.' She still spoke with the extravagance that was fashionable in her pre-war adolescence. It was as if time had stopped with the death of her husband at the beginning of the war, when she was twenty.

'Not exactly to see you,' he said, 'but I want to talk to you.'

'You must come for lunch. Come now, before I die of curiosity. I want to know all about it. What's brought you here? Not a rare bird because I should have heard, and we should be invaded by hundreds of dirty young men. How's darling Molly? You didn't come last autumn. I do miss you both.'

Her cottage was shady and smelled, George thought, like a good whole-food shop. She made tea deftly and seriously, then brought out a loaf, cheese and smoked fish. They sat together by an open window. The breeze moved the curtains and carried into the house the scents of the garden. George sat without eating, without thinking, just enjoying the peace.

'Darling, do stop being so mysterious. Tell me what it's all about.'

'Did you ever meet Tom French?' he asked. 'He came here a few times, although I think he stayed on St Mary's when he was last on Scilly. He was a birdwatcher. He was murdered about a fortnight ago, in Rushy, the village on the north Norfolk coast.'

She was not shocked. Very little shocked her.

'I've probably met him. I try to see most of the rarities. The birdwatchers all seem to know me, and I talk to them, but I don't know any names. Are you involved in it professionally?'

'Not really. I retired last year, you know. But I was asked to find out if the murderer was a birdwatcher and I agreed.'

'And what brings you here?'

'Peter Littleton.'

'Ah, of course, dear Peter. Did he know the poor boy?'

'He was a friend. But I think there were other connections.'

'And you've come here to find out what they were?'

'Something like that.'

'I'm not sure that I want to help you. Peter was a dear friend.' He must have shown his disappointment, his tiredness, because she grinned. 'But of course I'll talk to you about Peter. If I don't someone else will, and the islanders don't like him.' She smiled again, a wide mischievous smile. 'When he left, it wasn't with a whimper. They're still talking about it. He wrote a rude, if accurate description of his wife in red paint on the post office wall. You can still see it faintly even now. And he drove Ted Baxter's tractor into the harbour.

'Of course they never liked him. He was an outsider and a birdwatcher too, which made it worse. He lost his temper before he went. But those were childish things, hurtful but not vicious, and Barbara provoked him. I taught her, you know. Barbara Baxter she was then. Quite a pleasant little thing. A bit simple. Not at all academic. She tried her best, but she wasn't up to it. Of course, Ted Baxter blamed me for the poor school reports. Instead of letting her go with her friends to the comprehensive on St Mary's where she would have been perfectly happy, he sent her to a private school on the mainland. They didn't teach her anything useful and made her sulky.'

'Did you see a lot of Peter Littleton?'

'He used to come down quite often. For some intelligent conversation.' She smiled at herself. 'That sounds terribly arrogant and snobbish, doesn't it? We're just different, Peter and I. We didn't fit in. Ted Baxter is an intelligent man. His intelligence makes him a lot of money. But he isn't interesting. Peter would come to see me, perhaps one evening a week. We would listen to my music, talk about books. The islanders thought it was very strange that he took so much interest in me. When he went off as he did, they almost blamed me. Very medieval, as if I were a witch who'd cast a spell on him.'

'Did he ever mention a girl, Sally Johnson? She worked on Tresco. She would have been here two years ago.'

'I know that there was a girl. He never told me her name.'

'Did he tell you anything about her?'

'For that summer he talked about nothing else. No practical details like her name or where she worked. Just about how much in love he was. Madly in love like a teenager.'

George remembered fleetingly that Rob had described Tom's love for Sally like that. Charlotte continued:

'Then came the agonizing about whether he should leave Barbara. He felt he owed her something. She had given him four years on St Agnes and he loved the place. He had decided that he would leave her, when the girl disappeared. For a while he tried to find her, but she'd hurt his pride. He thought that she'd just decided that she didn't want to know him.'

It was tantalizing. He knew that Peter and Sally had been seeing each other that summer, that they had fallen in love, but there was still no proof.

'If I'm right about the identity of the girl,' George said, 'she was pregnant. Did Peter know that?'

'No,' she said, moved almost to tears. 'Oh, the poor darling boy, the poor girl. He never knew. He thought that she just ran away.'


Ted Baxter was as hostile as George had expected him to be. He was a short, squat man, built like a Welsh miner. When George arrived he was scraping the mud from his wellingtons at the kitchen door. It was teatime. He must have been impressed by George's air of authority because he asked him, grudgingly, into the house. When George explained why he was there, Baxter's hostility became focused not on George, but on his son-in-law. The farmer made no pretence at concern about the death of a birdwatcher, but although it was obvious that his only feeling for Peter was one of obsessive hatred, his attitude to his son-in-law's involvement in the case was ambiguous. He was worried that his daughter might, in some way, become implicated, but he was delighted that all his suspicions about Peter's character had been confirmed. He supposed, without question, that Peter was the murderer.

As bearer of such news, George was made almost welcome. Baxter ordered his wife to pour tea for George and in a musing, gloating way began to talk. The farmhouse was not a traditional cottage but a modern bungalow with large windows giving a spectacular view down the island to the sea. As George listened to the man talking, he looked out and thought that it was a perfect place to fall in love.

'I was against it from the start,' Baxter said. 'She could have done better than that layabout. She was as pretty as a picture. She could have had any man she wanted. She said that he'd been to Oxford, but you would never have known, the way he dressed and talked. They let anyone into the universities now. Degrees are two a penny. He had no job when he first came here, no prospects. He was one of those twitchers, sleeping rough on the beach. He met Barbara in the Tavern. She was working there that summer. She didn't need to work but she'd just left school, and was feeling bored. You know these young people. He got round her somehow with his smooth talking and his poetry, and his fancy ways.

'He came to see me, respectable enough, to ask if they could get married. I can tell you I was shocked. To be fair, he was willing enough when I said to wait for a year, but she wouldn't have it. She wanted to be married that summer, and nothing else would do. I should have been firm, told her to wait, but in the end I agreed. She's our only daughter and maybe we spoil her.

'It never worked out of course, not from the beginning. He was a clown. He couldn't settle to work. I run a serious business and he never could take it seriously. All the same, I could have put up with all that, Mr Palmer-Jones, if he'd been good to our Barbara. After they were married he hardly seemed to take any notice of her. He'd got what he wanted – her money and a home on the island here. We put them in the old farmhouse where we lived until we had this place built. It was comfortable enough – Barbara had it done out just as she wanted – but he never appreciated it. There was a garden at the back of the house, and he just let it run wild. I had to send one of my men down to clear it in the end. He took no care of the place.

'He never took Barbara out. He spent all his free time out on the island with his binoculars looking at bloody birds. And in the evenings, when it was too dark to see, he'd have his nose stuck in a bloody book. Barbara used to come round here, just to have someone to talk to. He was mad about those birds. Crazy. Look at the way he behaved when he left here. That wasn't the work of a sane man. Barbara's been on tranquillizers ever since that night. She still can't sleep properly without the tablets. That's what birdwatching does to a man. It turns his mind, and changes him into a lunatic. I won't have them on my land now. I can't bear to see them.'

'Do you know if Mr Littleton saw any other women while he was married to your daughter?' George asked, still looking at the magnificent view, wondering if the island had worked its magic twice for Peter. Was it here that he had first fallen in love with Sally, as well as with Barbara? Because, despite the lack of proof, he was convinced that Peter and Sally had been in love. He knew that Peter was Barnaby's father.

'Him?' Ted Baxter almost spat with disgust. 'He wouldn't have had it in him. Who would have wanted another woman when he could have had my daughter? I tell you. You don't know these birdwatchers. They don't care about anything else except their birds.'

'So there were never any rumours about Mr Littleton and another woman?'

'Rumours. There may have been rumours. There are always

192

rumours in a place like this. There have been rumours enough about Barbara and none of them are true. Not one of them. She was a good wife to him.'

The back door leading to the farmyard opened then, and a young woman walked in. She was wearing jeans and leather boots and a loose jersey. She had been riding. She was beautiful, in the conventional way that a model is beautiful. Her tan was too deep, her lashes too long to be natural. Her hair was wind-swept, but when she shook it, it settled back into its ordained shape. She raised her eyebrows at their visitor with an attempt at sophisticated curiosity, but when she spoke, the simple, friendly girl described by Charlotte Cavanagh showed through.

'Who's our visitor, Dad? Is there any tea in the pot, Mum?'

George saw no sign of the strain described by Ted Baxter, the dependence on tranquillizers. She looked healthy; pampered. In middle age she would grow fat.

'This is Mr Palmer-Jones, my love,' said her father, as if he were talking to an invalid. 'He's come to ask some questions about that husband of yours. You don't have to talk to him if you don't want to. We don't want you to upset yourself.'

'He's my ex-husband, Dad,' she said. 'And I don't care at all about answering any questions. What's he done? Been in trouble with the police again, has he?'

The last question seemed to be a malicious attempt to bring her father to anger. She shot a defiant look at him as she spoke. But Baxter misunderstood her, and thought that she was accusing him of telling the police about Peter's final fling on the island. He answered defensively.

'Why are you talking about the police? I promised that I

wouldn't go to the police and I never did. And I paid off Mary at the post office so she wouldn't make a fuss. He's never been in trouble with the police. Not because of me at any rate.'

'I didn't say because of you, Dad,' she said with another failed attempt at sophistication. 'He'd been in court before he came to the island that first summer.'

Before Ted Baxter could use this information as yet another indication of his opinion of Peter Littleton, George interrupted.

'Did he tell you why he'd been in court?' George asked, knowing already what the answer would be.

'Drugs,' she said flatly. 'He'd been in trouble for taking dope.'

'Did you know that when you married him?' Ted Baxter was flushed with rage but, in an attempt not to upset his daughter, he tried to restrain his anger. 'You knew he was a junkie and you married him. I've had a drug addict under my roof?'

'Oh, Dad,' she said condescendingly. 'He wasn't a drug addict. Everyone does it these days. It's nothing to make a fuss about.'

Ted Baxter, luckily, seemed able to find no reply to this, and George asked:

'Did he use drugs when you knew him, when you were married?'

'Not much.'

She spoke with regret, as if admitting an indiscretion. Perhaps she thought it was sophisticated to take drugs.

'I think sometimes the birdwatchers brought him some. I know that he smoked occasionally at parties.'

'Did you ever meet any of his friends?'

'I certainly did,' she said petulantly. 'They came to stay every spring and autumn. They made a terrible mess all over the house. There were sleeping bags everywhere. I even found one of those twitchers sleeping in the bath. I stuck it for two years and then I put my foot down. Peter brought them home for meals sometimes, usually when I was out, but I wouldn't have them to stay.'

'Did any of them become your friends?'

She tried to look amused.

'They hardly seemed to notice that I was there. They only ever talked about birds.'

'Did you meet Tom French or Rob Earl?'

'I remember Rob Earl. He's the good-looking one. He looks like that old-fashioned film star . . . What's his name? He was in all the westerns on the television. Rob got drunk at our wedding. I've heard of Tom French, but I can't remember what he looks like.'

'He had a party on St Mary's a year ago last September. Peter went to it. Did you go with him?'

'No,' she said definitely. 'I never went to any of the bird-watchers' parties. I was never made to feel welcome.'


George walked back to the quay the long way round, along the cliffs. The scent of gorse blossom was sweet and heavy, and the light was very clear. Gulls and guillemots, unusually lazy, sat in ledges on the cliffs, or glided below him. Further away, he could see his boat waiting for him and the boatman sitting on the sand, apparently asleep.

He sat on the short grass and tried to evaluate the infor-mation he had gained since coming to the island. There was really nothing new, nothing tangible. He knew now that Sally had become involved with some man while she was working on Tresco, and that she had left suddenly because she was pregnant. He could have deduced that from Barnaby's age. He had learnt that the police wanted to question her about drugs found at a party she had attended. Surely he could infer that the party had been Tom's. It coincided exactly with the date of Tom's court appearance. Why, then, was he so convinced that Peter and not Tom was the father of Sally's child? Because of the way that Sally and Tom's relationship had developed and because she had never allowed Tom to be considered the father. But he still had no real evidence of any connection between Peter and Sally, apart from the coincidence that both had been on Scilly and both had been in love. He had learnt that Peter had been prosecuted in the past for drug abuse, and that he still occasionally took cannabis. Did that have any relevance? Had he planted the drug on Tom at the party? That was aimless speculation.

The heat was making George drowsy and muddled his thoughts. He stood up quickly and walked back towards the boat. He had wasted enough time. Perhaps the young people would be back from Scotland and he had more questions now to ask them.

He was walking down the lane towards the quay when Charlotte Cavanagh caught up with him. She moved strongly and purposefully, like a man.

'George, my dear. I'm so glad that you're still here. I was afraid that I'd miss you. I've remembered something. It doesn't look very good for Peter, but I suppose that I should tell you. Peter had a rival in his love for the girl. He used to laugh about it and about how slow and timid this other boy was.

"She doesn't even know that he fancies her," Peter said to me. "And yet he's so lovesick that he doesn't think about anything else. Perhaps I should leave her alone, to give him a chance. He'd be better for her than me. But I can't do it." Oh George, I'm sure that the name of the boy was Tom. I'm certain of it. He was a birdwatcher and he was staying on St Mary's.'

So the trip had been worthwhile. He had made the vital connection between Tom, Peter and Sally. They had all been together on the Scillies and they had all been in Norfolk on the day of Tom's death. For the moment that was enough for him. In the small boat, with the breeze blowing against his face and the low sun reflected on the water, the magic of the Scillies began to work for him again and he was untroubled.

# Chapter Twelve

MOLLY WOKE TO THE smell of frying bacon and mushrooms. George was home then. She roused slowly from a deep sleep, comfortable because George was back. He had not come to bed; she hoped that he had slept in the train. He had a remarkable facility for managing without sleep, but she could not understand it, and she was anxious about him. She sat up.

The bedroom was appallingly untidy, furnished from auctions and jumble sales. Her clothes were spilling out of drawers and were piled on the unsteady wooden bedside table, which her eldest son had made in his school woodwork class. George's wardrobe was firmly shut and his side of the bed clear of debris, but everywhere was very dusty. Molly did not notice. It was never any different. She tried to tell, from the kitchen sounds, if George had had a successful trip. She dreaded his perceived failures because of the pain of his self-doubt, his loneliness and guilt, and on her own account, because the effort of getting through to him, to reassure him, drained and exhausted her.

She heard footsteps on the stairs, then the door opened

and George was bringing her tea. After all the years of marriage, she was still deeply pleased to see him. He opened the curtains and the sunlight almost blinded her, so that she still could not tell from his face if he was happy or disappointed. He cleared some of her clothes from the table onto the floor, then placed the tea beside her.

'Tell me what happened,' she said. 'Did you find out what you wanted?'

'Breakfast is ready,' he said. 'I'll tell you in the kitchen.'

He bent down and kissed her. She watched him go with relief, knowing that whatever had happened on Scilly, he was more at ease. She washed and dressed quickly, then followed him down. He had already eaten, but poured out coffee for them both.

'Did you find anything useful?' she demanded.

'I'll tell you in a moment, but first have you had any news from Ella or Mrs Black? Has Terry been found? Have Rob and the others arrived back from Scotland?'

'No to all the questions. I phoned Ella yesterday afternoon. The police seem to be doing a house-to-house search for Terry in Rushy and Fenquay and they're moving on to Skeffingham today, but they've told Mrs Black that they've no warrant for his arrest. They just want to talk to him. Ella hasn't heard from Pete, Rob or Adam at all. She's quite hurt. She's got the impression that they're phoning someone else for any information about birds.'

Molly looked at him over her gold-rimmed National Health spectacles.

'Well,' she said impatiently. 'It's your turn now. What did you find out?'

'That Sally Johnson has been lying to us. She left Tresco

a year ago last September, apparently because she was pregnant, although there may have been other reasons. She left
in a hurry. The day before she went she was at a party given
by a birdwatcher who sounds very like Tom French. Later
the police came to the hotel to look for her, because she had
been a witness in a drugs case.'

'So Tom was Barnaby's father after all, and that was why
he was so keen for Sally to marry him and move to Bristol
with him.'

'I don't think so. According to Charlotte Cavanagh, who
seems to have known Peter very well, Peter was in love at
that time, not with his wife, but with a stranger. Do you
remember that, when we first met Peter at the greenish
warbler, he mentioned in quite an offhand way that he only
became completely disillusioned with his wife when he met
someone else? I think that he was talking about Sally. Charlotte
said, too, that someone else was interested in the girl. Someone
called Tom.'

'But Sally had no legal ties with Tom. If she'd wanted to
live with Peter she could have done. Why didn't she? Did
Peter know that she was in Norfolk?'

'I don't know. I don't know what it all means. Perhaps now
that I know this much, Sally will tell me the rest. There's
another complication. According to Barbara, Peter's ex-wife,
Peter used drugs. Not often, but quite regularly. He even had
a conviction for cannabis abuse.'

'Is that significant? It isn't so unusual.'

'It's just another coincidence, isn't it? Tom, known never
to touch drugs, got charged with possession of cannabis. I'm
sure that Peter was at that party, but he got away. And talking
about coincidences, I want to talk to Bernard Cranshaw about

those letters, and about who told him that Tom French had been to court.'

'So you're planning to go back to Rushy today?'

'Definitely. I want to see Bernard Cranshaw, and I must go to the remand centre where Dennis Shawcroft, the chef from the White Lodge, is being held in custody. After all, he seems to have had something to do with Terry's disappearance. He may even know where he is. He certainly made every effort to stop the lad talking to us.'

'Clive Anderson came to see you last night,' Molly said. 'He wanted to know where Adam was. Adam hasn't been in touch since his accident, apparently. His school hasn't heard from him. He's supposed to be taking A-levels next week. He's allowed the time off for revision, but he should have been into the school to discuss an essay. Poor Mr Anderson. He was quite human. He's very worried about Adam, you know. He wasn't very happy that he'd disappeared to Scotland with the other three. He almost accused us of being negligent.'

'He's right,' George said. 'Does he think that Adam will come back to sit his exams?'

'He didn't say. I got the feeling that he came to get information, not to give it.'

'Do you think that he knows more than he'll admit?'

'It's impossible to say. That's why it was always so difficult to appear before him in court. His face was so impassive. You could never tell whether or not you'd got through to him. Last night he seemed very eager to find out exactly where Adam was.'

'Did you tell him?'

'I didn't know. They'll have seen the stork yesterday evening and could be anywhere by now.'

'I wish we knew whom Adam met in Fenquay on the morning of his accident.'

'You don't think that it was Clive Anderson?'

'I don't know at all. I want to talk to Sally about it. She may be able to give some description of Adam's companion.'

George was impatient to get to Norfolk. Molly packed in a disorganized, absent-minded way, growing flustered as George urged her to hurry. It was just the same before every trip.

When they reached Rushy George dropped Molly at the Windmill. It was Friday and already the cafe was full of twitchers talking about the weather forecast, the high pressure, the east winds and the possibility of migrants.

Before leaving home George had telephoned one of his contacts in the Home Office. He was expected at the remand centre, where Dennis Shawcroft was being held in custody. So, reluctantly, he left the enthusiastic birdwatchers to their speculation, and Molly and Ella to their gossip, and drove inland towards Norwich.

He had visited many such places before, but coming across the long, grey concrete walls, the threatening notices, the floodlights, after driving down a sunny, country road, there was still a shock, a sense of unbelievable incongruity.

The gate officer was expecting him, and was friendly, told a joke. That was another incongruity: humanity in such an apparently inhuman, functional place. He was shown into a waiting room, where three men and a woman were already sitting. In the corridor outside a prisoner was ineffectually pushing a mop over the tiled floor. George smiled briefly at the other occupants of the room. The men were at home there. Two of them were solicitors, George thought, and the third, as easily identified by his leather jacket as if he were wearing a uniform, was an officer of the CID. The woman, no more than a girl, was nervous. She was reading a file intently, making notes. She could have been a young solicitor, or perhaps a social worker. She had never been inside a prison before.

A middle-aged prison officer collected them and led them across a yard to a shabby, temporary hut where all the visits took place. A group of prisoners passed them in the opposite direction, and George saw with pity that the girl blushed at the obscenities and catcalls directed at her, apparently from the whole group. He thought: *Whoever killed Tom French will be sent here before the trial.* And he thought of all the people involved and, in a spasm of self-doubt, he wondered if he would ever find out.

Professional visits took place in small, private rooms, out of earshot of the prison officers. George had been classed as a professional visitor. The man was waiting for him, sitting at a stained table, his head in his hands. In the ill-fitting prison clothes he seemed smaller.

As he heard the door he looked up.

'You,' he said aggressively. 'What do you want? My bloody solicitor hasn't been to see me yet. Do you know anything about it?'

'No. I'm nothing to do with your solicitor.'

'What are you doing here then?'

'I want your help,' George said mildly. He sat at the table opposite Shawcroft and tried to make himself relaxed, receptive.

'Are you police?'

'No.'

There was a pause.

'What do you want to know?'

'I want to know about Tom French.'

'Christ!'

Dennis stood up, his hands flat on the table, and shouted, 'I've told them all I know about bloody Tom French.'

An officer looked in through the window to see if George needed help. George signalled gently that everything was fine. He leant back slowly and took a packet of cigarettes out of his jacket pocket. Slowly he opened it, letting the wrapping drop onto the table. He offered the packet to the angry man.

Dennis took the cigarette quickly, lit it himself, using the matches that George had thrown onto the table, and sat down. He inhaled greedily, and George knew that he was thinking that if he was quick, there might be time for another cigarette before the interview was over.

'Tell me then,' George said quietly. 'Tell me all you know about Tom French. Start by telling me why you frightened Terry away when you knew that I was asking about Tom.'

'That wasn't about Tom French. You were asking about dope. I didn't know who you were. I hadn't seen you then but I knew that someone had followed my mate and me from the marsh. You could have been the drug squad. I didn't scare that loony off. I just told him not to talk to you. You know what he's like. He could have told you anything.'

'So far as you were concerned, Tom French never smoked cannabis?'

'I've told you. I told you in the Lodge. No.'

'And if he had wanted to get hold of some, it would have been readily available?'

'I suppose so. At a price. But he didn't want to. I've been telling you. He never touched the stuff. He was always preaching at me about it. Once he'd started he'd never let it alone. He wasn't no saint. I've had to put him to bed a couple of times, he's been that drunk. But he'd talk to me as if he was a vicar. It used to get on my nerves. And it wasn't only me. He did it to everyone. He was kind, and he did put himself out for you, but he never let you forget it.'

Then George knew why it was done and who had done it. He did not know how or where it was done. He realized that it had been there all the time, that he could have known from the beginning. He remembered the little things – the insincerity in Rob Earl's voice when he was describing his friend, the phrase used by Sally when they had first met, a phrase which should have been followed up. There was no triumph in knowing. He gave Dennis another cigarette.

'So if you didn't frighten Terry, why did he run away?'

'God knows. Why did he do anything?'

Dennis was getting restless now, quickly smoking his cigar-ette, knowing that there was no chance of getting another. The prison officer looked through the window and tapped at his watch. They had lunch early. He was in a hurry to get the prisoners ready.

'Did you like him?' George asked, looking for the first time directly at the man. 'Did you like Tom French?'

Dennis stood up, already programmed by the routine of the prison.

'No,' he said. 'I don't know why. There was no reason why I shouldn't. But I couldn't stand him. I hated his guts.'

Impatiently the officer swung the door open, and George and the three men and the woman, who seemed to be almost in tears, were shepherded back to the gate, as if they, too, had been prisoners.

George drove slowly back to the coast. It was a different problem now. Before there had been a desperation to know, and that was all that mattered. Now he knew what had happened. First he had to convince himself intellectually that he was right, then he would have to do something about it. He stopped at the side of the road just outside Rushy. There was a line of birdwatchers on the shingle bank silhouetted against the sun. He looked through his binoculars to check that he was not missing anything especially rare, but they were lying back and talking.

At Fenquay, Sally asked him into the house in a whisper. She had just put Barnaby to sleep and was afraid that she would wake him. She looked strained still, and very tired.

'Barnaby's teething,' she said, when George observed that she was not looking well.

'You'll be worried about Peter too,' he said.

'I don't know anyone called Peter.'

'Sit down,' he said comfortably. 'I'll make us both some tea.'

She did as she was told, and was still sitting there when he returned. She took the mug and cupped her hands around it. She drank slowly and big, wary eyes stared at him over the rim of the mug.

'You don't need to say anything,' he said. 'Just listen and see if I've got it right. You went to work on Tresco. I don't know why. That bit isn't important. You found it difficult to settle. You'd done hotel work before, so you went to Scilly. It must have been beautiful in the spring. You would have arrived at about this time of the year. You felt out of place on Tresco and you didn't get on specially well with the other girls in the hotel – Annie sends her regards by the way. So on your days off you explored the other islands.

'I don't know where you first met Peter, but I would guess that it was on St Agnes. One of the lanes there is called Barnaby Lane, isn't it? It's an unusual name and it reminded me of St Agnes as soon as I heard it. Peter loved you very much. Then, towards the end of the summer, the birdwatchers began to arrive on the islands. One of them was Tom French. He took a cottage on St Mary's and intended to spend the whole autumn there. He was a friend of Peter's, so you came to meet him. Tom loved you too, but he didn't have Peter's personality, did he? Did you even notice, I wonder, that he was so infatuated with you?

'At the end of September Tom had a party. You already knew by that time that you were pregnant. You wanted to go to the party. You, who never made a fuss about anything, got so upset that you might have to miss it that Annie gave you the evening off. Did you mean to tell Peter that evening that you were expecting a baby? What happened? I think there was a police raid for drugs. The Scilly islanders are always worried that the birdwatchers will contaminate the morals of their young people. Peter was worried. He already had a conviction for drug abuse. A second, with a stiff Cornish court, could have meant a prison sentence. He planted what-ever cannabis he had on Tom. In that way he would also remove a rival from the scene.'

'No,' she said. 'No, it wasn't like that. I didn't tell Peter about the baby, because I didn't want to put any pressure on him to leave his wife. I wanted him to leave her for me, not for the baby. That night was my own personal deadline. If he didn't tell me that night that he wanted to come away with me, I was going to go on my own. That's what made it so special. He left the party before the police arrived. He was very sweet. We had a good evening. But he said that he needed more time to decide. I could understand. He took the marriage seriously, even though it wasn't working very well.

'I knew that he'd been to court before. That night he left the party early. He'd left his coat behind, and in the coat pocket there was some cannabis. When the police came I was terrified for Peter. Of course, they wanted to know who the coat belonged to. They didn't seem very efficient. I didn't think that they'd check. I persuaded Tom to say that the coat was his.'

'And Tom agreed. Just like that.'

She blushed. 'As you said, he was infatuated.'

'So that's why you always felt so obliged to him. It wasn't just that he looked after you so well through your illness. He'd been to court, been sentenced to three years' probation, to protect the man you loved. What did he want in return?'

'I didn't think about that then. I just wanted to stop Peter going to prison. I knew that Tom had never been in trouble before. I suppose I thought that he'd just get a fine and that Peter would repay him. He was Peter's friend.'

'What did Peter think about all this?'

'He never knew. He knew that Tom was up in court, I suppose. But he never knew that it was his dope which put Tom there. I don't expect he even missed his coat. He was always losing things. But I never saw him again, after that party, and as far as I know Tom didn't see him again either.'

'But Tom did want something in return, didn't he?'

'He never asked,' she said defensively. Then all in a rush: 'Yes, he did want something. He wanted company, affection, to be needed. All the things that most of the birdwatchers want.'

'Did he ask you to come and live here?'

208

'Not directly. I went to my mother in London when I left Tresco. It didn't work out, but I waited and had the baby there. I'd written to Tom, just to thank him, and I'd said that I was fed up at home. He wrote back, straight away, and said that he knew that there was a cottage to let in Fenquay. All that I told you about my childhood in Fenquay was true. I was so happy here. It seemed like, well, like a magic coincidence. So I moved. He seemed to take it for granted that we would be friends, more than friends. He was so lonely, and I was so depressed. I lost all my confidence after being in the hospital, and he was good for me. He took control, I didn't have to make any decisions.'

She paused, put her cup on the floor beside her, and when she looked at George again, there were tears in her eyes.

'I did try to make him happy. But it wasn't honest, it wasn't real. It seemed so wonderful when he talked about the job in Bristol. I counted the weeks until he was due to start.'

'And then,' George said, 'he changed his mind, wanted to marry you, and said, if you refused, that he would try to get custody of Barnaby or have him put into care. Did you know then why he did that?'

'No,' she said. 'It was awful, dreadful. I suppose I thought that he needed me too much. Or at least that he needed someone to look after. And he had grown very fond of Barnaby. He liked to make believe that we were a real family, that he was the father.'

'But in fact, just before you had your row, Tom had been to see Ella. Ella read him a letter she had just received from Peter. Peter was intending to come and live in Norfolk. Tom wanted you married and out of the way before you realized that Peter was free.'

'I didn't know that.' She spoke quietly, sadly. 'I didn't know that Peter was here. Not until . . .' She hesitated.

'Not until the evening after the film at the Windmill. The night when we found Adam Anderson in the well. The night you suddenly felt ill and had to go home.'

'Yes,' she said. 'I was so confused and miserable. I didn't want to believe that Peter could have killed Tom, but it seemed so odd seeing him there, after all this time. It seemed such a coincidence. He had been married and now he was free . . . I had been as good as married and now I was free. I couldn't understand why he hadn't been in touch with me. And then there were the letters.'

'I know,' George said gently, 'another dreadful coincidence.'

'You can't understand what it was like. Getting the letters was bad enough. Thinking that Tom's murderer was interested in me, worrying about Barnaby. Then, before I knew that he was here, it was dreaming about Peter that kept me sane. Just to know that somewhere there was someone I could care about honestly. And then to find out that he was mixed up in all this. I even thought that he had written the letters for some mad reason.'

'Did you know that he was in Rushy on the morning Tom died, and that he didn't let anyone know that he was here?'

'No, I didn't know,' she said, then quickly, hopefully, trying to persuade herself as well as George: 'I've been thinking. It is possible that he doesn't know that I'm here. Another coincidence. He doesn't know anything about Barnaby, so he wouldn't connect Tom's girlfriend and baby with me. Even if they mentioned my name, Sally's not unusual.' She grinned weakly. 'And in the village they call me Mrs French. I think they mean it to be kind. They know I'm not married.

'He didn't see me that night at the film. They must have been late coming in, because he wasn't there when the lights went off, and I left early to go and get things ready at the Windmill. I could see Rob Earl when I went out of the hall, and I could see that there was someone sitting next to him, but in the dark I didn't know who it was. He would never have been able to recognize me in that light. That evening, back at the Windmill, I didn't leave the kitchen. So you see, he might not even know that I'm here.'

George realized that for this instant she was more concerned that Peter might have rejected her, forgotten about her, than that he was a murderer.

'Yes,' he said. 'It might be as you say. But until we can find him and talk to him we can't find out.'

'Why? Where is he? He hasn't run away?'

'Not exactly. He's gone to Scotland to see a rare bird.'

'Do you think he killed Tom?' She said it conversationally, breathlessly.

'I'm sorry,' George said, wondering for a moment if he should tell her, 'I can't tell you, until I've talked to him.'

'I'm sorry,' she repeated. 'I should have told you all this before. I feel better now. But I was so worried about Peter. Has it caused you a lot of trouble?'

'Only a day trip to Scilly,' he said lightly. He continued more seriously: 'When you saw Adam in Fenquay on the day of his accident, you thought he might have been talking to someone in the coffee shop. Can you remember anything about the other person? Could it have been Peter for instance?'

She looked at him sharply, but answered honestly.

'It could have been anyone. I think it was an older person,

but I don't know why. I really didn't get a good enough view. I'm sure that it was Adam, though.'

'Will you be all right here on your own? Should I phone Jenny Kenning and ask her to come over? I'm sure that she's a good listener.' He looked at his watch. It was three thirty. Bernard Cranshaw would soon be back from school. 'I must go now.'

'I'm fine. Barnaby will be waking soon. I can talk to him. And I'm going out tomorrow. Ella has asked me to give her a hand at the Windmill. Sandra's gone to a wedding. It'll be fun and she's going to pay me.'

As they got up, and George prepared to go, he took her hand.

'I don't want to frighten you, but I want you to promise that you will be careful. Don't let anyone into the house, not even someone you know, or someone who seems quite harmless. And don't tell anyone that you saw Adam in Fenquay that day. That really is important.'

'Okay,' she said, not recognizing the seriousness of his voice. She was feeling happier after her talk with George. 'But don't worry. No one ever comes to visit me.'

As he left the house George could hear Barnaby talking loudly and incomprehensibly to himself, and rattling the bars of his cot for attention.

They had seen the black stork. They had seen it early in the morning after their night in the signal box. At the same time George would have been in the helicopter on his way to Scilly. Tina was nearly asleep and felt very hungry, but she shared with the others a secret elation, a deep uncomplicated joy at seeing the bird, which carried them, and her, further north, to new places and different birds.

She had resisted at first. It was only Thursday. She could still get back in time for lectures and an important tutorial on Friday, but the others would not hear of it. It was decided that if no rarity turned up elsewhere, they would stay in the Highlands until Sunday, and see some of the breeding birds. Peter especially was excited by this. So they went to the Cairngorms. In the Old Caledonian Forest they looked for crested tit and capercaillie. The sun slanted through the pines onto the moist floor of the forest. It was moss green and boggy, and there was a smell of pines and of water. Further up the mountain they saw ptarmigan, on the bare boulder scree there were dotterel, and away over a long, narrow loch they saw golden eagle.

Adam began to relax, became, even, good company, surprising the others with a quirky sense of humour. Tina became less pompous, stopped lecturing about statistics and theories, and started to enjoy the birds she was seeing. Peter and Rob showed off their birdwatching expertise. In an easy, tolerant way they were all getting on very well.

Each evening they made a phone call to get information.

'It's crazy,' Tina said defiantly. 'You wouldn't catch me coming with you to Cornwall to see something rare.'

'You would,' Rob said. 'I can tell. You're hooked.'

But they never phoned Ella. Rob had wanted to. He had argued that she was the best contact there was. She got to hear of everything, but Peter said that he wanted to forget Rushy for a while. It was good to get away from it. It pleased him to think that nobody in Rushy knew where they were.

# Chapter Thirteen

GEORGE DROVE SLOWLY DOWN the steep hill to Rushy. The village of red-tiled roofs, with its trees and gardens, seemed suddenly precarious, separated from the sea only by the marsh and the shingle bank. As he watched, the sun disappeared to be replaced by huge, solid storm clouds, which gathered out to sea. The place became tinted by a sinister, sulphurous light, like that in a sepia photograph. The village had never looked more striking. A motorist behind him sounded his horn, and George realized with embarrassment that he was driving too slowly, blocking the narrow road. Waving apologies he drove on, down into the strange brown light and the village.

He needed proof. Terry could have given it to him, so could Adam. Terry had been gone for nearly a week and George had begun to fear for his safety. He did not know when Adam would return. It occurred to him that it would help to look again at the marsh. He was beginning to think that he knew how the body had been moved, and a visit to the pool and the marsh track would confirm the feasibility of his speculation. He would collect Molly from the Windmill, and they could walk along the marsh track, and look at the pool on the way to Bernard Cranshaw's home.

But when he pushed open the door of the Windmill he realized that he had not eaten all day, and the smell of cooking was irresistible. Molly was still there, still drinking tea. She was incapable of boredom, and it was an entertainment for her to gossip to Ella, and to listen to the customers talking.

There had been a variety of people in the place. Jack sat with her first. He was back from a morning's fishing and described some of the technicalities of his craft. She listened, genuinely interested. Local people used the cafe, although it was a little way out of the village, and Molly listened unashamedly to the women talking. It mattered to her that the young girl with the bleached hair and the whining toddler was thinking of leaving her husband and moving in with her mother, and that the heavy, middle-aged woman with varicose veins was worried about having to go into hospital for an operation. When the women went back to Rushy to collect the children from school, to prepare tea for their husbands, there was still a small group of reed cutters and bait diggers, sitting with their backs to the birdwatchers. Their accents were so strange that although Molly listened and enjoyed the music of their speech, she could not understand what they were saying. But the birdwatchers still felt that the place belonged to them. They arrived, all day, in small groups, planning a weekend in the area, wanting to know if anything had been seen.

'Put it on the board,' Ella would say if she heard them talking about the birds they had seen. The board was an old school blackboard, salvaged when one of the nearby village schools had closed. It was covered each day with records of birds seen in the area and rare birds seen elsewhere, with witticisms and juvenile jokes and rude pictures of bird-watchers. It was the means by which information was transferred. Each evening Ella would edit it, with a duster, censoring any items of which she disapproved, giggling despite herself.

So when George arrived at the Windmill after his visit to Sally's, Molly was still sitting at the counter, comfortable, unobtrusive. He felt a pang of guilt and gratitude, because he had known that she would still be there, because she was so reliable. He smiled at her and she smiled back to tell him that she did not mind, that in fact she had been quite enjoying herself.

'Is there anything about, Ella?' he asked, just as all the other birders had done.

'I don't think that there's anything special. But look on the board!' This last phrase was shouted in the tone of exasperation a mother uses when reminding a child to close a door.

Obediently he read the board while she made him sausage and chips and tea. There were a couple of bluethroats at Wells, a golden oriole on Salthouse Heath, good birds, but nothing special enough to bring a group of experienced birdwatchers back from Scotland before the weekend was over. They needed a real rarity. He had an idea.

They walked from the Windmill out onto the marsh. George took Molly's hand and described his visits to the remand centre and to Sally's home.

'So that's why she always felt so obliged to Tom,' Molly said. 'It must have been horrible.'

'It can't have been easy, being in debt to Tom,' George agreed. He continued carefully: 'I'm beginning to develop an idea about what might have happened to Tom. My discussion with Sally helped to confirm it.' Tentatively he explained his feelings about the case. 'Do you think that it could have happened that way?'

'I think you're right,' she said after a pause. 'I don't like it, but I think that you're right. Why do you want to look at the marsh again?'

'Because I haven't properly considered the practical details of my theory. It didn't occur to me, until I drove back from Fenquay, where Tom might have been killed. It's too late to tell if I'm right. There will be no sign left now. But we can check if my murderer could have moved the body to the pool. If it just isn't practically possible, I'll have to think again. I want to find Terry's shortcut into the White Lodge.'

The marsh pool was closer to the track than George had remembered, and the body had been found in the water nearest to the track. There was a narrow sandy footpath from the track to the pond.

'Your idea would work very well here,' Molly observed.

George nodded distractedly and turned his attention to the track. It was pitted with ruts, where tyres had worn two grooves in the sand and the pebbles, but between the two grooves was a relatively level area of grass. He nodded again. It would be possible. He could be right.

They followed the track to the road, then walked along the opposite hedge, away from the village. George was looking for Terry's shortcut into the White Lodge grounds. It was, when they found it, quite obvious, and they wondered why they had not noticed it before. A small gate in the hedge led from the road into the Lodge park. Two wooden planks had been laid across the ditch to make a bridge for easy access. It must have been used quite regularly by the hotel staff.

'So you could be right,' Molly said. 'We've not seen anything to disprove your theory. Do you still need to see Bernard Cranshaw?'

'I need to talk to him to eliminate him. Practically, it's just possible that he killed Tom. I'm certain that he wrote the letters to Sally. But I don't think that his is the sort of obsession which would lead him to kill. He just seems very lonely and frustrated, but you're the expert. I'll be glad of your opinion. In any event he may be able to give us some information. He was out on the marsh early that morning, and he might have seen something.'

'According to Peter Littleton, he's mad enough to kill,' she said. 'When we were at Scarsea last weekend, he told me that Cranshaw was out on the marsh taking pot shots at him.'

'Was anyone else there when Peter Littleton told you?' he asked.

'No, I don't think so.'

'Did he say if anyone else was on the marsh when Cranshaw was supposed to be shooting? What I mean is, was there anyone to confirm Peter's story?'

'I don't know,' she said quietly.

It seemed that they had arrived at the Cranshaws' in the middle of some domestic dispute. They could hear Mrs Cranshaw as soon as they reached the front gate. The window was open and her words were clear and shrill. There was no anger in her voice. It was cold and relentless, the voice of a woman with a justifiable complaint.

'You never think of me. I thought you were different from your father but you're not. You're just the same. After all I've done for you. So, you've even started drinking. Just like him. He never talked to me unless he was drunk, and then it was only curses. I never thought you would take to drink. I thought you would have had more consideration for your mother.'

There was a scream, so high-pitched that for a moment they could not tell if it was a man or a woman. It was Bernard Cranshaw.

'Shut up,' he shouted. 'I can't stand any more. Leave me alone.'

There was the sound of breaking glass.

Molly was too used to family quarrels to be embarrassed.

'Come on,' she said. 'If we don't get in now, he'll walk out.'

George, uneasy at the intrusion, knocked at the door. A sudden silence followed the sound of his fist on the door, and they realized that throughout Bernard's emotional outburst Mrs Cranshaw had continued talking. Only now, with the prospect of strangers to entertain, did she stop.

She came to the door to let them in. There was a pause before she opened the door, and Molly could see that she had used the time to repair her make-up. She wore bright, irregularly applied lipstick and there were two feverish spots of rouge on her cheeks. She had the face of a marionette.

Molly automatically took charge.

'We've come to see your son, Mrs Cranshaw,' she said briskly. George, despite the tension of the situation, was amused at the ease with which she assumed the role of social worker. 'You won't mind if we come in?'

It would have been impossible for Mrs Cranshaw to refuse, but she seemed, in fact, quite pleased to see them. She followed them into the front room, where Bernard Cranshaw was sitting, and began once more to talk. Cranshaw hardly noticed that they were there. He had thrown his glass into the fireplace and was watching the remains of the drink run down the tiles and into the carpet. It was obvious that he had not long been home from school. There was chalk dust on his jacket. His face was very flushed. Molly turned and faced Mrs Cranshaw so that it was impossible for the older woman to come any further into the room.

'Thank you very much,' Molly said. 'We'd like to talk to Mr Cranshaw on his own if you don't mind. I'm sure you're very busy.'

Mrs Cranshaw was about to argue, but Molly smiled. It was a gesture so firm and decisive that it was as if Mrs Cranshaw had been slapped. Looking very old, she turned and left the room, giving a brief, contemptuous glance towards her son. He had begun to pick up the glass, a fumbling and ineffectual attempt to appear normal.

'Leave that now,' Molly said gently. 'We can clear that up later. We want to talk to you.' She sat on the chair next to his and with a gesture of friendship reached over and touched his arm. George, still uneasy and embarrassed, stood apart and watched.

Cranshaw's face was still red, and a nerve in his forehead twitched, so that his eyebrows moved in a ridiculous appearance of surprise. He had very thick eyebrows. He was breathing heavily as if he were still angry, but he was making a tremendous effort to grow calm. Molly was talking softly, about the weather and teaching, and living in Rushy, waiting for some of the tension to go, waiting until he was able to talk rationally to her. Then he interrupted her.

'How's Mother?' he asked. 'I must have frightened her. Shall I go and see her?'

'She's well,' Molly replied. 'You can explain to her later.'

'She won't understand. She doesn't listen.'

'It must be very difficult to live with someone who doesn't listen.'

'It's impossible. I know that I should make allowances. She hasn't had an easy life. Father was never here. She brought me up practically all by herself. But I can't go on being grateful. I try to explain that I make sacrifices too, but she doesn't listen. If it wasn't for her I could have married. Other people have so much freedom now. These young people, the children in school, some of the teachers even, they have so much freedom and they just abuse it. It's wicked.'

'Is that why you wrote the letters?'

'You know about the letters?' he asked quickly. Molly nodded.

'I've been so worried about them. I knew that you would find me.' He fell silent, studying the stain on the carpet and the splinters of broken glass. George was fascinated by the conversation; he was afraid to move for fear of breaking the spell of understanding between the two. Because he knew that somehow Molly did understand this man whose moods and anxieties were, to him, incomprehensible. If he were mad, she seemed capable of bringing reason to his madness.

'You wrote the letters,' she said, in the form of a question, 'because you thought that they had too much freedom?'

'I wanted them to pay,' he said angrily. 'They hurt me so much and I wanted them to pay. He didn't care how much it meant to me, my Saturday mornings with the children.'

*Not those letters!* George screamed silently to himself. *I know all about those letters. What about the others, the letters to Sally?* But Molly allowed Cranshaw to continue talking.

221

'They liked me, they really liked me. It wasn't like the children at school. Some of the little ones used to hold my hand. Then he started coming with us onto the marsh. I was pleased. I was glad to have him there. But he started lecturing to me in front of the children, laughing if I made a mistake. He said that I couldn't see properly and that I was getting old. Not in so many words, but that's what he meant. He had no right to criticize. I saw them together on the marsh one day, him and that woman from Fenquay. She was wearing one of those dresses that you can see right through, and nothing underneath. I was in one of the hides and I could see them. They had no shame. They even had her child with them. I knew then that I had to do something about it. They weren't the sort of people to look after the village children.'

'So you wrote to the children's parents and told them that Tom was a drug addict. How did you know that he had taken drugs?'

'I heard some of the birdwatchers talking about Tom French. A group of the young ones, no more than children themselves, were in one of the hides. They had the flaps open and I could hear what they were saying. He thought that he was their hero, but they could see through him, just like I did. They said that he lectured them about taking drugs, but he'd been in court for it himself. It was a sign. Don't you see?' He looked eagerly at Molly. 'They'd given me the information I needed. It was a sign that I ought to act.'

'So,' Molly repeated, 'you wrote to the parents. But what about the other letters, Bernard, the letters to Tom's girlfriend, to Sally Johnson? You wrote to her too, didn't you?'

'It was for her own good,' he said wildly. 'Don't you see?

That man was corrupting her. She's a good woman, a beautiful woman. She didn't need him, I had to warn her off.'

'But after he died, Bernard? What was the point of writing to her then?' George thought that Molly was losing a little of her social worker's self-control, but perhaps the hint of accusation in her voice was intended.

'I enjoyed it,' the man said simply. 'I did it when Mother was in bed. It was exciting. It made me excited to think that I was writing to her.'

'Didn't you think that she might be frightened?'

'That was all part of it. I imagined her lying in bed, frightened. Because of me.'

'But you haven't written to her for a while now. Did you realize that it was wrong, that it was hurting her, and that you would have to stop?'

He shook his head. 'I couldn't write to her. I had an accident and hurt my arm so that I couldn't write. But it didn't stop me thinking about her. I lie awake every night and think about her.'

His eyes were gleaming with the memory of his pleasure and desire. George watched with distaste, then looked at Molly, whose face expressed only interest, understanding. *How does she do it?* he wondered. *She seems almost to be encouraging him, by sitting there so calmly and acceptingly.*

'Do you like seeing people frightened, Bernard?' she said. 'Other people?'

He shook his head. 'It was only her. I didn't write to anyone else. I couldn't forget her. I dreamed about her.'

'But what about the birdwatchers? I think you like making them frightened. Didn't you shoot at them on the marsh to make them scared?'

He laughed with sudden delight and George realized how disturbed he was. 'That's different,' Bernard said. Then, more calmly, 'I never meant to hit them.'

Molly persisted, her voice still gentle but very firm. 'When we came in, you and your mother were having an argument. You were very angry. Do you often get angry?'

'No,' he said very quickly, 'not very often.'

'Perhaps when you get angry,' she persisted, 'you do things that you regret. Perhaps then you feel ashamed and you lie about it, and then it's difficult to explain what you did and why you did it. Has that ever happened, Bernard?'

Reluctantly he nodded his head. It was as if Molly still held him in her spell. He had to tell her the truth.

George was puzzled. He was certain who had killed Tom French, so what could Bernard Cranshaw have to confess?

'Why don't you tell me all about it?' Molly's soothing voice broke into his thoughts.

Cranshaw mumbled now. He had become quite inarticulate. Even the gestures, the fidgeting and sniffling, were those of a naughty boy.

'The day that Tom French died . . . ?' he began.

No, George thought, swept by a sudden panic. It can't have been him. I can't have been wrong. Instinct and reason had led him to the same conclusion. If he was wrong, he would lose faith in his judgement, in himself.

Cranshaw finished his sentence in a rush of words:

'The day that Mother fell down the stairs, I pushed her. I lost my temper.'

'Tell me about it,' Molly said.

'I was up and dressed. She got up to go to the bathroom. She saw me and started talking to me. She didn't want me to go out on the marsh. She was standing at the top of the stairs. It seemed so easy. I pushed her.'

'And you've been worrying about it ever since,' Molly said. Then, with a very subjective unprofessional expression of bitterness:

'I don't suppose that your mother would let you forget it?'

He was calmer after the confession, the nerve in his forehead was still. 'You will help me, won't you? I'm worried that I might do something dreadful, that I might properly hurt her.'

'Of course I'll help you,' she said. 'But first I want you to help us. We want to find out who killed Tom French. Can you tell us anything about that, anything at all? It would help Sally too.'

'He was killed with a telescope,' the man said suddenly and clearly. 'I found it. It was covered with blood. I didn't touch it.'

George wanted desperately to interrupt and to take over the interview, but he felt that it was only Molly who held the man's concentration.

'Where was it?' Molly asked. 'By the pool on the marsh where Tom's body was found?'

'No, it was in the Lodge park, quite near to the hotel, under a bush. I didn't feel like going out onto the marsh that day. I was upset. I was looking for owl pellets. That's how I saw it.'

So it was there, George thought. I was right. That's where it happened.

'Are you sure that you didn't touch it?' Molly asked. 'The police searched that area very carefully, and didn't find it.'

'Well, they wouldn't have done,' he said scornfully. 'It had gone. When I went back later that morning it had gone.'

Now George found it impossible to keep quiet. Molly had been asking all the right questions, but he could not sit and watch any longer.

'Why,' he asked in as controlled and quiet a voice as he could manage, 'didn't you tell the police about this? Or you could have told me.'

Bernard Cranshaw accepted the interruption as a matter of course.

'I couldn't tell the police.' He was panicky again. 'They would have found out about Mother. I couldn't have had the police around here.'

'Tell me about the telescope,' George said quietly. 'What kind of 'scope was it? Did you recognize the make?'

'It was a new one,' the man said eagerly. 'Not like mine. I always wanted a new one.' His face clouded over. 'Mother said that it would have been a waste of money. But I would have looked after it.'

He stood up suddenly, walked to a cupboard in the corner, and lovingly brought out his telescope. It was solid brass and beautifully cared for.

'This is mine,' he said. The one I saw was new. One of the short ones, that you need a tripod for.'

'What colour was it?' George asked. 'Was it with a tripod?'

The man shook his head.

'I can't remember the colour. Grey or green. It was very messy. I was upset. I didn't see a tripod.'

He seemed to lose all concentration then, and sat nursing the old brass telescope, rubbing patches of dull or tarnished metal with his handkerchief, comforted by the ritual activity.

Molly pulled his attention back into the room. 'I think you and your mother need a little break from each other, don't you? I've got an old friend who works for social services here. I believe we could arrange some respite care for Margaret. She could treat it as a little holiday. She'd enjoy the company and it would give you a break.' A pause. 'And I think we should give your doctor a ring. As you said, you need some help too. You've been under a lot of stress for years.'

'Will you tell the police? About Mother and the letters.'

'Sally wants the whole thing forgotten,' George said. 'And it's up to your mother to make a complaint, not us.'

Molly waited with the Cranshaws until a place had been found in a care home for Bernard's mother, but George left. Outside it was sticky and humid, and the storm clouds he had seen earlier in the day had spread, so that the sky was dark. There seemed to be no air and no light. His knowledge seemed to him an intolerable burden, but until the group of birdwatchers returned from Scotland there was nothing that he could do. Bernard Cranshaw had given his theory more weight, but he had no real proof. He started out for the village.

In the Cranshaws' house, there was a burst of activity. Suddenly everything seemed more normal, less tense. Molly helped Margaret to pack her bag. The woman had been reluctant at first, but Molly had explained that this wasn't permanent, not unless Margaret wanted it to be. There'd be company, activities, and she'd be well looked after. In the end, she'd seemed almost excited, waiting until the social worker arrived.

It was so dark that Molly switched on the electric light. Bernard helped his mother out to the social worker's car, and held her for a moment, with real affection.

'I'll come and visit! As often as you like.'

Margaret turned her face to be kissed.

Back in the house, Bernard sat, still polishing the telescope. The doctor had agreed to see him at home. Molly didn't want to leave him alone until then.


As George walked back to the Windmill he devised a plan.

Ella had opened all the windows and the door of the snack bar, but inside it was hot and steaming. A group of young people stood laughing around the blackboard. George took Ella into the kitchen and spoke to her. When they returned her eyes were gleaming with excitement. She was singing loudly and tunefully.

George joined the lads and they became quieter, respectful. 'Anything about?' he asked.

A large, unkempt boy with painful acne shook his head. 'I suppose it's getting a bit late to expect much now.'

George grinned: 'I think that the middle of June is a good time for a real rarity, for something really special.'

He looked at the debris of cameras, telescopes and binoculars on the tables. Without exception all the telescopes were short, fixed-focus models.

'Do you know if anyone has had a 'scope repaired lately?' he asked generally. 'Mine seems to be out of alignment and I wasn't sure where to get it mended.'

There was a lot of advice about where best to have optical equipment repaired, but no useful information.

As he left he called to Ella: 'Molly and I will be spending tonight at the White Lodge. Let us know if anything turns up.'

From the hotel George phoned the police station. It was an embarrassing phone call and he nearly lost his temper several times. He spoke first with a polite, rather slow-witted sergeant and then to an arrogant detective who, but for his prejudices, would have been reasonably intelligent. George, ignoring the man's sneers about amateurs and the Home Office, explained his interest in the case. He tried to explain that he had received some information which he was certain would assist the police in their inquiries.

The news about the telescope and its description seemed at last to force the detective to take George seriously, but he insisted that they had a prime suspect: Terry Biddle who had disappeared from the village and seemed to be on the run. With a great gesture of generosity, the detective agreed to send a constable out to speak to Bernard Cranshaw some time the next day, but he made it clear that he would prefer to concentrate his efforts on finding Terry Biddle. Finally, he said that while a telescope was a possible murder weapon, the only forensic evidence was that it was a smooth cylindrical object. George just restrained himself from shouting that he had seen a copy of the police report, and the detective rang off.

That night George and Molly had a quiet meal in the hotel restaurant. Each was preoccupied. George was considering the details of his plan, not allowing himself to consider the final outcome. Molly was thinking of Bernard Cranshaw, and wondering how the thing would end. The doctor had been sympathetic. He'd insisted that Cranshaw take some time off work. Molly hoped they'd done the right thing in not telling the police about the man's anger and his loss of control. There'd been violence enough in this small village. When she and George did speak the conversation seemed hushed, intimate, because outside, even with the thick curtains drawn, they could hear the sound of rain and thunder. Later the electricity supply failed and the dining room was lit only by candles and the flashes of lightning.

Terry was terrified by the storm. He watched the huge clouds roll in from the sea like giant waves. He did not understand what was happening. He had no memory of any other storm. The house he had built was no protection against the noise of thunder and lightning and the rain. He crouched under the dripping gorse bushes and the rain ran in a stream across his feet. The wind blew straight into his face and lifted the corrugated iron roof at one corner so that it banged. He felt cold and miserable. Then there came a gust of wind so strong that it lifted the roof away from the bushes and Terry watched with horror as it was carried down the hill, bouncing and twisting as if it were no heavier than a piece of cardboard. Now there was nothing between him and the sky and the lightning. He forgot his discomfort and felt only terror. His fear of the storm was stronger than any vague, previous fear.

He remembered suddenly and vividly Mrs Black and the solid house in the village. He thought of warm food and he wanted to go home. He ran down the hill, exposed, the only person in the world, it seemed, who was out in the storm. On the road between Skeffingham and Rushy a van driver stopped and gave him a lift home.

When the electricity went off Mrs Black lit candles and thanked heaven for the coal stove. There was a knock on the door and she carried a candle with her to answer it. It would be the police, she thought. Who else would be out on such a night? But even as she went to answer it, daring not to hope, she thought that it was a sheepish knock, not a policeman's knock. Terry stood there, grinning, pushing his dripping hair away from his eyes with his fist.

'I'm sorry,' he said automatically, the grin becoming guilty. Then with excitement: 'I ran away.'

He was surprised because she did not scold him. She held him to her just for a moment, then took him in and ran him a bath, and fed him. He talked about running away, and the house he had built. He had already forgotten the storm. She listened and then talked to him about his reasons for running away. They were sitting in the dark by the fire. She talked to him about Tom French, taking him back to the morning of the murder, slowly gaining from him information which he never knew he had. She tried to telephone George Palmer-Jones, but there was no reply. Only then did she contact the police station. When a police car came to take Terry away, she went with him.

Ella sat by the telephone all evening. It rang incessantly. The birdwatchers had discovered her home phone number years ago and she had never been able to discourage them from using it. It was always busy on Friday nights, when they were deciding where to go for the weekend, but tonight, it was exceptional. She played her part well. She had always been a good actress. George would be proud of her.

# Chapter Fourteen

No one ever knew for certain who started the rumour of the blue-cheeked bee-eater. Later, George Palmer-Jones denied all knowledge of it. He just shrugged his shoulders and smiled, reminding his friends of other rumours: the gyrfalcon in South Wales, the black-throated thrush in Lancashire. Ella's version of the story was uncharacteristically vague. She claimed that someone had phoned her from the village on the Friday evening and that she had written the details on the board. She had passed on the information from the board as she always did.

Whatever the origin of the rumour, by late that Friday evening the news that a blue-cheeked bee-eater had been seen near Rushy had become widespread. The species had not been seen in Britain since 1951, but that had been in the middle of June and it was perfectly possible that it should occur again. And the rumour was so detailed, with its exact position, the names of the observers and the time when it had been seen, that it was accepted without question. The names of the observers were unfamiliar, but the story was that the bird had not been seen at Rushy, but on a local authority reserve a couple of miles inland, so it was assumed that the observers were the reserve wardens, or knowledgeable locals, not twitchers. Afterwards, when the hoax had been discovered, it was decided that the story had been too cleverly constructed, too plausible, for the rumour to have been created by accident.

On the Friday night the news was received and passed along the grapevine with intense excitement. Anxious parents consulted timetables, packed up sandwiches and let schoolboy sons, rude and uncommunicative in their fear that the bird might have gone, spend their first night away from home. Students waited until pub closing time, walked through evening streets to motorway exits, and began to hitchhike to Norfolk. Responsible family men cancelled family plans, filled their cars with students and schoolboys and drove across the country, revelling in the irresponsibility of the night-time drive, the madness and the expense of it all. That was the attraction of twitching: the escape from anxious parents, lectures and essays, work and families, the knowledge that, despite all the effort and the movement, in the morning the bird might have gone.

By dawn on the Saturday morning the big car park at the Windmill was full of cars. There were even two minibuses and a coach. A few people slept, curled up in sleeping bags on the back seats of their cars, but generally it was a social occasion, a time to drink coffee from a flask and catch up on news. At dawn they drove in convoy to the place where the bird had been found, an area of disused gravel pits, small ponds with a patch of deciduous woodland, which had been designated a nature reserve by the council. A systematic search was organized throughout the area, but nothing was seen. By the time the warden arrived at nine, his visitor centre was besieged by hostile twitchers who wanted to know why they had been deceived into visiting a reserve which supported only common breeding birds. His bewilderment and obvious lack of ornithological knowledge were so genuine – he repeated endlessly: 'I'm sorry, I'm a mammal man myself' – that finally most of them left him alone. It was only when this crowd of birders drifted back to Rushy, to the Windmill and the pub, that the village realized it had been invaded.

The warden, an elderly man near to retirement, shut himself in his office and tried to ignore the succession of battered cars which arrived all day, and the aggrieved drivers who wanted to know where 'it' was. At last he stuck a notice on the gate – 'There is no rare bird on this reserve' – and went home early.

Rob Earl, Peter, Adam and Tina heard the news of the blue-cheeked bee-eater on the Friday evening, when they made their regular phone call to their contact in Norwich. The news came as a welcome relief. It had been an aimless day, yet no one had felt able to take the decision to go south. They had watched a pair of Slavonian grebes on a small puddle of a loch, and Adam especially had found the experience dissatisfying. He longed for the expensive telescope and binoculars left behind at home. He had borrowed an old pair of binoculars from Pete Littleton for the trip to Scotland, but they were heavy and unfamiliar. He had used Rob's telescope to look at the grebes, and although Rob had insisted that there was nothing wrong with it, Adam found it impossible to get a clear image of the birds.

It seemed that the whole world was out of focus. The

previous days had been pleasant but they had been dreamlike, unreal. Now he had to come to terms with the fact that he was at risk. More than that, he had to do something about it. Tina and Rob had begun to bicker about the practical details of the trip. There was a quarrel about who had paid for the last tankful of petrol. Only Peter seemed content, unwilling to consider returning south before the Sunday night.

Rob made the phone call from a public box outside a small bar in the village where they were staying, while the others waited inside. The landlord and the locals had not responded to the young people's overtures of friendship, making it quite clear that they disapproved of Tina's presence in the place. When Rob came in chanting and singing like a football supporter, waving his arms above his head, indifference turned to active hostility and they were forced to make their plans sitting in the car.

Of course, there were few plans to make. Despite Peter's initial lack of enthusiasm it was inevitable that they would go for the bird. Peter drove and Rob and Adam sat in the back of the car, consulting the field guide by the light of a flickering match. Tina could not sleep. She was feeling increasingly irritated by these men with their futile hobby, their insane enthusiasm. She had enjoyed the stork, but Rob had been wrong; she did not share their obsession. When they arrived at the reserve early on the Saturday morning she was too tired even to leave the car. They waited until nine o'clock when the warden arrived, and it was obvious that nothing had been seen. Then they went to Peter's cottage to sleep.

They were still asleep at midday when George Palmer-Jones called to see them, but the door was unlocked so he went inside. Tina had taken the bed and the bedroom and the men were asleep on the sitting-room floor. They did not stir when he looked in on them. George returned to the kitchen. He made a pot of tea, emptied the packet of biscuits he had brought with him onto a plate, and carried everything on a tray into the sitting room. With this peace offering he woke them. They were not angry, or even surprised to be woken, and sat half-dressed, half-covered by their sleeping bags, to drink tea and to talk. They thought that he had come to find out about the bee-eater. There was a lot of good-natured speculation about the root of the rumour.

'I've just come back from Scilly,' George said conversationally.

'Why?' Rob asked quickly, aggressively. 'What's been seen there? Why weren't we told about it? Was it suppressed?'

'I didn't have time for birdwatching.' There was a silence.

'Why did you go to Scilly?' Peter asked quietly.

'I had some information and I needed to check it. I had to find out if there was any real connection between you and Tom French. I saw Barbara. She doesn't send her love.'

'The only connection was the one that you know about. Tom and I were both twitchers. We were friends.'

'No,' George Palmer-Jones said. 'The real connection between you and Tom French was a girl. A girl called Sally.'

'But I don't understand,' Peter said 'I haven't seen Sally since the autumn before last. She left very suddenly. She didn't write. I don't even know where she is.'

'Is that true?' The question was put to them all. Adam would not meet his eyes. He looked blank, as if he were embarrassed to be listening to the conversation. Rob shrugged his shoulders. Peter looked quickly at his friend.

'Of course it's true. I tried to find out where she was from the hotel, but they didn't seem to know either. She hadn't given them any notice that she was leaving.'

'You *are* talking about Tom's Sally, Sally Johnson?' Rob asked. George nodded and Rob continued: 'I don't think that I've told Peter about Sally. I certainly didn't realize that Peter knew her before Tom did. I wasn't on St Mary's when Peter must have been going out with her, and I was never very good at writing to him. So far as I know it's true that Peter didn't know that she was here.'

Was he, George thought, being a little too accurate? If George had asked a different question would he have received more information?

Peter interrupted George's thoughts.

'I don't understand,' he repeated. 'How do you all know Sally? Does she live round here? Did Tom know her?'

'I would have thought,' George said, 'that by now you would have gathered that Sally was Tom French's girlfriend. She lives at Fenquay.'

Peter ignored the implication of deceit.

'Tom always fancied her,' he said slowly. 'He had a cottage on St Mary's, the summer she worked on Tresco. But I never thought that she liked him. Vanity I suppose. Is that why she ran away? Because she couldn't face telling me that she liked him best?'

'No,' George said. 'She ran away because she couldn't face telling you that she was pregnant.'

Adam blushed, polished his glasses, wished that he was somewhere else. Rob tried to restrain a grin.

'Barnaby!' he said. 'Peter is Barnaby's father! I can't imagine Peter as a daddy.'

George continued seriously:

'For some time the police thought that Sally had murdered Tom. They may still suspect her. It's a logical supposition. It was common knowledge that they had been arguing. Tom had found out from Ella that you had left Barbara and were thinking of living for a while in Rushy. He was terrified of losing her to you. He tried to persuade her to marry him. He threatened that he would have Barnaby put into care, then said that he would apply for custody of the child himself. I would have expected him to contact you, if he was that desperate. I'm surprised that he didn't attempt to persuade you to stay away.'

Once again Peter ignored the question implied in the last sentence.

'Why did she stay with him?' he asked. 'If he treated her so badly, why didn't she leave him?'

'Are you sure that you don't know? It was because she felt obliged to him. He did her a favour. Perhaps you remember that the last time you saw her was at a party, Tom's party.'

Peter nodded.

'You left early to get back to St Agnes, and you left your jacket behind. In the pocket you had left some cannabis. Presumably you had obtained some for your own use. When there was a police raid, Sally persuaded Tom to say that the jacket belonged to him. She knew that you had a previous conviction for possession of cannabis, and she was afraid that you would go to prison. He pleaded guilty to the charge and received a probation order. Sally felt that it was her fault. Tom was able to use considerable emotional blackmail to tie her to him. Of course, you should be grateful to him. Local authorities prefer not to employ teachers who've been to prison.'

Peter seemed shaken and dazed, though not by George's harsh observation. He asked: 'How old is Barnaby?'

'I'm no expert. About twelve months, I should think.'

'She was waiting for me to make up my mind to leave Barbara. I kept putting her off . . . How has she managed to bring him up? What has she done about money? What does he look like?'

'Perhaps you should ask Sally those questions. She's working for Ella at the Windmill today. Barnaby will be there too.'

Peter was almost panic-stricken. He seemed to have lost all confidence.

'I can't go now. You don't realize what I've done!'

Then, more calmly, he said: 'You're right of course. I'll go to see her this afternoon and arrange to meet her, so that we can talk.'

He took little part in the remainder of the conversation, and made no pretence of following what was being said.

George turned to Adam:

'I must know what you were doing on the morning of your accident. If you were with someone that morning you must tell me who it was. I don't think you understand how important it is.'

His voice was almost pleading, but Adam refused to respond. He blinked and shuffled in a graceless, adolescent way.

'I'm sorry,' he said at last. 'I just can't tell you.'

'I'll be around all day,' George said. 'If you change your mind, come and see me.'

Adam smiled sheepishly. Rob pulled himself out of his sleeping bag and stretched.

'Does this interrogation mean that you still don't know who killed Tom French? It's very impressive, all this information about Sally and Peter, but it doesn't help much, does it?'

'I shouldn't say that,' George said carefully. 'All investigation is basically a matter of eliminating the irrelevant. And it all helps me to get a clearer picture of Tom French. You didn't like him, did you?'

'What makes you say that?'

'Some of the things you said about him. No. More accurately, it was the way in which you said them. Why didn't you like him?'

'When I told you that he was generous and kind, all that was true. He was like that. But he wasn't sincere. He wasn't kind through friendship. It was to prove that he was a kind person.'

Adam seemed about to interrupt, but only shook his head and let Rob continue.

'I suppose that he was desperately insecure. He assumed an almost god-like interest in other people's moral welfare. He intruded. It was impossible to shake him from the belief that he was right. He never listened to what other people said. He just carried on talking, or rather lecturing. He was good at lecturing.'

Rob paused and considered before continuing: 'But that's not a fair picture either. With people who didn't pose any threat, like children or old ladies, he was perfectly natural. I could never understand him.'

'Why didn't you tell me that you felt like that about him?'

'It didn't seem . . .' He searched for the right word. ' . . . appropriate. And it was only my impression of him. I know that I'm not the most tolerant person in the world. Other people seemed to like him, especially if they weren't bird-watchers. Perhaps he needed to keep his reputation as the great twitcher. You know what they say: "Once a twitcher, always a twitcher." Even other birders seemed to get on okay with him. He was quite a legend with the youngsters, you know. Tom French who put Rushy on the twitchers' map.'

'But he did,' said Adam. 'He did make Rushy a very special place, pretty well all by himself. And I did admire him. Even though he didn't manage to get out much, he was still an excellent birder. The rest was just his attitude. He was shy, I think. He didn't know how to speak to people.'

'Now don't get me wrong,' Rob said. 'I didn't want him to die. I was really shocked, and I want you to find out who did it. I'm just trying to be honest about him.'

George began to pile empty cups onto the tray.

'Have you come across anyone lately who has had any trouble with their 'scope, any focusing problems? Or do you know of anyone who has recently dropped or damaged a telescope?'

Rob and Peter shook their heads. Adam looked quickly at Rob, but before he had the opportunity to speak Tina came into the room. She had dressed and was carrying her sleeping bag in a striped canvas bag over her shoulder.

'I'm going home,' she announced aggressively. 'I've had enough of all this madness.'

George immediately became charming.

'I can understand just how you feel,' he said reasonably, 'but I would ask you to reconsider. I do believe that I can reach some conclusion about Tom's death very shortly, and anyone who knew him well may be able to help me. Please stay until Sunday. Perhaps I can tempt you: I have a close friend who's a member of the Rushy ringing group. He was planning to cannon-net some waders on the beach early tomorrow morning. Perhaps, you'd be interested in going along to help?'

Tina's aggression dissolved.

'It's ages since I've done any cannon-netting. Do you think he'd mind if I went with him?'

She put her canvas bag on the floor and sat on it. 'Is there any tea in the pot?'

When George Palmer-Jones left to return to the Windmill, Adam Anderson found himself going too. Adam wondered, briefly, at George's skill at persuading people to do what he wanted. He was touched, but faintly irritated by the older man's concern. It would do no good.

The storm of the night before had disappeared, leaving the ditches full and the grass wet. It was a still, clear day, with a faint mist over the sea. Ella was looking out for George and called him to her as soon as he entered the Windmill.

'Mrs Black has been trying to get hold of you,' she said. 'Her Terry came home last night. She's frantic because the police are still holding him at the station and she thinks that you might be able to help. She says that she's got the information you wanted. Very mysterious she was. She wouldn't tell me what it was all about, but she said that you would understand.'

'Where is Mrs Black now?'

'Back at the cottage. She says that she's got a solicitor to look after Terry. She's desperate to talk to you, and she's gone home to wait for you.'

'Do you know where Molly is?'

'She'll be back in five minutes. She's just given Jack a lift home in your car.'

'Can you ask her to keep an eye on Adam?'

'I'll keep an eye on that young man.'

George smiled, and a little reluctantly walked back to the village.

Sally started to walk from Fenquay to Rushy. There was no bus at the right time on Saturday, it was a fine day and it was not far to walk, even with Barnaby in the pushchair. But just outside the village a butcher's delivery van stopped, offered her a lift and took her all the way to the Windmill. She saw this good luck as an omen. It would be a good day. She felt light-headed with expectation, with a teenage, romantic anticipation that all that lay ahead would be happy and fulfilling. Overnight she had convinced herself that George Palmer-Jones thought that Peter was innocent.

She knew that he had given her no grounds for that belief, but she had no doubt at all that it was so. Peter was innocent, and the only reason he had not come to see her was because he had not known that she was living in the area. Soon, perhaps even that day, he would return from Scotland, George would tell him all about her and Barnaby, and they would begin their life together again. All her fears had vanished. Rushy was clean and fresh after the storm and in the still air was the scent of lilac and cut grass. It was a day for hope and for dreams to come true.

Ella had never before seen Sally so elated. The younger woman filled the place with a giggling good humour. She was singing as she worked and she made silly jokes. Barnaby too seemed to have caught his mother's excitement. The kitchen door had been left open so that he could play on the short grass outside. He had found a bright, striped ball, almost as big as himself, and he rolled over with it on the grass, laughing helplessly. Ella fed him chocolate biscuits and fizzy drinks.

Ella was glad to have Sally there. During the day the Windmill filled steadily with depressed and tired twitchers who had travelled from all over the country to see the blue-cheeked bee-eater. Sally worked faster than Sandra, so that the birdwatchers at least could not complain that they had to wait for their food. Ella had passed on the information about the bee-eater to most of them, and although nothing directly was said to her, she could sense their disappointment and frustration. She did not want to give them further grounds for complaint, and Sally distracted them from their depression and anger. Most of the twitchers had little contact with women, so to be teased and flattered by a pretty woman made them feel good. It was a novelty. In some way it compensated for the wasted trip to Norfolk.

Sally worked deftly and quickly, but she did not concentrate on what she was doing. Each time the door opened and a new group of birdwatchers pushed past the rucksacks into the crowded building she looked up to see if she recognized a new arrival. Because she was sure that Peter would come to find her that day. In Scotland he would have heard the rumour of the rare bird. He would have come home. Each time she had to turn her disappointment into a bantering call of welcome.

It was in the middle of the afternoon when the young birdwatcher came in to give her the message from Peter. It was a quiet time and Ella had taken Barnaby for a walk in the pushchair to give him a chance to sleep. Sally had watched the door open, turned back to cutting sandwiches to hide her sadness when she did not recognize the arrival, and then looked up again as he approached her. He was short and fat. She had never seen him before.

'Excuse me,' he said. 'Are you Sally Johnson?'

She nodded.

'Peter Littleton asked me to give you a message. He would like to talk to you. Could you meet him in the north hide in about an hour?'

Before she could answer or ask any questions the boy left, smiling over his shoulder at her as he shut the door. She had no opportunity to gloat that she had been right, to dream about the meeting, to picture how he would look and what she would say, because Ella came in, loud and real, demanding immediate attention.

'It was so cold out there,' Ella said. The fog had come in from the sea, quite suddenly. Over the village it was very warm and clear, but across the marsh the weather was raw and damp. She shook the drops of moisture from her dark curls to prove it, and insisted on a hot drink for herself and Barnaby.

Sally felt an irresistible urge to talk about Peter.

'Ella,' she said suddenly, 'do you know Peter Littleton?'

'Of course I do,' Ella answered with possessive pride. 'He was one of my first twitchers. He's a dear.'

'I used to know him very well,' Sally said. 'Oh Ella, he's come back from Scotland, and he wants to meet me in about an hour. Do you mind?'

'Now don't be silly. Of course I don't mind. Has he been in then? Did I miss him?'

'No, he sent one of the birdwatchers with a message.'

Ella protested at first when Sally wrapped up Barnaby and put him in his pushchair to go with her to see Peter, but Sally was insistent. She said that there was a very good reason why Peter would want to see Barnaby too, and Ella finally seemed to understand. She held the door open for Sally to negotiate the way out of the building, and gave a faint, romantic sigh as she waved them out into the fog.

It was with some surprise, then, that Ella saw George Palmer-Jones and Peter Littleton come into the Windmill thirty minutes later, and it was with some anger that she said to Peter:

'You've not left that girl and that baby out there on the marsh in this fog?'

She noticed that he seemed unwell, ill at ease, and as she spoke all the colour drained from his face.

'What do you mean, Ella?' he asked quietly.

'Sally,' she said impatiently. 'You sent a message that you wanted to see her out on the marsh. She took the baby with her.'

George looked questioningly at Peter, who shook his head.

'I was going to ask her to meet me outside,' he said. 'Then the fog came down and I thought it wouldn't be fair, so I waited until I knew it would be quieter here, and built up my courage to come in.'

'Do you know who brought the message?' George asked.

'No.' Ella seemed not to sense that it was important. 'Sally just said it was one of the birdwatchers. Because the message came from Peter, I presumed that Rob had been in. Did you see Mrs Black?'

'Yes. I suppose Molly and Adam are out on the marsh?'

'I think so. I gave Molly your message. Adam sat out on the bank for a long while talking to the other lads, then they both went off towards the village.'

'What about Rob Earl or Tina? Have you seen them?'

'That Tina was in earlier. She was looking for you too. She said something about arrangements for going ringing tomorrow. She hasn't been gone long. She went out soon after Sally and Barnaby. I haven't seen Rob at all.'

George turned, without a word, and went out. Peter hesitated for a moment, then followed him. Ella shook her head and hoped that Barnaby would not catch a cold.

Sally found her way to the north hide quite easily despite the mist. There was a solid boardwalk, and it was easy to push the chair along it. The mist made the encounter more exciting. Far away there was the heart-rending call of a foghorn and the hollow sound of the pushchair on the boardwalk echoed around the marsh. She had thought that he would be in the hide to meet her and when it was empty she was a little disappointed, but she sat to wait. She opened the flaps, but could see nothing outside except for a small pool of water. The noise of the foghorn was repeated very close to her by the boom of a bittern, and the sound shocked her. The fog seemed to be growing thicker and as she sat waiting, with nothing to do, she began to feel uneasy. Barnaby was unusually quiet and would not respond to her games. She longed to hear footsteps along the boardwalk, for Peter to climb the ramp into the hide, and yet she became more and more convinced that he would not come.

It never occurred to her to go back to the Windmill. She

did not think that she might see Peter another time. More than anything in the world she wanted to see him now. Perhaps she had made a mistake, and this was not the north hide. Perhaps Peter was waiting for her in the other hide, thinking that she did not care and had refused to meet him. She imagined his distress at her callousness, and it became suddenly so real, so intense that she felt that she must find him and comfort him. She was convinced that he was waiting for her in the other hide and that he needed her. Although she had only a limited idea of the position of the hides, she pushed the chair down the ramp and onto the boardwalk. She realized immediately that the fog was much thicker than it had been on her arrival.

'Peter! Peter!' she called. 'It's Sally. I'm here. Where are you?'

She tried to keep the panic from her voice, but Barnaby began to whimper.

She followed the boardwalk further into the marsh. The noise of the pushchair wheels on wood was solid, reassuring. She tried to shake away her panic. She was quite safe. She was not even lost. All she had to do was to turn round and follow the walk back to the Rushy road. She would try to find the other hide. If the boardwalk came to an end, she would turn back and return to Rushy. Perhaps Peter had decided that it was too foggy to bring her out. She would just check the other hide and then she would go back. But when she stopped walking, when there was no sound of the pushchair wheels rattling on the wooden planks, her panic returned. In the silence she heard strange noises. She peered into the fog and saw strange shapes.

It was in one of those moments of silent panic that she

heard the footsteps on the boardwalk behind her. She bent over the pushchair as the tension left her, in a thankful collapse.

'Peter!' the tears of relief rolled down her cheeks. 'I thought you weren't coming. I've been so scared.'

There was no reply.

'Peter, can't you hear me?'

The voice that answered seemed closer than the footsteps. It spoke, with quiet hatred, a list of obscenities. That such words could be spoken with such control made the speaker inhuman, quite unnatural. Sally screamed and the voice laughed.

Then it was just like her nightmare. As she ran along the walk, the sodden reeds tangled around the pushchair's wheels and caught at her legs. She was wearing jeans and as they got wet they clung to her legs and restricted her movement. She could hear the footsteps behind her come closer and closer. The path was becoming narrower and less firm under-foot. She knew that the pursuer would catch up with her. Then the chair wheel caught in a rut, it skewed off the path and tipped over. Barnaby was crying, quietly, as if he were frightened to make too much noise. As in her dreams, she bent down to take him into her arms to comfort him and to wait for the person who was following her.

The murderer must have reached her as she bent over the pushchair. She felt something tight about her neck and as she gasped for breath the picture of Barnaby's face, white and crumpled with distress, turned for a moment into Tom's face.

Just before she fainted she heard a woman's voice.

'Adam,' Molly shouted. 'Adam, don't listen to those voices. Don't listen to them. Listen to me.'

Adam had a leather strap around Sally's neck. Barnaby was crying, but Sally was still and quiet. The boy turned and saw Molly, and dropped his hands from Sally's neck. George and Peter arrived then, but neither Molly nor Adam saw them. While George skilfully cared for Sally, and Peter awkwardly comforted the baby, Adam held out his hand to Molly as if he were drowning. She took it and held it tight while he cried.

# Chapter Fifteen

THE NEXT DAY THEY all sat on the lawn behind Sally Johnson's cottage. Sally was supposed to be resting and lay back on an ancient, precarious deckchair. The bruises on her neck were starting to show, but she did not appear to be ill or upset.

Barnaby sat on her knee. He was very quiet and held her tight. That night he had not slept. He was sucking his thumb.

The others were sprawled on the grass. Rob was lying on his back in his usual pose of total relaxation. Tina sat with her hands around her knees. She looked tense, tired, but she had been ringing early that morning with George's friend. Peter sat at Sally's feet, not touching her, not even looking at her very often. George and Molly were a little apart from the rest.

There was a sense of sadness, of shock, but also of excited curiosity. It reminded George Palmer-Jones of a funeral. The relatives are mourning the loss of a person they knew well, but are eager to hear the contents of the will.

Only Molly seemed utterly depressed, empty. She had gone

to the police station with Adam and had been up for most of the night. It was she who spoke first, breaking through the conversation about Tina's ringing expedition.

'You mustn't hate him,' she said. 'It wasn't Adam. Not the Adam we all knew. He heard voices. They told him to kill Tom and try to kill Sally.'

There was a pause. Molly was remembering the night in the police station.

'Tell us all about it, George,' Sally said gently. 'I don't understand what happened. Why should he have wanted to kill Tom? Tom was always kind to Adam. They didn't even know each other very well.'

The others were relieved. No one had wanted to bring up the subject for fear of distressing Sally, but they had all wanted to know. They all wanted to talk about it.

'Of course he's mad,' George said. 'Whatever long words Molly may use to describe him, he's mad. That's why I took so long to realize what had happened. I was looking for a real motive, a strong motive, but there wasn't one.

'Adam killed Tom because he didn't like him. Sally told me, when we first met, that Tom was patronizing towards the younger birdwatchers and that they resented it, but I was shamefully obtuse and I didn't follow it up. I always knew that Adam was disturbed – he was always too controlled and calm – and I knew that he was very frightened, but I thought, as you know, that he was frightened of someone else.

'All Tom's birdwatching acquaintances tried to be kind about Tom, everyone said how generous and likeable he was. It was only when I interviewed Dennis Shawcroft, one of the chefs at the White Lodge, that I had an objective impression. Then I realized how much someone as disturbed and insecure as Adam would be affected by his attitude. It took me all that time to see that the motive might have been one of pure dislike, fuelled by Tom's insensitivity.

'It came to me quite suddenly. Something triggered Adam to action. When I realized what that was, the whole thing became obvious. But still I had no proof and I hadn't been able to talk to Peter and Rob to eliminate them. The only witness was Terry Biddle and he had disappeared. All I could do was to make sure that it did not happen again, and I did try to keep Adam with me, but then Terry Biddle came back. His landlady, Mrs Black, wanted to see me urgently, so I had to leave Adam with Molly.' He looked apologetically at Sally. 'Of course, if I'd known what would happen . . .'

Sally smiled. George Palmer-Jones took his wife's hand and said very softly, just to her: 'You've talked to Adam. Do you mind telling them what happened?'

'Birdwatching was the only thing that Adam was good at,' Molly said. 'His father had made him believe that he was useless, and birding was the only thing that mattered to him. The day of Tom's death he had gone to Rushy convinced that he was going to find a rare bird, something so rare that it would make him famous. But when he went into the field, Tom French had already found the rarity.'

'Tom French found the bimaculated lark?' Rob asked.

George interrupted: 'That was the trigger, you see. Once I linked Tom French to the bimaculated lark, Adam had to be the murderer.'

Molly continued: 'Tom must have seen the bird almost as soon as he left the hotel building, and he followed it to the edge of the park, where you all saw it later in the day. Adam found him there, watching it. Adam believed implicitly that he was meant to find the bird, and that Tom French had in some way tricked or betrayed him by getting there first.

'If Tom had let him play a part in it, had consulted him about the bird and shared it with him, perhaps Adam would never have lost control. It's impossible to say, irrelevant even. Adam was very disturbed and would have broken down at some time. But Tom irritated Adam. He lectured to him about the lark. He talked to Adam as if he were a child, as if he knew nothing about birds. Adam says that he did not mean to kill Tom when he hit him. He lost his temper. Tom would not stop talking.'

'So Tom French found the bimaculated lark,' Rob repeated. He was very impressed, almost envious. He turned to George: 'You see, it's like I said. "Once a twitcher, always a twitcher." He wasn't played out after all.'

There was a silence. It was a tribute to Tom's ability as a birder.

George continued his explanation.

'Because of the way the body was lying, we knew that Tom hadn't been killed where he was found. We couldn't decide how the murderer carried the body to the pool. It's about three-quarters of a mile from the White Lodge, too far for one person to carry a dead weight. But Adam was seen with the body by one person. That person was Terry Biddle who works in the White Lodge, in the kitchens. He has a learning disability, but it seemed that his evidence was reliable. He knew Tom. Terry told us that he had seen someone with Tom's body going up the marsh track, but then Terry ran away before he could give us any details.

'The next day Molly saw Terry again, but still she couldn't persuade him to describe the murderer.

'Unfortunately, I'd given Dennis, who is rather an unpleasant person, the impression that I was interested in the presence of cannabis on the hotel premises, and he told Terry not to speak to us. Before I could dispel the misunderstanding, Terry disappeared. I gather that he saw a birdwatcher in the village, it reminded him of what had happened to Tom, he was frightened and ran away.

'It was only on the night of the storm, when Terry came home, that he told his landlady, Mrs Black, exactly what he had seen. She tried to phone me that night, but I was in Rushy, and she couldn't get in touch. She tried to explain to the police what Terry claimed to have seen, but she must have been upset and not very articulate, and they could not link the bicycle with Adam. If they had, we might have saved Sally an unpleasant experience.'

'Bicycle? I don't understand.' Sally once more accepted the implied apology.

'Often when he went birdwatching, Adam used to take a small, fold-away bicycle. Terry saw a young person pushing the bicycle with Tom's body bent double over the front. The young person was wearing binoculars. It would have been hard work, pushing the body like that, and it would have been dangerous, but it would have been possible. He couldn't have done it, though, if he'd been carrying a heavy telescope at the same time. His is an Optylon. It's short, but very heavy. He left the telescope where it was, planning to return for it later. We know now that Bernard Cranshaw found it, but he was feeling so guilty about having caused his mother to fall down the stairs, and so frightened of the police, that he did nothing about it.'

'Someone else with mental health issues.' Rob was unsympathetic.

George nodded.

'Perhaps. But not as dangerous as Adam.'

'I don't understand why Adam moved the body,' Peter said. 'It seems a crazy risk to have taken.'

'He had to move it away from the bimaculated lark, because he was desperate to claim the lark as his own. If he had left the body where it was, one of the birdwatchers was certain to find it. Because of the lark, everyone would know that Adam had been in the area. Besides, Adam didn't want to detract from his glory in finding the bird. The drama of a body might have done that. It was well hidden in the pool, and he timed his announcement of the bird just as the fog was clearing, so that as soon as it was possible to see anything all the birdwatchers were drawn away from the marsh.

'I'm still not quite sure why Clive Anderson asked me to investigate the case. Perhaps something about Adam's manner made him suspicious. Perhaps, like us, he just thought that Adam was very upset.'

Rob interrupted: 'But when he found the bimaculated lark he seemed so normal and natural. He must be a bloody good actor.'

Molly shook her head.

'By then he would have convinced himself that he had found it, that he hadn't killed Tom, that his voices had been the killer's. Last night he kept saying: "They killed Tom."'

George continued with a steady, detached voice, as if he hoped that an explanation of the facts would calm Molly, and that he could replace some of the emotion with reason:

'When Adam came for a meal with us, I told him that somebody had seen the murderer on the marsh track with Tom's body. Perhaps he thought that we suspected him, or at least that we had a description of the murderer. He felt that he had to divert attention away from himself.'

'So he wasn't pushed down the well,' Tina said. She was angry. 'I was so sorry for him. He seemed so frightened. I thought he needed me to protect him. And it was all acting. He climbed down.'

'That's not possible.' Rob was adamant. 'I can't believe it. You said that he was terrified when they got him up, and he couldn't have climbed down there. Not without a rope.'

'He used a rope,' George said. 'His father was quite famous as a mountaineer, and he used to take Adam with him, when Adam was younger. There's a mark in the wood of one of the uprights on the windmill. It puzzled me at the time. It was caused by the rope biting into the wood. Adam must have doubled it around the post, so that he could pull it after him. Then he would have thrown it down into the well. Of course he was terrified. It was dark down there. Perhaps he panicked when everyone arrived at the party, but nobody heard him. I presume that by then he had pulled down the rope and thrown it away. It would have been impossible for him to climb out on his own.

'If you remember, we thought it strange that he'd left his binoculars and telescope at home that day. I should have realized then that the whole thing was planned. He was afraid of losing them or damaging them. But I liked him. It stopped me thinking straight.'

George remembered that night and the white, sobbing boy. If only he had known then. He knew that the boy had been ready to confide in him. If only he had said the right words, had had the ability to inspire a little trust. But then nothing, really, would have been very different. He had a sudden vision then of the remand centre where Dennis Shawcroft had been held, the long walls and the smell and the uniforms. The hospital would not be very different.

'But why me?' Sally said suddenly. 'I don't understand what he had against me!'

She coddled Barnaby close to her in a fierce, involuntary gesture.

'Your involvement in it confused me all the way through. It was an unhappy coincidence, but it was all, in a way, provoked by Tom, who tried too hard with people, who couldn't relax with them. You couldn't tell me about Peter because you were frightened for him, and you couldn't explain why you were so obliged to Tom because Peter was involved. Bernard Cranshaw wrote unpleasant letters to you because he hated Tom, and because he was jealous of him, and, in a way, of you. You both represented a freedom which he could never attain. But he seemed to me too weak to hurt Tom. Even when he was trying to scare the birders off the marsh he never really meant to hurt them. When he tried to hurt his mother he only bruised her. And his hatred for you and Tom was too close to love for him to contemplate doing you any real harm.

'Adam has always been too controlled. He would never let off an air gun, or have an argument. He kept his resentment to himself.

'His attempt on Sally's life was another attempt to protect himself. Our belief in his story depended on our being convinced that he was pushed. If we believed that he was pushed, our attention was directed away from Adam as the possible murderer. But Sally had seen Adam in Fenquay on the day of his supposed accident, and he was on his own.

He also had a coil of nylon rope with him. In fact Sally didn't see whether or not Adam had a companion, and she didn't see the rope. But he didn't know that.

'I think that he brooded about Sally spotting him in Fenquay and began to see her as a real threat. He was with us when we were discussing Sally's relationship with Peter and decided to use that knowledge to lure her out onto the marsh. After I'd left him in the Windmill he went and sat on the shingle bank, and began talking to some young lads. There were a lot of strangers in Rushy that day, come to see the bee-eater. Adam pretended to be called Peter Littleton and asked one of the boys to give the message to Sally. Then he set off in the opposite direction, with Molly following him.'

He smiled at his wife.

'He gave me the slip,' she said ruefully. 'I'm not as young as I was. I followed him inland, right out of the village. He took that narrow lane which goes to the church, and then turns into a footpath, and eventually joins the Dereham road. You know that all the roads out of Rushy climb a bit. I was getting short of breath. I stopped and looked back over Rushy and saw that the mist was moving in from the sea. When I looked back, Adam seemed to have disappeared. I thought for a while that he was hiding, for a joke.

'Then I saw him running down the main road towards the marsh. I knew I'd never catch him, but I walked down the hill after him. I heard him, in fact, before I saw him. The track into the marsh forms a sort of embankment and he must have climbed down into the reeds. By that time I'd walked out of the sun into a thick mist, and he didn't see me. I don't think he would have noticed me anyway. He was talking to himself. It was quite horrible. I heard mud and shingle splashing into water. He must have climbed onto the track ahead of me. I suppose that he could hear Sally further on. Of course, I had no idea she was there. You all know what happened next.'

Sally leant over and took Molly's hand. Barnaby stirred and smiled. Peter took him and held the baby over his head. Barnaby giggled and pulled at Peter's hair.

They went then, leaving Peter, Sally and Barnaby in the garden together.

Again, the notion of a funeral returned to George. Like distant relatives who leave hushed voices and reverent thoughts in the church, they began to talk normally of ordinary things. Away from the influence of Sally and the cottage, Rob and Tina were making plans to return to Southampton. They began to laugh together at a private joke, and George realized how little the whole business had affected them. He had thought that Tina was attached to Adam. He had been concerned for her, but they were young and tough. They would have no nightmares.

Rob swung his cheap, nasty binoculars over his shoulder and said:

'Right. Back to Rushy now, I think, and the Windmill. To find out if there's anything about.'

George, who was driving, was not offended by this command, or by the young people's resilience. He would have nightmares enough for all of them.

# COME DEATH AND HIGH WATER

Read on for an extract from the next book in the
George and Molly Palmer-Jones series

# *Chapter One*

CHARLIE TODD, HIDDEN BEHIND black leather and helmet, began the steep descent to the shore. He felt like Mr. Toad at the start of his wild, outrageous adventure, and bent low over the handlebars of his motorcycle. It was easier to imagine, when he was going downhill, that he was riding a more powerful machine, and Charlie Todd was a great believer in the imagination. Imagination, after all, had made him a fortune. He looked down over the river. The mud was turned into golden sand by the September afternoon sun, and the island, tear-drop shaped at the mouth of the estuary, was deceptively clear. It looked very close. He could see the Land Rover moving slowly over the rocks at the south end. John would be on his way to collect the weekend guests. Charlie was not looking forward to the committee meeting, but as he did not like to cause disappointment, he quickly put all thought of it from his mind. The lane was narrow, the typical Devon hedges a tangle of bramble and hawthorn, and for a while he was forced to concentrate on the road. There was no need to hurry because John would wait for him, but he did not want to cause the others too much inconvenience. Not today. He drove round a sharp bend, through a small, overgrown wood, and once more the estuary was spread before him. He had bought the island nearly five years before, and since then had spent every summer there. He supposed that he should feel sad at the prospect of leaving it behind, but Charlie Todd never felt regret. He looked forward with commitment and passion and enjoyment to his new venture, was totally immersed in his new enthusiasm. But because he was a great believer in imagination, it did occur to him that the others might be a little sad that the island was to be sold.

'Mummy, do you have to go out now?' The girl dribbled grimy tears. 'You promised last night that you'd help, then you went to that meeting. Daddy wouldn't let me wait up for you.'

Pamela Marshall looked at her watch. She would already be five minutes late for Jerry. She would not usually have worried about that, but today she had to talk to him before they met the others.

'I *am* sorry, darling. Perhaps Daddy can help. He'll be home soon. Or Edward. It's his chess night, isn't it? He'll be in at five.'

'None of them can do French as well as you.'

Sian hated French and worried about it. Pamela looked at her watch again, and then at the immaculate kitchen, cluttered already with school bag, dirty sandwich box, gym kit, and then at her unbelievably untidy, bedraggled daughter. She stifled her irritation.

'I can't stop now, darling. You know it's my Gillibry weekend, but I'll be back on Sunday afternoon. Forget about

French tonight. Do your other homework, and I promise that I'll help you on Sunday night.'

Sian smiled and Pamela's irritation disappeared. Her daughter might be untidy and not very academic, but she was no disgrace to her. She was at least pretty.

'I must go now,' she said, 'or the others will have to wait for me. There's plenty in the freezer. If Daddy does happen to be late, just help yourselves. Or perhaps it would be nice if you and Edward could have a meal ready for him when he gets in.'

She kissed her pretty daughter on the forehead, tied her expensive, hand-knitted Guernsey casually around her neck, and hurried away before her son or her husband could distract her further.

With relief Jasmine Carson locked the front door of her flat behind her. Despite its comfort and convenience she hated it. For thirty years she had taught biology at a private girls' school and her rooms there had been her home. They had been high ceilinged, impressively proportioned. When she retired it had seemed sensible to buy somewhere appropriate to her needs, and she had chosen a ground-floor flat in a new well-appointed block on the sea front. She had always been congratulated on her common sense and while she had been tempted to move somewhere older, to a cottage perhaps with a garden, she had resisted in favour of central heating and a built-in kitchen. Now she was too proud, too afraid perhaps of making a worse mistake, to move again, and knew that the flat would be her home until she died. She supposed that she would get used to it. Already she could bear what had seemed the unbearable heat of the communal areas, and she presumed that the other residents, most of them elderly, would come to realize that she had no interest in the lives of their children who lived in Milton Keynes or Johannesburg, would stop showing her photographs of apparently identical grandchildren.

She drove inland from Gillicombe, the seaside town which she had made her home. The road followed the bank of the estuary and as the tide ebbed, the island became an island no longer, different from its surroundings not in substance but in kind, a lump of sandstone surrounded by muddy sand. That is my real home, she thought. She felt as tensely excited as a young girl off to a dance, hoping that her lover would be there, expectant of adventure, new experience. Then:

Romantic old fool, she thought. What's so special about the place anyway? Fifty acres of sandstone at the mouth of the estuary, and it only becomes an island at high tide. Not a proper island. Not remote at all. Only three miles from the biggest tourist town in North Devon.

But whatever she made herself think, she knew that the pain of rheumatism in her hips and her spine disappeared as she drove along the river to meet the Land Rover, and that the real reason for tolerating the dreadful flat on the sea front was that at night, from her bedroom window, she could see the light of the Gillibry buoy.

It was a pleasant walk down the hill from the main road to the quay. A breeze blew from the sea. The two young men had hitch-hiked from Gillicombe, but were content to walk the last mile.

'I don't understand,' said the tallest, lazily, 'why you keep coming to the island. You were never that keen on ringing, even when we were kids. Now you hardly ever bother to come out with the North Devon Ringing Group. I don't even know if you've still got a valid ringing permit. But you're still a member, still pay the subs, and now you're on the committee.'

'I'm on the committee,' said the other, Mark, 'because you co-opted me.'

'I mean, I understand why it's so important to me. I've got that boring job in the shop, most of my friends – like you and Jon – have gone away to college, and there's not much else to do round here. But you're different. You're into all sorts of things – music, politics. You've loads of friends at university.'

'I suppose so. But it is special, Gillibry, isn't it?' He seemed ashamed then of being so serious, and when a motorbike – apparently without a silencer – drove so fast down the lane behind them that they had to climb into the hedge, he was pleased to be distracted.

'Wasn't that Charlie?' he asked.

Nick, the tall one, shrugged.

'Probably. He's an appalling driver. He'll get himself killed one day.'

'What happens to the island if he dies?'

'Didn't you know? He's left it to the observatory in his will. It's the sort of grand gesture he's good at.'

There was a pause for a moment, before Mark spoke again. 'He's like a kid, isn't he? Everything's done on impulse. He sees something he wants and he has to have it. Otherwise, he throws a massive tantrum.'

'Just as well for us that he took a fancy to the island.'

'And,' Mark went on, 'that he was rich enough to buy it when it came up for sale.'

'It's an odd way to make a fortune, writing daft children's stories. Have you ever seen them?'

'Yeah. they're really good. My sister's kids think they're brilliant. It's just as well he became such a famous author. His family would have disowned him otherwise. They always treated him as the black sheep, didn't they? They said he was letting down the family name. Until he got rich. Then they decided that he was just eccentric.'

Nick shifted the rucksack on his back. He had his own view of the Todds.

'It's your first committee meeting, isn't it?' he said. 'I hope that you don't find it too boring. They're all the same. Nothing ever happens.'

Jerry Packham lingered over his work, pleased at last with the result. His bags were ready and subconsciously he listened for Pam's car, for the change of gears on the steep lane. He knew that she would be late. She always was. It was one of her ways of stressing the nature of the relationship between them. She would be expecting him to be waiting at the gate for her as usual. But today he was reluctant to leave. He wondered for one mad moment if he should tell her that he did not want to come, that he was too busy, that he wanted to finish the series of paintings, but he knew that he did not have the courage. He would finish the affair, but not yet. She had dominated the partnership so completely that he hesitated to take the lead even in separating. Besides, he wanted to see Charlie.

He had first illustrated Charlie's stories for a joke, before they were published. Charlie had lived in his village then, and they had shared the same local. Charlie had been convinced even then that the stories would make his fortune.

Jerry had never been to art college. He had left school at fifteen and become apprenticed to a sign writer. When the man retired he had taken over the business and expanded it. He had begun to design menus, posters, had even tried a set of postcards and found that they had been easy to sell. The sign writing became less important. In his spare time he enjoyed sketching and had been persuaded to sell the results through the numerous gift shops in Gillicombe. The illustrations had been fun to do; he had let himself go. There had never been any formal arrangement between himself and Charlie. He had never really believed that the books would be accepted for publication, and when they were, it seemed right that they should come under Charlie's name, that Charlie should get all the publicity and most of the money. The television serial had made the stories famous, and Jerry had taken no part in that.

It had been one of Jerry's birdwatching friends, George, who had suggested that Jerry should get an agent to negotiate a better contract with the publisher.

'Those books are made by the illustrations,' George had said. 'They're superb. Without them, I doubt if Charlie would have been published at all.'

So he had received a more generous proportion of the royalties in the most recent series of books. He had become used to seeing his drawings reproduced in comics, on children's sketch pads, on sweet packets. He was comfortably off, but he was bored by the characters in Charlie's books. Each story seemed the same as the last. It was time to try something new. He had been offered other commissions and had decided that he should tell Charlie that he would not be available to work for him, at least for a while.

Now he was working on a children's encyclopedia of the countryside. It was very different from the illustration of Charlie's fantasies, but he was enjoying the precision and the subtlety of it. He was looking at a recently completed colour plate of leaves and trees when he realized that the doorbell was ringing, and he hurried, rather pleased with himself, to meet Pamela.

As he looked down over the island, Doctor Derbyshire experienced, as he always did, a sense of achievement and of pride. Charlie might have financed the observatory, but the idea had been his. Without his organization, his persistence, Charlie would have grown bored with the negotiations to purchase, would have given up the project. Charlie was like a child and the doctor knew how to handle him.

Mrs. Derbyshire drove her husband to the quay. He disliked driving. He fussed over his luggage and made her check again that his favourite jersey was packed. She sighed with maternal irritation. He had not been happy since his retirement from general practice. She was grateful for the island. It stopped him mooning around the house, sulky and petulant as a schoolboy. That had been a dangerous time and she had been worried. The planning and the intriguing had given him life again, given him a future.

Paul Derbyshire looked at his watch and then over the shore. The Land Rover was on its way. John was a reliable boy. He looked forward to the committee meeting, planned his chairing of it. The committee were all well-meaning, enthusiastic people, but needed a strong chairman to give them proper direction. His wife watched his enjoyment with satisfaction, and planned a private, pleasant weekend. They were a happy couple but she understood nothing of the complexities of his affection for the island. She saw it as a toy, a distraction. It kept him busy.

But it's the only contact I have with real beauty, he thought as he waited for the Land Rover. It's the daughter I never had, my creation.

She would never have imagined him capable of such lyrical folly. She waved at the other birdwatchers and drove off to her knitting and a nice glass of sweet sherry.

When John Lansdown first moved to the island, every trip to the mainland was a challenge. There was no track. The Land Rover was driven south from Gillibry over steep green rocks, through seaweed-filled pools on to the shore. There, the sand could be soft and the gullies deceptively deep. If the tide had not ebbed sufficiently there was a danger of being stuck halfway across the channel. It had made him nervous. The Land Rover was his responsibility. Now he knew the way and was used to the Land Rover. Only in thick fog was he still wary. Automatically he counted the seals on the sandbank and estimated the number of waders on the shore. He hoped to persuade the others to try the new cannon net and would need to know what they could expect to catch. His reaction to the September committee weekend was ambiguous. The committee members were competent ringers and knew the observatory system. Some of them were friends. It was easier, perhaps, than having a group of strangers to stay, certainly easier than the schoolchildren who were the observatory's usual visitors, but he always felt that he was on trial throughout the weekend and that the committee was assessing his competence to run the place. He knew that

Elizabeth felt the same. She supervised all the domestic arrangements in the observatory, and though it was organized like a youth hostel, she cooked three meals a day for the visitors. The thought of Elizabeth brought back the pleasure of anxious excitement which he had been feeling since she had told him that she was pregnant. She had insisted that no one else should know. He wanted to tell everyone he met – it felt like a validation of their relationship – but she had a kind of superstition about it. It was natural, he supposed, because of the miscarriage she had suffered when she was married to Frank. He was certain that nothing would go wrong. How could it, when things were going so well for them? They both loved the island. In the precarious world of natural history he had a secure job. Charlie Todd might be an eccentric neighbour, but he subsidized the Gillibry Trust's funds so that although John and Elizabeth were not well paid, they received more than they would have done from any other conservation charity; and their home was reasonably warm and well maintained.

He turned the Land Rover sharply, and then he could see the people waiting for him at the quay. What can they be talking about? he thought. They're all so different. What can they have to say to each other?

Carefully, aware that they were watching, he drove the Land Rover from the sand on to the stone slipway. It had been a jetty once. Ships had sailed from there to the Armada. Now the estuary had silted up. There was sand and saltmarsh, and the people waiting there with their bags and suitcases looked slightly ridiculous. He jumped down and opened the back of the Land Rover.

'We've been discussing the paddock heligoland,' Miss

Carson said immediately. 'When I was on the island last I was appalled. It should be repaired at once. Charlie says that he can give us some wire mesh. Perhaps we could organize a working party.'

Of course, they would have that in common. They were passionate ringers. He thought that Jasmine was the school-mistress of stand-up comics and cartoonists. She was big-busted and formidable in thick woollen stockings and lace-up boots. She climbed without fuss, without a hint of rheumatism, into the back of the Land Rover.

'If you want us to do the work, it'll have to be soon. Mark goes to college again at the end of the month, and I'm very busy.'

Nick spoke aggressively, more loudly than was necessary.

How ungracious he is, John thought. He does do more than his fair share, but he enjoys it. I hope that he's not going to be rude all weekend. Elizabeth does hate it.

But Miss Carson was disposed to be conciliatory.

'Of course,' she said. 'You know that we depend on you and Mark. We must talk again about attracting new, younger members.'

That, too, was a perennial item on the agenda. We must attract new members, but we will not accept their new ideas or give them any responsibility. The observatory had recruited a number of schoolboys over the years, but only Mark and Nick were left. The others had drifted away, disillusioned by the slow pace of change on the island, the refusal to accept new ways of doing things, tempted by girlfriends, rare birds, beer. John wondered sometimes why Mark and Nick stayed. He suspected that Nick might enjoy the alliances and plotting as much as the older members did, but Mark was different.

He had a wild and wicked sense of fun, a wide circle of friends, other interests.

As he always did, Charlie Todd climbed into the front seat, the only comfortable seat of the Land Rover, without giving anyone else the opportunity of doing so. John was never sure whether this lack of courtesy was caused by Charlie's usual absentmindedness or by cunning. It was probably absent-mindedness. He was a small, round man with curly white hair, like a doll's wig, and a perpetually dazed but happy expression. People spoke to him slowly as if he were deaf, or very old, or a child. He could have been any age from fifty to seventy.

'George phoned up,' Jasmine Carson barked suddenly. 'He couldn't get through to you. He won't be able to get here until tomorrow, but he said not to pick him up. He'll walk out straight after the tide.'

The others climbed in then, Pam Marshall and Jerry Packham taking care to sit on opposite sides of the Land Rover, Paul Derbyshire peevish about leg room and the splash of oil on the seat. It was all the same as every other committee weekend.

The south of the island had been leased to the council and was managed by its Recreation Services Department. This meant little more than that the litter bins were emptied occasionally and that the area was open to the public. In the summer families walked over to experience a tide on a real island, to picnic on the beach or on the grass. There was nothing else to do there and no one was there now. John noticed briefly that Pam was looking as glamorously well-kept as always, that Jerry was not staring at her with his usual rapt attention, then with an irrational progression of thought, wondered if Liz would marry him now. He knew her so well, yet could not predict how she would react if he asked her again. He was frightened of upsetting things between them. It was her secrecy, her power to surprise which attracted him so deeply.

Through use a track had been worn from south to north over Gillibry and the island rose steeply away from the shore. The observatory was at the far north end, at the point of the tear-drop, like the figurehead of an old carved boat. It looked down over the rest of the island. In contrast Charlie's house was hidden in a fold in the ground, surrounded by the only trees which would grow on Gillibry. It was just more than halfway along the track, in a natural bowl, so that the cliffs to the east and the west of it were high and rocky, but the house was sheltered. In the summer flowers grew in the garden. The house itself was a prefabricated wooden chalet which Charlie had imported specially from Sweden. It was incongruous with bright paint and shutters and could have been taken from one of the illustrations of his books. The house was known on the island as the Wendy House. No one could remember who had named it.

# A BIRD IN THE HAND

**Ann Cleeves** is the author of more than thirty-five critically acclaimed novels, and in 2017 was awarded the highest accolade in crime writing, the CWA Diamond Dagger. She is the creator of popular detectives Vera Stanhope, Jimmy Perez and Matthew Venn, who can be found on television in ITV's *Vera*, BBC One's *Shetland* and ITV's *The Long Call* respectively. The TV series and the books they are based on have become international sensations, capturing the minds of millions worldwide.

Ann worked as a probation officer, bird observatory cook and auxiliary coastguard before she started writing. She is a member of 'Murder Squad', working with other British northern writers to promote crime fiction. Ann also spends her time advocating for reading to improve health and wellbeing and supporting access to books. In 2021 her Reading for Wellbeing project launched with local authorities across the North East. She lives in Northumberland where the Vera books are set.

You can find Ann on Twitter and Facebook @AnnCleeves

# THE TWO RIVERS SERIES

## Discover Ann's latest lead character Detective Matthew Venn

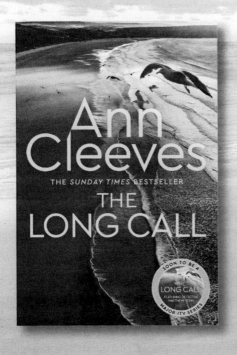

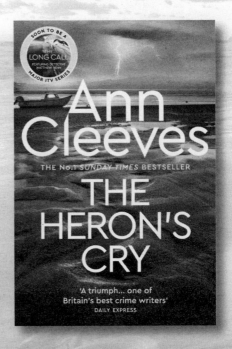

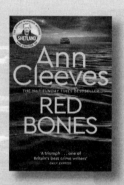
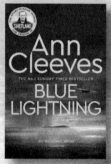
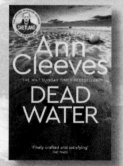

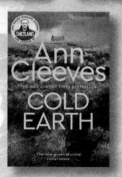

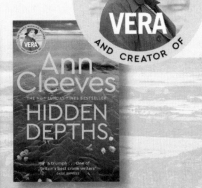
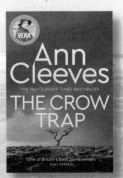

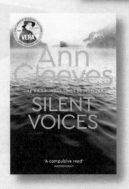
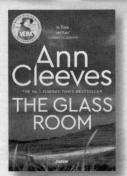
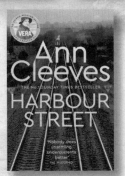
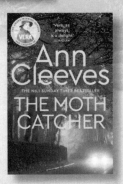
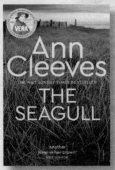

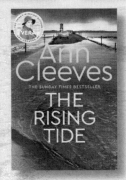